HOME

A Post-Apocalyptic/Dystopian Adventure

The Traveler Series Book One

Tom Abrahams

D1607844

A PITON PRESS BOOK

Home

The Traveler Series Book One

© Tom Abrahams. All Rights Reserved

Cover Design by Hristo Kovatliev

Edited by Felicia A. Sullivan

Proofread by Pauline Nolet

PITON PRESS

http://tomabrahamsbooks.com

OTHER WORKS BY TOM ABRAHAMS

THE TRAVELER SERIES

CANYON

WALL (SUMMER 2016)

MATTI HARROLD POLITICAL CONSPIRACIES

SEDITION

INTENTION (OCTOBER 2016)

JACKSON QUICK ADVENTURES

ALLEGIANCE

ALLEGIANCE BURNED

HIDDEN ALLEGIANCE

PERSEID COLLAPSE: PILGRIMAGE SERIES NOVELLAS

CROSSING

REFUGE

ADVENT

For my homies: Courtney, Sam, and Luke

"The probability of apocalypse soon cannot be realistically estimated, but it is surely too high for any sane person to contemplate with equanimity."

— Noam Chomsky

CHAPTER 1

OCTOBER 12, 2037, 11:56 PM

SCOURGE +5 YEARS

EAST OF RISING STAR, TEXAS

Marcus Battle checked his scope. Though the green and black optics revealed nothing, he knew something — or some*one* — was out there. A trip alarm three hundred yards from his front gate told him he wasn't alone.

He was flat on his stomach thirteen feet in the air, hidden between the pine slat walls of his son's oak-mounted treehouse. The muzzle of the twenty-inch barrel of his rifle rested at its edge in the middle of a wide gap at the corner.

It provided Battle with both good reconnaissance and an excellent spot from which to stop intruders should they get too close. Intruders were always trying to get too close. He always stopped them.

Battle fingered a piece of mint chewing gum from his breast pocket and popped it in his mouth. He checked the scope again. Nothing.

He slipped his finger off the trigger of his DPMS Prairie Panther King's Desert Shadow semiautomatic synthetic .223. He called the rifle "Inspector" after the lead character in the *Pink Panther* movies. He named all of his weapons after movie characters.

Battle checked his watch. It was almost midnight. Until he identified the intruder or intruders, this would be a long night. Since the Scourge five years earlier, there were a lot of nights like these.

He smacked his gum, relishing the mint. He tried to pop a bubble, but the piece was too small. The gum got stuck on the back of his front teeth and he had to flick it free with his tongue.

Then he heard footsteps.

Really, it was the sound of leaves rustling and crunching under the pressure of someone running. Somebody was sprinting toward his gate. He checked the scope, scanning the oak-dotted landscape that hid his property from the main highway.

He shifted left and then right. Then he moved left again and saw a green figure moving swiftly toward the gate. It disappeared behind an oak and then flashed between two more. The darkness was a challenge with night-vision scopes. Too much light and they didn't work; too little light and they didn't work.

Battle let out a long breath and touched his finger to the trigger. He pressed the rifle into his shoulder, tracking the intruder, anticipating its line to the gate.

"As far as the east is from the west," he whispered to himself, "so far has he removed our transgressions from us."

Battle set his jaw. He was about to pull the trigger when a woman screamed.

"Help me!" she cried breathlessly, her plea echoing into the cloudless, moonless sky. "Help me, please!" The woman was running away from the gate now, parallel to the front fence that surrounded the central two acres of his property. She was running west, straight toward him.

Battle knew this could be a trap. She could be bait intended to lure him from the security of his perch. Then, somewhere not far away, hidden amongst the oaks, men would lay in wait to pounce. Still, a voice in his head told him to wait before pulling the trigger.

The closer the woman got to the treehouse, the more genuine her fear seemed to be. She was tripping over herself, unable to maintain her balance as she worked the fence line. The lack of moonlight made it nearly impossible to see anything without the scope.

Further south amongst the oak trees, there was more rustling. There were at least two men running and grunting. One was running faster than the other. He called after the woman.

"Get back here!" he growled. "You belong to me!"

Battle shifted his weight and scanned left again, pulling into focus a bright green image. He saw the faster of the men on the gravel path outside the gate. He gripped a shotgun with both hands, like an infantryman, and had a handgun holstered on his right hip. His chest was heaving as he stood at the gate.

"You can't run!" he yelled. "I'm gonna get you. This time I'm cutting off a—"

Thump! Thump!

The seventy-seven-grain hollow-point bullets took one tenth of a second to drill through the man's sternum once Battle pulled the trigger. Immediately expanding on impact to increase the damage, the bullets dropped him where he stood, still clutching his own rifle.

Pop! Pop! Pop!

Battle pulled his eye from the night scope to avoid the muzzle flashes' blinding bursts of green light from the return fire. His eyes searched the darkness.

Pop! Pop! Pop!

The bursts of white light were about seventy-five yards away and directly south of the treehouse. From the sound of the gunfire, Battle figured it was a .45 semiautomatic pistol. The magazine probably held ten or fifteen rounds.

Pop! Pop! Pop! Pop!

The slower man was either out of bullets or he had five more. It didn't matter. The four bursts of light confirmed his position. He'd be dead in less than three seconds.

Battle saw the final two flashes. He glanced in the scope and spotted movement against the side of an oak.

Thump! Thump! Thump!

Pop!

The hollow points hit the man's neck in a tight pattern near his collarbone. The shock of the impact caused an involuntary twitch, and he pulled the trigger of his Glock once as he hit the ground. The slug bore into the oak next to him.

Battle listened to the quiet: no rustling, no wind, only the soft whimper of the woman. He elbowed his way to a spot at the corner of the treehouse, where he could peer straight down. He pointed Inspector straight at her, his finger behind the trigger guard, and used the scope to find her.

She was curled against the fence, her body as small as she could make it. Her face was buried beneath a long mop of hair. He could see her back heaving and trembling as she breathed. He took a deep breath, almost swallowing the gum, and made a judgment call.

"Stay there!" he yelled down to her. "I'm coming to help you."

"No!" she called back, looking upward in the general direction of his voice. "No! Don't, please."

"I'm not going to hurt you," he promised her and inched back into the treehouse. She repeated her lack of interest in his assistance. A moment ago she was asking for help, now she didn't want it. Maybe it was a trap. Maybe she *was* bait. However, he'd cut the line and she was floating free.

Battle dropped back onto his rear and unscrewed the bipod from the bottom of the rifle. He pushed himself to his feet, slinging Inspector over his back. He grabbed a pair of head-mounted thermal goggles and tucked his Sig Sauer P226 into his waistband. The Sig was nicknamed "McDunnough", after Nic Cage's character in *Raising Arizona*.

Between the fifteen rounds left in Inspector's magazine and the ten .357 bullets in McDunnough, he was loaded for bear, or whatever else he came across.

At the trapdoor entrance on the western side of the eight-by-eight treehouse, Battle climbed down the pine planks nailed into the oak's trunk. Rung by rung, he moved quickly and silently until he hit the leaves clustered on the ground. He was mere feet from her, but was separated by the five-foot-tall wooden picket fence that ran in a rectangle around his central two acres. Thick aluminum mesh, sturdier than chicken wire, filled the spaces between the pickets.

"Just stay there," Battle said in the most comforting voice he could muster. It had been years since he'd tried to comfort anyone but himself. "I'm going to come around through the gate. I'll come around and help you inside."

"No," she whimpered. Even a few feet from her it was hard to make out much more than the whip of her hair as she protested. "Please don't." Her voice trembled with a vibrato that under other circumstances might have made Battle laugh.

Battle flipped the thermal goggles over his eyes and turned them on. Everything was awash in orange. Her pupils, pinpricks as they were, glowed back at him like a deer on the side of the road. Goosebumps rose on his neck. Her fear was palpable.

"It's okay," he said, holding his hand up. "I won't hurt you."

He marched toward the gate, his feet crunching the leaves as he stepped. The woman said something to him as he walked away, but it was warbled and unintelligible. He could only imagine what the men had done to her. He didn't want to imagine it.

At the gate, he opened a waist-high box and punched in a code. The wrought-iron gate hummed along its track as the motorized chain pulled it open.

He stepped through the opening and knelt at the body of the running man. His eyes were fixed open and he stared back at Battle as he rummaged through the man's pockets. He didn't find much: a pack of Camel cigarettes, a lighter, a flask, and a box of shotgun shells.

Battle checked the rifle, a gas-operated Browning Silver Hunter. He shook his head at the impracticality of the weapon in a post-Scourge world. It was beautiful, with a walnut stock and a satin finish. But it was a stupid weapon carried by what Battle imagined was a stupid man.

He laid down the Browning, which he'd already decided he'd call "Lloyd" from the movie *Dumb and Dumber,* and checked the hip holster. It was empty.

Empty?

Battle closed his eyes and thought back to the moment he saw the holster from his position in the treehouse. It wasn't empty, he was sure of it.

He scrambled to his feet and started backing toward the gate. When he reached the threshold, he spun to reach for the access panel. But something solid and heavy crashed into the side of his head, knocking the optics from his eyes. Battle stumbled, momentarily dazed as another thick volley hit him in the side of the head and he tumbled to the ground, the weight of Inspector pulling him awkwardly to one side as he fell.

He was on his side, the rifle half underneath his body, when a steel-toed boot slammed into his ribs. Battle tried scrambling away but wasn't fast enough.

"You killed my brother," snarled the attacker, kneeling down with all of his weight onto Battle's bruised ribs. "I'm gonna kill you." Still leaning onto Battle, the attacker gripped his neck with his left hand and pushed a handgun into his cheek with his right.

Battle's right arm was pinned underneath his body, but his left arm was free. He whipped his hand to the small of his back, groping for McDunnough.

"You're like a bug on its back," the attacker sneered, jabbing the muzzle at Battle's face. "A little baby bug. Say goodbye, baby bug."

That taunt gave Battle the instant he needed to pull the Sig from his back and, in one fluid motion, jam it into the attacker's chin and pull the trigger. The point-blank blast knocked him onto his back. Battle rolled over, sliding the rifle from his back as he got to his feet, and wiped the blood splatter from his face. He tucked the Sig into his waistband and stepped to the chinless attacker to kick the handgun from his cold, dead hand. Battle winced against the pain in his side, raising the rifle's scope to his eye as he moved aggressively back to the woman.

"Who are you?" he demanded, Inspector leveled at her head. "Why are you here?"

"I—I—" She held her hands in front of her face.

"Who are you?" Battle shoved the rifle at her. "Were you bait?"

"Bait? No. No. Please."

"You asked for help, then you said no. Then I get jumped, almost killed. What do you want?"

"I wanted help," she whimpered. "I wanted help. They were chasing me. I escaped. They chased me. I escaped." She shook her head, her hands still blocking her from the muzzle.

"Who are they?"

"They're bad men," she said. "Bad men."

"Why did you tell me not to help you?" Battle's finger was on the trigger, his left eye pressed to the scope.

"I knew you hadn't killed all of them."

"How did you know?"

"Two were chasing me. Two were farther behind."

"Two?"

"Yes."

"So there were four of them?"

"Yes."

Battle spun around, his pulse quickening. He adjusted his grip on Inspector and scanned the tree line, his eye darting from oak to oak. Nothing. He spun back to check the woman.

She still cowered against the fence, her hair and hands blocking her face.

"Come with me." He reached down and grabbed her arm, pulling her to her feet. "We need to move."

She hesitated. "I think I sprained my ankle."

"We'll worry about it later. You need to cope."

At a pace that had her tripping over herself, Battle led her to the gate. He shoved her past the opening and, scanning the oaks, backed his way behind the gate. He thumbed the electronic lock and the tall wrought-iron fence slid past him, clanging as it locked into the closed position.

"We need to get to the house." He tugged her along the crushed gravel driveway toward the front door of the main house. She limped, almost hopping as she moved. She asked Battle to slow down. He ignored her.

The drive split at the eastern edge of the house. Part of it continued straight back to the detached three-car garage. Battle followed the fork to the left, in front of the house. He pressed an electronic code on a panel at the front door and pushed on the heavy, solid mahogany wood.

He stood in the entry, scanning the property one more time, and shut the door. He made a mental note of the weapons he'd left outside; Lloyd the rifle, and the 9mm that nearly killed him. He'd have to wait until daylight to retrieve them.

"I'm going to search you," he warned. "I'm not going to hurt you. I need to make sure you don't have any weapons."

She didn't respond. Her arms were folded across her chest. She was shivering and trying to keep weight off her bad ankle.

"I need you to lower your arms," he said. "I'm going to run the back of my hands along your body."

She dropped her arms and flinched when he touched her. He carefully searched her as he would any potential threat. Satisfied she was weapon-free, he turned his back on her and stepped back to the front door to flip a series of switches on the wall. The entryway and a long hallway lit with a soft yellow glow. He pressed some numbers on a keypad.

"The alarm is now on," alerted the monotone security system.

He put his hand on the small of the woman's back, leading her toward the kitchen. She was wearing jeans and a white T-shirt. Both were filthy. Her feet were bare. Battle imagined she hadn't bathed in a while.

He helped her to the kitchen and punched the dimmer switch near the entry. He pointed to the lone barstool at a large white and gray granite island.

He moved around to the opposite side of the island while she took a seat and swiveled to face him. She pulled her hair behind her ears using both hands and looked up at him.

Battle set the rifle on the island in front of him, but kept his hands on it. He was a safe enough distance away from her should she try something, and still close enough to have a conversation.

She was the first person in the house, other than him, in more than seventeen hundred days.

CHAPTER 2

AUGUST 5, 2032, 10:35 AM

SCOURGE -2 MONTHS

EAST OF RISING STAR, TEXAS

"You know you're crazy." Sylvia Battle stood at the bottom of the largest oak tree on their fifty acres. She was looking up at her husband and his latest creation. "He's never going to come down from there."

Marcus Battle slung his canvas tool bag over his shoulder and sat on the edge of the trapdoor, his feet dangling. He'd just finished affixing the second hinge to the door.

"Him?" He laughed and slid his body into the opening, pulling the door closed behind him, then descended the fresh pine planks that served as a ladder on the trunk of the tree. "I may never come down."

He skipped the final couple of rungs and jumped to the ground, the tool bag slapping him on the side.

"Careful." Sylvia laughed, wrapping her arms around her man. "You've got a bag full of dangerous tools there."

"I'll show you a dangerous tool," he smirked and planted a kiss on her lips.

"You taste like sweat."

"I'll show you sweat."

"Enough, Marcus." She slapped him on the chest. "You're filthy."

"I'll show you—"

"Got it." She shoved him and turned to walk toward the house. "You coming in?"

"Yeah. I need to check the barn first. I'll take a shower before I head into town to get some replacement supplies."

"I thought you did that already," she said, stopping to plant her hands on her hips. "It's an hour each way to Abilene. How long will you be gone?"

"Three hours or less. I'm a fast shopper. I'll stick to the list. I've got a rotation going. Out with the old and in with the new."

"Sir, yes, sir." Sylvia stood at attention and saluted him.

"I'm not a sir." He rolled his eyes. "If you're going to salute me, at least get it right."

"Sorry, Major Battle." She giggled. "That always gets me. Major Battle. You should have stayed in a little longer, then you'd be Lieutenant Colonel Battle. So much better."

"You wouldn't let me stay in," he reminded her.

"Whatever." She waved him off and walked straight for the main house. "I'll see you inside."

Marcus loved watching her walk. Her shoulders were back, her hips swinging slightly back and forth. She disappeared inside the house, and he made his way to the barn, one of three structures on their fifty acres. He'd fenced in the central two acres and added an electric gate. He didn't like his wife and kid being alone in the middle of nowhere when he traveled, and the fence and the gate gave him a slight sense of security.

Inside the fence was the barn, the main house, the three-car garage, and a garden. He also had added a treehouse for his son's birthday. Wesson was about to be nine. He was the center of their world. If it weren't for Wes, Marcus knew he probably would be lieutenant colonel. He'd probably still be active, probably be in Syria or Iran. Or he'd be dead.

Instead, he was swinging open the large barn door and stepping inside a two-thousand-square-foot guardian against the end of the world. The barn contained a cache of goods that could keep his family alive and thriving for years if everything went to hell.

Having served six tours of duty in three war zones, he knew what hell was like and believed he could never be too prepared.

Along the back of the eighty-foot-long wall of exposed beams, Marcus had constructed a series of twelve-foot-high shelving units. The unit stretched for forty feet and featured six shelves, each two feet apart. He'd divided them into four ten-foot sections; dry goods, canned goods, toiletries, and first aid/hardware. He even managed a stash of antibiotics and corticosteroids. A former army medic who'd become a pharmaceutical sales rep had given him samples on trips through Abilene. They were common, broad-spectrum drugs with a decent shelf life, and the rep told him the drugs lasted long after the marked expiration date. Even if they lost some potency, Marcus thought it better to have something on hand in an emergency. TEOTWAWKI was definitely an emergency. Marcus would always pay for lunch in exchange for the supply.

It took him three years to fully stock all of the shelves, and as items were set to expire, he'd use them and purchase replacements. Marcus knew Sylvia thought at first it was a big waste of time and money, though she'd stopped complaining when a freak winter storm had blown through central Texas, crippled the power grid, and left the roads to and from their property impassable.

It was that storm that convinced her to let him buy a trio of Norcold freezers that ran on solar, natural gas, or electric current. They weren't cheap, but they could lengthen the life of their food storage by months. He kept two of them stocked with ground hamburger, chicken breasts, pork loin, and venison. The venison he'd hunted and dressed himself. There were even a couple of packages of boar sausage.

One of the three freezers, all of which were in a row against the western wall of the barn, was dedicated to water. It was filled from top to bottom with gallon jugs of frozen well water. If by some chance his well became contaminated or the pipes froze, the frozen jugs in the freezer would be the only potable water available. Once thawed, it might last his family a week or two. It was better than nothing. He used and refilled the jugs every month.

The eastern wall was lined with weapons. Inside a sliding locked cabinet that stretched most of the wall's twenty-five feet were wall racks replete with rifles, handguns, a shotgun shell press, boxes of ammunition, a composite bow and quiver, and a couple of dozen high-precision arrows.

Marcus also had a gun safe in the master bedroom closet of the main house, in which he kept his favorite sidearm and a sawed-off shotgun, which he jokingly called his "room broom". This armory was for the end of days he was certain he'd see in his lifetime.

As he always did, he checked the lock on that cabinet first, tugging on it before spinning the combination numbers on its bottom. He turned to his left and walked along the warehouse-style storage racks along the back of the barn. He scanned the shelves along the bottom, the items that expired more frequently, and pulled out his cell phone.

"Open notes," he said into the device. "I need AA and AAA batteries. Also I need another two boxes of Sudafed, three tubes of Neosporin, and five bottles of aspirin."

He walked the remaining shelves, checking expiration dates on bags of rice and cans of beans, soup, and tuna, before finishing his rounds with the freezers. His list wasn't as long as he'd anticipated, which was good. He'd spend less time at the store and less money.

Marcus closed the barn doors as he left, walking by the large natural-gas-powered generator that abutted the edge of the barn. Each of the three buildings had a dedicated emergency generator that automatically engaged in thirty seconds.

They were connected to a natural gas line that ran underneath his property. He'd reached an agreement years earlier to lease a section of his land to an energy speculator. When the play hit gas, the operator installed a gathering line exclusively for Marcus's use.

Central Texas was a huge source of natural gas, accounting for a large part of the fifty-eight thousand miles of pipeline that ran through the state. Unlike a lot of landowners, Marcus kept his mineral rights when he bought the land. That move allowed him to earn royalties on whatever was found beneath his property: oil, gas, a mixture of the two.

The speculator had been more than happy to accommodate Marcus's insistence on a free, virtually unlimited and uninterrupted flow of natural gas rather than paying out residuals on the find.

The in-kind deal allowed for the gas to flow from the well to a nearby field treatment plant that removed the sulfur, helium, and water from the otherwise dry gas. That gathering line, much narrower than the pipeline, carried clean gas directly back to the Battles' property.

Sylvia told Marcus she wasn't sure about the arrangement. She didn't like the idea of a gas well and the aboveground mechanics operating on her land. She thought her husband was foolhardy for turning down the monthly four-figure payout the residual would provide.

Marcus had insisted she think long term. Between the natural gas and the solar panels on the roofs of the barn, house, and garage, they were living off the grid. They had no electric bill, and when the worst happened, they'd be living like nothing happened. At least, that was the plan.

Marcus stepped onto the porch and opened the front door to his home. He was immediately leg tackled by his son.

"Is it finished?" The boy looked up vertically at Marcus, his eyes wide.

"Yes," Marcus said. "You'll be able to play in the fort until you shove off to college."

The boy buried his head in Marcus's legs and squeezed.

Marcus was right about so many things. His son shoving off to college someday wasn't among them.

CHAPTER 3

OCTOBER 13, 2037, 2:14 AM

SCOURGE +5 YEARS

EAST OF RISING STAR, TEXAS

Battle couldn't take his eyes off the woman slurping hot broth behind the steaming bowl she held to her face. She'd bathed and was wearing an oversized faded TCU T-shirt. The purple horned frog was barely visible from the wear. Her shorts, also Battle's, were cinched with a drawstring as tight as she could knot it. Her purplish, swollen ankle was expertly wrapped in an Ace bandage.

Her hair, still wet, was an auburn color, something he couldn't tell when she was dressed in the grime of the chase. Her face was drawn, her eyes sad, but there was something beautiful about her. The pain etched into the thin lines on her brow and her temples made her appear paradoxically vulnerable and resilient in a way Battle hadn't seen since Aleppo, a lifetime ago.

He shook off the thoughts of the battlefield and offered her more milk. She nodded from behind the bowl.

"You don't want to eat or drink too fast," he warned. "You're back out on your own in a couple of days. I don't want you sick."

She lowered the bowl and took a gulp of the milk before wiping her mouth with the back of her arm. "How do you have this? I haven't had milk since before the Scourge."

"It's powdered milk. I keep it in a vacuum-packed container and mix it with water when I need it. It's okay, but I really should have stopped using it a couple of years ago."

She held the glass at her lips and put it down. "Maybe I should have water."

He shrugged and glanced at the glass. "I haven't gotten sick. There's an aftertaste, that's about it."

She picked up the glass and took another sip. "Thank you."

"You said that. It's not a big deal. And you can't stay here long."

"You said that."

Battle walked back to his refrigerator and pulled out a bottle of well water. He uncapped it and took a swig. "You haven't told me your name."

She ran her finger through the bowl and licked it. "Lola."

"Lola, huh? I'm Battle."

She squeezed her eyebrows together, deepening the furrow between them. "Battle?"

"Yes. Who were those men?"

She traced the inside of the empty bowl with her finger, her eyes avoiding contact with his. "They're part of the Cartel."

"What's that?" Battle took another swig and leaned on the counter.

What little color flushed her cheeks vanished. She spoke slowly, every word sounding calculated. "You don't know what the Cartel is? You don't know who they are?"

"No."

"How is that possible?" she asked. "They control everything, at least for two hundred and seventy thousand square miles."

"What do you mean *everything*?"

"Everything," she repeated, her eyes lifting to meet his. "They run the water, the gas, what little power we have. They control the food supply and the roads."

Battle studied her face, the concern in her eyes, and the barely visible tremble in her lower lip. "Never heard of 'em."

"Then how do you have all this?" she asked, waving her hands around the room. "Power, running water, cold milk, and hot soup?"

Battle considered the limitless number of answers to that question and chose the easiest. "I just do."

"And they let you?"

"Nobody *lets* me."

"It's been five years since the Scourge started," she said. "How have they not taken this from you? How do they not know you and you not know them? I can't be the first person to come here."

"You're the only one who's lived to talk about it, except for the one who got away tonight."

She sat up and backed her body away from the counter. "So you kill everybody."

"Yes."

"Wh—"

Battle held his finger to his lips. He needed to think.

These weren't random scavengers or thugs. They were organized criminals with bosses. How the Cartel hadn't found him until now was miraculous. But the blessing was over. The one who got away would be coming back with reinforcements.

"Wh—" Lola tried again. He shushed her again.

He didn't have much time. He needed as many answers from Lola as he could get: who she was, how she'd become involved with the Cartel, how she escaped, what she knew about the men he'd killed and the one who escaped. Any actionable intelligence was critical to their survival.

"They're coming back," he told her. "They'll kill both of us unless you tell me everything you know about them. And I need to know everything about you. Understood?"

Lola nodded and tears welled in her eyes.

***

OCTOBER 13, 2037, 7:42 AM

SCOURGE +5 YEARS

EAST OF RISING STAR, TEXAS

They sat on the back porch, the sun casting its earliest shadows from the east. Battle looked to the right, seeing the orange glow peek through the tangle of oaks and mesquite beyond the fence line.

Neither he nor Lola had slept while she'd carefully unpacked her story. Battle struggled to understand her. At times she spoke in fragments and non sequiturs. He knew she was leaving out details, but conceded to himself those were left in her head.

He slid his palms along the cracked arms of his Adirondack chair. She rocked back and forth, rhythmically pushing with the ball of her uninjured foot in the high-back chair next to him.

"So after you left Louisiana," Battle coaxed, "you moved west into Texas and found shelter in Tyler."

She nodded. "After my husband was killed, we couldn't stay there. Louisiana was always supposed to be a waypoint for us anyway. I didn't know anybody. The shelters were overflowing. It was lawless there, and that was before the Cartel."

"What did you do in Tyler? You still haven't told me how the Cartel kidnapped you."

She stopped rocking. "My son, Sawyer, he — I — we did what we had to do."

"And the Cartel?"

"They moved north from the border and east from Arizona, I think," Lola said. "I don't know, really. There are so many rumors and legends about them, I'm not sure what's true. I still can't believe you don't know about them."

"I don't have television," he said. "And I rarely listen to the radio, shortwave or otherwise."

"Why?"

"There's nothing out there for me. My world starts and stops here. I need to focus on protecting what's mine, not concern myself with the outside world." Battle shifted in his seat and then redirected the conversation. "This is not about me, right now. I need to know about you and the Cartel."

Lola looked north, toward the vegetable garden directly behind the house, and shuddered. "My son," she said, swallowing against what she was about to tell him, "he stole from them."

"What did he steal?"

"An orange."

"An orange?" Battle looked at Lola. A tear rolled from the corner of her eye down her cheek. He was surprised she had any tears left. "That's it?"

"Yes," she said and sniffed. "He was hungry. Food distribution wasn't for another day and—"

"Food distribution?"

"Yes," she said. "I told you, they control everything. Everything."

"So he stole the orange..."

"From a man in our apartment building," she said. "He wasn't home. His door was unlocked. Sawyer always saw the man with food, so he snuck in to take an orange. The man walked in on him."

"I'm assuming he was Cartel." Battle pinched the bridge of his nose and rubbed the lack of sleep from his eyes. "The man. That's why he always had food?"

Lola nodded and buried her face in her hands. Battle let her cry without interruption or consolation. He started to reach for her a couple of times, but stopped himself. He waited until the emotional wave subsided.

"What did they do?" he asked.

"They made us their slaves."

"You were already a slave, though," Battle reasoned. "Weren't you?"

"We were more like indentured servants," she corrected him. "We got paid. We worked at a laundry. It was the only job I could find for us. It was enough to survive, most of the time. When Sawyer stole from them, when he took one orange so he wouldn't go to bed hungry again, they took our jobs from us. They made us work on one of their farms, in the fields. Sunup to sundown. They moved us to a commune. Thirty-two people in a room. Sixteen beds."

"How old is he?"

"Thirteen."

"When did this happen?"

"Six months ago."

"Where is he now?"

Lola's face lost all expression, her eyes fixed in the distance. She began rocking again, faster than before, her foot pumping up and down. Up. Down. Up. Down. Battle thought she hadn't heard the question, so he repeated it.

"Where is he now?"

Nothing.

"Lola!"

Her eyes fluttered and the rocking slowed. She turned to Battle and looked him in the eyes for long enough that Battle had to glance away.

"He's still with them," she said. "There were four of us who tried to escape. Two were…they didn't make it out of the commune. Sawyer and I made it out. We ran. We ran…so fast…"

"How far did you get?"

"We were gone for a couple of days, I think," she said. "We fell asleep. Somewhere not far from here. Maybe a couple of hours. They found us. Followed our tracks maybe, or moles ratted us out, I don't know. But they found us.

"They grabbed me first," she said, her lower lip quivering again. "Sawyer kicked one of them and that distracted them. I got free and…"

"And what?"

"He told me to run." She popped up from the rocking chair and turned away from Battle, balancing herself on her good leg. "Sawyer yelled for me to run. I didn't want to. A mother shouldn't—"

"You ran."

Though her back was to Battle, he could see her head nod, backlit against the rising sun. Her shoulders trembled and she sobbed.

Battle slowly rose and stepped closer to Lola. His hands felt foreign to him, as if they were someone else's, and he reached out to place them on her heaving shoulders. She flinched when he touched her then turned and threw her arms around him. He froze for a moment before pulling her into his body and holding her.

His fingers could count her ribs against her back. She was muscle and bone. Lola had suffered since the Scourge. Battle felt guilty for his relative fortune.

She pulled away from him, gripping his arms as she stepped back, the thick callouses on her fingers grazing Battle's triceps. "I went back for him. I didn't run far. I turned around and followed them. There were five of them. One of them was on a horse. The rest of them were walking. They had Sawyer tied to the horse."

"So he's alive."

"I think so," she said. "I wasn't able to follow them for long before one of them spotted me. The one on the horse took Sawyer and ordered the rest of them to catch me. He yelled after them that they might as well not come back to the commune if they didn't get me."

"And they chased you here?"

"Yes. I had maybe a five-minute head start on them. I ran for an hour maybe. In circles. Finally, I saw your gravel road and thought I might find a hiding place."

Battle smirked. "I guess you did."

"Thank you again."

"Don't thank me," Battle said, looking toward the sun, which was clear of the nearest oaks in a cloudless sky. The air was crisp. He took a deep breath. "I was protecting myself as much as I was saving you."

Lola folded her arms across her chest. Goosebumps popped on her bare arms, products of the early morning cool and the darkness that lay ahead.

"So what's your plan?" Battle asked. He knew the answer.

"I've got to find my son," she said. She looked up at Battle, her eyes pleading with him. "Will you help me?"

Battle took a step back from Lola and looked at the limestone pavers beneath their feet. He focused on the worn brown leather toe of his boot. "Sorry, Lola. Not a chance."

***

OCTOBER 13, 2037, 8:17 AM

SCOURGE + 5 YEARS

TEXAS HIGHWAY 36

BETWEEN RISING STAR AND ABILENE

Salomon Pico was heading northwest toward Abilene. He slowed from a jog to a walk, out of breath and beginning to taste the dryness in his mouth. He needed to slow down. He shook the last couple of water drops from his canteen and clipped it back onto his belt.

His feet were sore and the sting of blisters were bubbling on the back of his booted heels. He had another eight hours of walking, he guessed, but he wasn't sure if he wanted to make it.

The posse boss told him not to come back if he didn't have the woman with him. Three of his Cartel brothers had heeded the warning and wound up dead. He'd run instead. Whoever their killer was, he was too much for Salomon. The slightly built, wiry henchman was only good in a pack. When the last of his brothers died, he knew he needed to bug out.

He rubbed the back of his neck, then ran his sweaty hand up along the back of his bald head. The sun was rising in the East. It would be warmer soon and the walk would be tougher. Even in October, Abilene could have its hot spells.

He licked his cracked upper lip, feeling the bristle of his thick mustache, and pounded his feet along the edge of the asphalt one step at a time.

Salomon Pico knew there would be hell to pay at the end of the long walk. That, as much as his exhaustion, fueled his decision to walk instead of run. He needed time to think of the best way to handle his failure.

Pico was low on the Cartel totem pole. He didn't even have a rank or a title. Nobody answered to him. He was a grunt and he knew it.

However, Pico reckoned that being a low man on the only totem that mattered was better than being atop a heap of losers. That was how he saw the world after the Scourge — Cartel and losers.

He adjusted his jeans, which were riding up his crotch. The sweat was chafing him in uncomfortable places. The jeans didn't fit right anyhow. He hadn't owned the right fit of jeans in over a year. Grunts couldn't be choosers. They were grunts.

Or better yet, Pico secretly told himself, he was a runt. He suckled at the smallest tit, if and when it was available.

His mind drifted as he walked, back to the days before the Scourge. He had a 2019 Camaro, a condo in Fort Worth, and a girlfriend who danced at a local club where he tended bar. He'd occasionally delve into the criminal world. A petty thief, Pico had a knack for cracking safes. It was a skill that paid enough to keep his girlfriend with him long after he knew she wasn't interested anymore. It was a sad relationship but exactly what Pico thought he deserved. He thought about that Camaro, imagining himself behind the wheel and cruising the interstate. The windows were down, or better yet, the air-conditioning was cranked. The music was cranked. Maybe old ZZ Top. "La Grange". His woman in the seat next to him, her hand on his leg.

He was so enraptured with the mirage he didn't see the man in a cowboy hat riding horseback and galloping toward him.

"Pico!" the man yelled, snapping the grunt from his daydream. "Where are the others?"

Pico focused on the man, looking up at him as he gathered his wits about him. His own pitiful reflection stared back at him from the man's reflective sunglasses. "You have some water?" He plucked his empty canteen from his hip and waved it at the man.

"I got water," he said, dismounting from the horse, landing awkwardly on a club foot. "But you gotta tell me what happened to the others. Why are you out here wandering on the highway?"

"There were…problems."

"What kind of problems?" The man took a canteen from his saddlebag but kept it at arm's length. He balanced himself against the horse, tugging on the leathers above the stirrup iron.

"She ran down some road to a house." Pico eyed the water. "It was more than a house. It was like a fort. There was a guy there." He reached for the canteen.

The man pulled it back. "What guy?"

"I dunno." Pico licked his lips. "He was like Mad Max. He ambushed us."

"So they're dead."

"Yes."

"And the woman?"

"I dunno."

"Because you left."

Pico hung his head. "I had no choice. He would have killed me."

"And…" The man slid his free hand onto his holster.

Pico tried to rearrange his jumbled thoughts, sensing the clock was ticking fast. "And if he'd killed me, then I couldn't come back and tell you where she is," he spat. "I couldn't have led you to them. I couldn't have helped you—"

The man held up his hand, pulling it from the holster. "I got it." He reached out with the other hand, giving Pico the canteen. "You make a good point. I'm surprised, but you did the right thing, Pico."

Pico uncapped the canteen and poured the water into his mouth, as much of it running down the sides of his face as his throat. He gulped and gasped. He only stopped when he choked.

"Easy there, Pico." The man adjusted the wide-brimmed brown cowboy hat on his head, tilting it lower on his forehead. The Cartel posse bosses wore brown cowboy hats. It was as much a warning to others as it was a privilege to the men who wore them.

Pico stopped coughing and caught his breath. "Thank you, Queho. Thank you."

Queho leaned on his good foot and took back the empty canteen. "Don't thank me yet," he said. "I ain't decided if you're living long term. I'm just not killing you here and now."

Pico thanked him again and went to shake Queho's hand. Queho stepped back.

"We're not friends, Pico. You work for me. How it's always been and how it's always gonna be." Queho stuffed the canteen into the saddlebag, gripped the pommel, and pulled himself onto the horse. "Get on," he ordered without offering a hand.

Pico clumsily reached with one hand onto the cantle on the back of the wide saddle. He stuffed the other hand under the saddle and gripped the gullet. With what little strength he had left, he managed to heave himself on the back of the horse and swing a leg over to the other side.

"I didn't think you'd make it," Queho said. He chuckled and dug his spurs into the side of the horse, yanking the reins to turn it around. The horse snorted, shook its head, and trotted northwest back to Abilene.

"We should be there in fifteen minutes or so," Queho called back to Pico. "You're gonna need to tell the men what you told me. Give us details. Tell us what you know about the fort."

"When are we going back?" Pico had his hands behind him, white-knuckling the back of the saddle. As the horse picked up speed, he held on tighter. He wasn't about to ask Queho if he could hold onto him.

"When I say." Queho pulled tight on the reins, stopping the horse. A stray mutt, mange creeping along its back and ears, was walking in the dirt some twenty yards to the right of the highway. Queho pulled a revolver from his hip and leveled it at the dog, tracking it as it slugged along, head dragging. "It'll be soon."

Pow! The shot rolled along the open plain like thunder. The dog dropped dead, the single bullet ending its sad life before it could yelp.

"I hate dogs," said Queho. He holstered the six-shooter and spurred the horse.

Pico affixed his grip as they gathered speed, his eyes on the dead mutt bleeding out in the dirt.

CHAPTER 4

AUGUST 5, 2032, 12:04 PM

SCOURGE -2 MONTHS

ABILENE, TEXAS

Bible Hardware was located at 333 Walnut Street between Third and Fourth Streets in historic Abilene. Family owned and always stocked, Marcus Battle preferred Bible to the other places in town.

He pulled his 2025 F150 up to the curb in front of the store, parking in front of the painted green awning that hung at the entrance. He looked across the wide street at the back of the main post office. The fenced parking lot was dotted with white mail trucks. He walked through the open glass double doors. A woman sat in a swivel chair at the entrance, surrounded on three sides by a large blue counter. Marcus said hello, grabbed a basket, and shuffled down the aisles, checking his phone for his list.

Shopping Bible Hardware was like stepping back in time. The store hadn't changed all that much since it had opened ninety years earlier. There was something comforting about the familiarity of it, though the irony of shopping there for the end of the world as he knew it wasn't lost on Marcus.

A kind older man named Don walked up to Marcus and patted him on the back. "Can I help you?" He laughed when Marcus turned around. "Oh, Marcus! I didn't recognize you with that ball cap pulled over your head."

"Hi, Don." Marcus took his hand and gripped it. "I'm good. Only got a few items on the list today."

"What's the date?" Don asked, stuffing his hands into the front pocket of his work apron.

"For what?"

"TEOTWAWKI?"

Marcus chuckled and dropped a package of AAA batteries in the basket. "I couldn't tell you, Don. That's a question for Sunday mornings. I want to be prepared when it comes."

Don winked. "Seems like Sunday morning would be the best time to get prepared. We haven't seen you in a few weeks."

"No excuses," Marcus said. "We just haven't made the time. We should, I know. It's good for us, and our boy loves Sunday school."

"No judgment," Don said. "I promise. But we'd love to see you."

"I got it. I shop at a place called Bible Hardware, I'm bound to talk about church, right?"

Don winked again, gave Marcus a thumbs-up, and backed down the aisle. "Let me know if you need anything. Say hi to Sylvia for me."

"Will do, Don." Marcus waved goodbye and found the AA batteries. He dropped several packages into his basket and rounded the corner, looking for LED lightbulbs. Even though they didn't expire, he liked keeping a stockpile of five for every bulb in the house. He needed a couple to round out the requisite stockpile.

He cut through the pesticide aisle and found Don helping a woman who wouldn't stop scratching her head.

"Hey, Marcus," Don said. "You got any pets?"

"No." Marcus made a wide berth around the head scratcher. "Why?"

"This young lady here is the fifth person this week to come here looking for flea prevention."

"Is that unusual?"

"It is because all the vets are out," Don answered. "Apparently there's some sort of flea outbreak."

"Hadn't heard about it."

"Something about the unusually warm summer all over the country."

"It's always hot down here." Marcus inched past Don and stopped at the end of the aisle. "So I wouldn't have figured."

"True enough." Don winked and turned back to the itchy woman.

Marcus finished his shopping and plunked the loaded basket onto the counter. He still had a half hour to grab some refills at the grocery store and hit the ETA he'd promised to Sylvia.

"No flea dip, Marcus?" the clerk asked, scanning the batteries, some six-inch-long galvanized plumbing pipe, and a rubber mallet. "You're about the first one today who hasn't had it in their basket or asked me where to find it."

"I didn't even know you carried it," he said, reaching for his phone. He slid it over the payment panel at the edge of the counter and waited for the total.

"There's been a run on it," she said, finishing up the scan. "Crazy, right? We can't keep it in stock. I hear it's a problem all over the world. Fleas are the new locusts." She laughed.

Marcus closed his eyes, recalling the exact words from Exodus. *"And the Lord said to Moses, 'Stretch out your hand over Egypt so that locusts swarm over the land and devour everything growing in the fields, everything left by the hail.'"*

"Wow, Marcus," she said, nodding her head. "Had no idea you were so well versed with the good book."

"I don't advertise it."

"Let's hope it's not the end of days." She chuckled. "It would be awful if the good Lord promised no more locusts and tricked us by swapping them out for fleas."

"Glad I don't have a dog." Marcus bagged his bounty himself and gathered the bags.

"I have three cats," she said and stuffed a paper receipt into one of the plastic bags. "They've got flea collars. Seems to do the trick. Plus they're inside only. That helps."

"I bet it does." Marcus smiled. "See you next time." He carried his bags out through the open doors, stepped from the curb, and tossed the bags into the bed of the truck. His cell phone buzzed.

"I'm on time," he said preemptively.

"It's not that," Sylvia said. "I need a few extra things at the grocery. I'll text you the list."

"Does it include more wine?"

"It does," she purred. "Hurry back."

"Will do. Send me the text. Love you."

"Love you."

Marcus knew these were the salad days.

CHAPTER 5

OCTOBER 13, 2037, 10:15 AM

SCOURGE +5 YEARS

EAST OF RISING STAR, TEXAS

"They're coming back," Battle insisted. "From what you've told me about these guys, they're not for letting bygones be bygones. They sent a search party to find you and your son. They're not going to look the other way at losing three of their men."

He drove the spade into the dry Texas dirt and shoveled out another load, making the hole another couple of inches deeper. Lola stood behind him, her arms folded across her chest.

"You're only making my point for me," she whined.

"How so?" Battle grunted mid-dig. He was a machine, standing in the hole he'd been digging for the last two hours. They were on the back edge of his acreage, hidden behind a cluster of mesquite. He stopped to grab a swig of water from a large bottle and wiped his forehead with the back of his gloved hand.

"If they're coming back, we shouldn't be here. We should run. And if we should run, we should go find my son. I can't do it without you. I'm hurt. I don't have the strength or the ability to kill people, so..."

Battle blinked against the sweat in his eyes and turned back to his job, stabbing the dirt with the shovel, pulling up the dirt, and tossing it to the edge of the hole. Stab. Pull. Toss. Stab. Pull. Toss.

"Are you listening to me?" Lola leaned forward to press her point. "We shouldn't stay."

"I'm not going anywhere." Stab. Pull. Toss. "This is my home." Stab. Pull. Toss. "I'm alive because I stayed here. I'd be dead if I left." Stab. Pull. Toss.

"My son will die if you don't."

Battle stopped and planted the spade in the dirt at his feet. "I understand that's a possibility. But you have to understand something. You are not my responsibility. My responsibility to others died with the Scourge. Like I said, you can stay a week or so, until you can walk, and then you have to go."

"You're really kicking me out? Throwing me to those — those *wolves*?"

"I saved you from the wolves."

"Not if you're kicking me out. Not if you're refusing to help me find my son."

Battle used the handle of the shovel as leverage to step from the hole. He moved a step from Lola and stuck a gloved finger in her face.

"I didn't ask for this," he jabbed. "I almost shot you on sight last night. Maybe I should have. The longer you're here, the more danger I face. You have to understand, the world of compassion and helping thy neighbor died with two-thirds of the world's population. I'm a nice guy. But I don't have a death wish."

Lola's arms were locked at her sides, her hands balled into tight fists. "If you're not going to help me, you might as well have pulled that trigger. I'd just as soon be dead than live in a world where even a *nice guy* has lost his humanity."

She limped back toward the gate at the back fence. Battle watched her huff off for a beat before returning to work.

Stab. Pull. Toss. Stab. Pull. Toss. Stab. Pull. Toss.

"This is exactly why I stay to myself," he mumbled to himself. "Exactly why. I should have killed her. I wouldn't have known any different."

In the months after the Scourge had ravaged his family and countless others, Battle considered assimilation. He thought about inviting others to stay with him, to form a survival cooperative. He'd clear more land, expand the farming capabilities of his acreage, and indoctrinate up to a half dozen people into his way of thinking and doing.

He prayed about it. He did the mathematical calculations. Ultimately, he decided against it.

There was no way to vet the people he'd invite. Since returning from war and retiring from the military, he'd chosen to live a Spartan life.

His job had allowed him to live anywhere. He and Sylvia had bought property in the middle of nowhere, and when she was seven months pregnant, they'd moved from base housing at Fort Hood to their land near County Road 133 in Eastland County, Texas. The closest town was Rising Star, less than two square miles in size with a population of seven-hundred sixty-two.

"We don't have any neighbors," Sylvia had said, standing in the middle of the fifty acres with both hands on her belly. "And we barely have any trees."

"I can plant some. I'll put them all over the place. They'll be good cover."

"Neighbors?"

"Trees."

"What about neighbors?"

"We don't want any. That's the whole point of this."

Sylvia hadn't loved it. She'd missed her army wives and weekly margarita nights. Marcus traveled too much, and she was alone at least a half dozen nights every month. But she'd willingly given up civilization to have her man with her most of the time, in whatever circumstances.

They'd lived in a large Winnebago for close to two years while Marcus oversaw construction of the main house, the barn, and the garage. Aside from a week in Eastland Memorial Hospital when their son was born and one weekend a month in an Abilene hotel, they'd survived in close quarters.

"It's better than sleeping in a bunker," he'd frequently said.

"But not better than a latrine," she'd frequently replied.

Sylvia had been a saint of a woman. What woman wasn't when she supported the man she loved? For all the nights he was half a world away, she'd take him and their baby cuddled together in a twenty-five-by-seven-foot home on wheels.

A couple of nearby farmers stopped by during the construction. They were busybodies, nothing more. Neither offered help nor friendship.

One woman from a church in Abilene had brought a peach pie a week after they finished construction. Sylvia had met her at Bible Hardware and had opened up to her about their plans.

That was the one and only time she'd come by the place, though they had seen her every once in a while on Sunday mornings. Her name was Marge.

It was by design that Marcus had no friends or trusted neighbors before the Scourge. As such, he had none after it. The prospect of trying to trust people during desperate times had been too daunting and unpredictable for the skeptical soldier to risk.

Stab. Pull. Toss. Stab. Pull. Toss. Stab. Pull. Toss.

Battle stood elbow deep in the five-foot-long hole. He reckoned it was big enough for the task and climbed his way out. A few feet from the hole he grabbed the hand grips on a wheelbarrow and heaved it forward. The front brace creaked its disapproval of the weight, as did Battle's knees. He slogged forward to the edge of the hole.

Rather than dumping the contents into the hole, he grabbed each of the men by their legs and dragged them over the edge, rolling them into what would be their collective grave.

All three of them, one on top of the other, heaped into the hole. They were starting to stiffen, which made the task tougher. Once they were inside, he said a prayer for them and began the burial process.

Stab. Pull. Toss. Stab. Pull. Toss. Stab. Pull. Toss.

"You prayed for their souls?" Lola had returned. She was leaning up against a thirty-year-old oak without any foliage. "Why would you do that?"

Battle stopped shoveling and let out a sigh. "Why wouldn't I?"

"They tried to kill you."

"All the more reason I should pray for them."

She pursed her lips and used her back to push herself from the tree before taking several steps toward Battle. "You still believe?"

"In what?"

"God?"

Battle laughed. "Of course. Why wouldn't I?"

She wiped her reddened nose with the back of her hand. Her eyes were swollen. "Why would you?"

"God tries us," Battle said. "He challenges us. He hurts. He lifts us up. To me, God is never more present than in the darkness. I don't need God's strength when everything is good. I need it when I'm faced with a bunch of dudes from the Cartel coming to my house wanting to hurt me."

Battle turned back to look at the bodies half covered in dirt at the bottom of the hole. Tangled together, their limbs were indistinguishable from one another. The men had had mothers and fathers, maybe siblings and spouses. It was possible they even had kids. The Scourge had affected them too. They did what *they* had to do to survive, just as he had done. Though there was no excuse for enslaving a woman and her son, Battle wasn't judging them for that. He killed them because he had to kill them. Only God would judge them for why they made the decisions they'd made, just as He would someday judge Battle.

"You were crying?"

Lola nodded.

Battle looked at her for a moment and then turned back to the shovel. He adjusted the gloves on his hands, pulling them tight on his fingers, and dug into the shrinking pile of dirt and roots at the edge of the hole. Stab. Pull. Toss. Stab. Pull. Toss. Stab. Pull. Toss.

"How can you have mercy on their souls and not mine?"

Battle ignored her at first. He wanted to finish the job. Stab. Pull. Toss. Stab. Pull. Toss. Stab. Pull. Toss.

"Bat," she repeated more loudly, "can you have mercy on their souls and not mine?"

Stab. Pull. Toss. Stab. Pull. Toss. Stab. Pull. Toss.

"Hold on a second." Battle drove the shovel into the dirt and walked over to his guest. His chest was heaving up and down, his pulse quickened, as much by the challenge of the work as the challenge from Lola.

"You pray for them," she said, "but you'll kick me out and let me die. Let my son die."

Battle wondered why she was pushing. Did she sense a weakness? Was she trying to manipulate his faith? He knew she was desperate. He'd be desperate too. He couldn't relent. He couldn't go on a fool's mission, abandoning his home in the hopes of finding a boy who may not even be alive.

"It isn't like that," he said through a clenched jaw. "You can't judge me for how I live my life. You can't make assumptions about why I do what I do. If you don't like it, you can leave now. I've broken every rule I've made for myself by letting you live, by letting you stay. If you keep pushing me, I will break. And I'll send you back into the wilderness with nothing."

Lola didn't argue with him. She didn't pout or turn back to the house. She dropped to her knees, there in the leaves and dirt, and clasped her hands in prayer. She asked God for help. She asked He keep her son safe. She asked He help her navigate the road ahead. She asked He protect her host, despite his obstinacy.

By the time she rose from her knees, Battle was finished burying the dead. He had one hand around the shovel and the other placed on Lola's back, leading her toward the house.

"I need your help," he said. "We have to prepare for the possibility of an attack. Prayer can only do so much."

***

OCTOBER 13, 2037, 10:46 AM

SCOURGE +5 YEARS

ABILENE, TEXAS

Queho hopped from his horse, landing on his good foot first. He adjusted his hat, slid his sunglasses up his nose, and loosely looped the reins over a waist-high wooden post outside the Cartel's Abilene headquarters.

"Hurry up," he called to Salomon Pico. "We got stuff to do." He stepped onto the cement curb under the large green awning in front of the building. His club foot ached, as it did every day, as he pushed his way through the double glass doors. He didn't acknowledge either of the grunts standing guard at the entrance.

"You don't look good, Sal," one of the guards said to Pico.

Pico stepped slowly onto the curb. "Don't ask."

"Where's everybody else?" the other guard asked.

Pico waved him off and followed Queho with a push through the entrance. "Don't ask."

Pico walked into the dimly lit building, thankful for the blast of cold air greeting him. Smoky and stale, the HQ resembled a saloon as much as it did the place where the Cartel ran much of Central Texas. He found Queho off to the right, joining a group of cowboy-hatted posse bosses, but kept his distance until Queho called him over.

Queho shifted in the high-back wooden chair. He was one of five posse bosses sitting at the round table, along with an area captain named Cyrus Skinner. He wore a white hat and was blowing smoke from his nose, a cigarette hanging from his thick lower lip.

"Tell them what you told me," Queho instructed.

"Which part?" Pico asked.

Queho looked around the table and locked his eyes on Skinner, who sat across from him. "The part about Mad Max."

Pico shrugged and shrank against the eyes of the bosses. He swallowed hard.

"Tell us about Mad Max," Skinner growled. His voice was a deep gravel pit. "This single man who killed three of our brothers."

"I-I-I never s-s-saw him up close," Pico stuttered. "It was dark. But I saw his shadow. He was fast and strong. He shot straight."

"You never saw him?"

Pico shrugged again. "Like I said, boss, it was dark. I only caught a glimpse of him."

"And you're sure it was only one man?" asked Queho. "You told me you were sure."

"I'm sure."

Skinner took another long drag, the smoke circling his hat. "How is it we didn't know about this man?" His eyes moved from Pico to sweep the table. "We've been in control of this area for more than three years, ever since the US got out of Texas. How did we not find this man and take care of him a long time ago?"

The brown hats shook back and forth. The men wearing them had no answer for their captain.

Skinner took another long, slow drag and then slammed his fist on the table. His face contorted with anger and his lips curled. "WHY DID WE NOT KNOW ABOUT HIM?!"

All the bosses but Queho buried their heads behind their brown hats. None of them had an answer. Queho, though, looked Skinner in the eyes.

Pico took a step back from the table, partially hiding in the shadow cast by an overhead beam.

"We got about two hundred seventy thousand square miles to look after, Skin, and a good quarter of that falls under your command," he drawled. "I ain't gonna apologize for missin' one badass dude in the middle of nowhere on some backward county road."

Skinner flexed his fist and stared at the back of his hand as he spoke. "I hear you, Queho. But there's no excuse for losing three men to one badass dude. Especially when we were trying to wrangle a woman and her kid after they escaped right out from under our noses."

"You got a point. I think the question now ain't what we did or didn't do, it's what we do now. We got the boy back. Now we need to go get the woman and erase the badass Mad Max."

Skinner popped another cigarette between his lips and lit it. He sucked his chest full and held it before exhaling. "What's your idea?"

"Let's hit him fast. Big firepower. A lot of men."

"How many men?"

Queho looked around at the other posse bosses. As he met their eyes, one by one they looked away. His lips wormed into a smile. They were gutless.

"I'll start with every posse boss at this table," he said. "And I'll take four of their men."

"Twenty men?" Skinner took the cigarette between two fingers and flicked the ash onto the floor. "That it?"

Queho shook his head. "No. I'm going too. And I'm taking Pico. He knows where the place is and knows the rough layout."

Skinner nodded and let the cigarette droop from his lip. "That makes sense. Pico, what do you think?"

Pico looked at Skinner. "I think—"

"I don't care what you think," Skinner cut in. "You're going."

Pico slipped back into the shadow, digging his hands deeper into his pockets.

"Thanks, Skin." Queho chuckled. "Pico knows he's needed. He knows he doesn't have a choice."

"What else do you need?" Skinner puffed.

"I'll give you a list." Queho pushed back from the table and stood. He shot a look at each of the other bosses. "I'm in charge," he said to nobody in particular.

"When are you going?" Skinner raised one eyebrow higher than the other. "You said you wanted to hit him fast."

"Tonight," Queho said. "We go tonight."

CHAPTER 6

OCTOBER 2, 2032, 2:00 AM

SCOURGE +/- 0 DAYS

EAST OF RISING STAR, TEXAS

Sylvia couldn't sleep, which meant Marcus couldn't sleep. The bedroom television was turned to cable news.

"...appears to have begun in Iranian refugee camps. The pneumonia is believed to come from a deadly bacterial strain scientists have isolated to Yersinia pestis. *It's airborne, spreads rapidly, and can kill its host within forty-eight hours in extreme conditions. Reporter John Mubarak brings us the latest from a camp north of the Iran-Turkmenistan border near the city of Ashbagat."*

"Do we have to watch this?" Marcus was bleary-eyed, having spent much of the previous week finishing the fence line security system. He'd worked twenty hours a day, testing and retesting. He buried his head under a pillow.

"This is important," Sylvia said, aiming the remote at the television to increase the volume. "They're saying it's like a plague."

"...journey through the mountains of northeastern Iran to reach this camp was challenge enough for the thousands who braved it," said the reporter. *"Now that they're here, they're facing a graver danger in this tent city with close quarters. A deadly disease international doctors have nicknamed* the Scourge *is ravaging those at their most vulnerable."*

Marcus adjusted his pillow so he could see the screen. "The Scourge? That's a little dramatic, isn't it?"

"For the world's biggest prepper, I'd figure you for taking this as dramatically as it's being presented."

"I'm not saying it's not bad, I'm saying the name of the illness is over the top."

"It's only over the top if it's not killing your family."

"Maybe."

"The illness begins with a fever, a headache, and weakness, quickly deteriorating into pneumonia. If medication isn't administered within the first twenty-four hours, the mortality rate is an astonishing ninety-five percent."

Marcus sat up in bed. "That's scary."

"In camps like this, an airborne illness is the worst kind..."

Marcus reached for his iPad at the side of his bed and tapped open the browser. "What did he say the name of the disease was?"

"It's pneumonia," said Sylvia.

"No. What kind of pneumonia?"

"I don't know."

"Rewind it."

Sylvia rewound the report to the beginning of the reporter's introduction. The woman on the screen was sitting on the news set with a large graphic behind her emblazoned with the words *A New Plague?* She hit play.

"...bacterial strain scientists have isolated to Yersinia pestis. *It's airborne..."*

"Yersinia pestis," Marcus said and typed the words into his tablet. His lips moved as he read through the results, his eyes widening with every finger scroll.

"What is it?" Sylvia paused the television again. "What does it say?"

"It says it really is the plague," Marcus answered. "It's the pneumonic plague, a bacterial pneumonia spread by rats and fleas. There is no vaccine, but fast treatment of it with ampicillin or tetracycline usually knocks it out."

"The reporter said fast treatment works."

"Still..."

"Still what?"

Marcus clicked off the iPad. "There are so many of those refugee camps over there. Five or six in Turkmenistan, another half dozen in Afghanistan, which is crazy. Who wants to flee to Afghanistan, right? That's how bad it is in Iran. And that's not counting the countless hordes who've left Syria and are living in slums outside its borders. Then there's the Ukrainians. They've fled Russian control and have gone north to temporary shelters in Belarus or headed west into Moldova, where hundreds of thousands are living in tent cities there."

Sylvia leaned into Marcus and put her hand on his chest. "What does all of that have to do with pneumonia? Belarus is nowhere near Turkmenistan."

"All of these places have volunteer doctors," said Marcus. "They hop from one hot spot to the next, doing good, getting medicine and supplies to those who need it."

"And?"

"And all it takes is one of these do-gooders to get infected in one bacteria-laden camp and, without knowing he or she is sick, carry it to the next one."

"Spreading it."

"Yes."

"That *is* scary," Sylvia said. "I mean, I knew it was scary. That's why I was interested in watching the report. But now, knowing it's even scarier—"

"You wished you hadn't watched it?"

She gently stroked his face. "No. I'm glad you watched it with me."

"Me too."

"You don't think it'll get this far, though, do you?"

Marcus took his wife's hand and pulled it around his neck, rolling onto his side to face her. "I wish I could say no. But I can't. That's why I'm doing what I'm doing. I've never thought a catastrophe *might* happen. I just wondered *when* it would."

CHAPTER 7

OCTOBER 13, 2037, 11:30 AM

SCOURGE +5 YEARS

EAST OF RISING STAR, TEXAS

Lola nodded at a pair of photographs stuck to the kitchen refrigerator. "What was your son's name?"

Battle was washing dishes and she was drying them. He looked over his shoulder toward the fridge. "Wesson." He turned back to the sink and squeezed the suds from a sponge. "Wes for short."

She opened a cabinet and slid a plate on top of a stack. "Why Wesson?"

"Two reasons. It's my wife's maiden name. And I've always like Smith & Wesson."

"It's a nice name."

"Thanks."

"What was your wife's name?"

"Sylvia." He handed her another dish and filled a cup with water.

"Pretty name."

"Thanks." He handed her the cup. "We need to get going. We've wasted too much time."

"Eating?"

"They're coming back. I need to be ready. And as long as you're here, you need to be ready. You can help me."

"Fine." She put the cup in the cabinet and closed the door. "What are we doing?"

"Follow me." Battle dried his hands on a dish towel and led Lola from the kitchen back to the front entry hall.

"I'm going to run you through the basics of how we're set up here. You don't need to know everything, but I'll run you through the basics in case they attack, we get separated, and I need your help."

"Okay."

Battle stepped to the wall next to the front door. "These switches are critical. They control power to the house. Typically, I'm running on solar. That's this switch. If the solar drains too low, the power flips to natural gas. Generators power up within thirty seconds and everything goes back to normal."

Lola looked at Battle as if he were speaking Persian. "You don't get your power from the Cartel?"

"No."

"Everybody gets their power from the Cartel. They control the grid."

"I'm on my own," he explained. "I haven't been on the grid in years. I'm solar with a natural gas backup."

"What about water? Don't you have to pay them for your water?"

"I'm on a well. My septic system is okay. I have three tanks. One is full. I also collect rainwater in a cistern to irrigate the garden out back."

"Internet?"

"I don't have it. I was on satellite. I stopped paying for it right after my family — I disconnected it. I don't need to know what's going on beyond my land. It takes away from my focus."

"Wow."

"What?"

"I had no idea…"

"What?"

"That anyone was living like this. Clearly the Cartel didn't either. What do you do for food, other than the garden?"

Battle rubbed his eyes in frustration. "I'll get to that. Let me finish with the power source controls."

Lola raised her arms in surrender. "Fine."

"This switch over here shuts off all power. Don't touch that one."

Battle handed her an umbrella to use as a cane as they walked, not having the patience for her measured limp. He opened the front door and led Lola from the main house, the gravel crunching under their feet as they followed the path around the left side of the main house to the barn. He swung open the doors and ushered her inside.

He closed the doors behind them and planted his hands on his hips. "You said the Cartel controls power."

Her eyes on the massive shelves against the back wall of the barn, Lola answered, "Yes."

"So the infrastructure is in place — water, power, television, Internet?"

"Mostly. Power and water are expensive and can be intermittent. The power goes off a lot, in fact. Television is limited. It's all reruns and messages from the Cartel, no commercials. And the Internet is filtered."

"What do you mean?"

"Google doesn't work. There's something blocking it. I don't know. But you can use it to pay bills to the Cartel. Stuff like that."

"What happened to the government?"

"The Cartel *is* the government."

Battle let that sink in.

In the days after the Scourge, the government had collapsed, leaving a power vacuum? A criminal element had clearly taken over and essentially grabbed power from the surviving people, subjugating them or enslaving them. This was Hell.

"Who exactly is the Cartel?"

Lola turned her attention from the shelves. "I don't know how to answer that. They're just…they're the Cartel."

"Is it drug lords who filtered north? Biker gangs? Mafia? Who *are* they?"

"I guess all of the above? I really don't know. I only know you're either in the Cartel, you pay the Cartel, or you owe the Cartel. That's it, really."

Though Battle didn't like that answer, asking the question again wouldn't get him closer to understanding what and who it was he'd unwittingly alerted to his existence. He walked Lola toward the shelves.

"This is the stockpile." He waved at the vast floor-to-ceiling racks, trying to suppress a grin. "I've got maybe another eight or nine years' worth of supplies."

"That long?"

"I planned for three to four years," he said, walking along the racks. "When my household shrank to one, that extended my supply."

"How long did it take you to collect it?"

"Years. That said, we have to protect this. Without it, life becomes much tougher."

He pointed out the freezers and then led her across the barn to the armory wall. Lola trailed behind him, looking up at the high beams, taking in the size of the barn.

"Why did you do all of this?" she asked. "You couldn't have known the Scourge was coming."

He stopped and turned to face her. "I knew something was coming. A plague, a nuclear attack, zombie invasion, something... I'm cynical enough to know you can't give man anything nice without him breaking it. It was only a matter of time."

"You got lucky. You were paranoid."

"I was prepared, not paranoid. And I wouldn't call this lucky. I prepped. I planned. I prepped some more. And the only reason you're alive is because of that simple fact."

"Point taken," she said, lowering her head. "I'm sorry. I shouldn't have said that."

"Apology accepted. Let's move on. Do you know how to fire a weapon?"

"Yes. Well, kinda. I've shot a .22 at a shooting range before. I took archery at summer camp when I was a little girl."

Battle nodded his approval. "Good. That helps."

He opened the doors to the twenty-foot cabin and revealed the weaponry he'd stashed for a moment like the one he imagined was coming before the sun rose again.

Lola's eyes widened and she covered her mouth with her hands. "Holy mother —"

"Yeah," Battle cut in. "This is what will keep us safe."

***

OCTOBER 13, 2037, NOON

SCOURGE +5 YEARS

ABILENE, TEXAS

"I don't think you should take everybody tonight," Salomon Pico said. He was standing over a crudely drawn map of Mad Max's property. At least it was as close to a map as he could gather from the little time he'd spent there in the dark. Queho and the other posse bosses stood around him while he explained what little he knew.

Queho looked at him. "Why not? What's wrong with attacking him tonight? It gives him less time to prepare."

"He's already prepared, Queho," Pico said without looking his posse boss directly in the eyes. "It doesn't matter how much time we give him."

Queho shifted from his club foot to his good one. "Go on…"

"I think we should start by testing his defenses," Pico said. "I assume he's expecting us. *I* would be expecting us. If we hit him with everything tonight, we get one shot. But if we poke at him tonight, we find out what he's got going on. Then we go at him again tomorrow night with better information."

Queho ran his fingers along the cartoonish sketch on the table. "You surprise me, Pico. I wouldn't have pegged you for smart. But what you're suggesting, this idea of yours, it's smart. I like it."

Pico stood a little taller, lifting his chin. "I think—"

"You already told us what you think," Queho cut in. "I'd stop while you're ahead."

"How many men, how many horses?" asked one of the other bosses, a tall, heavyset man named Rudabaugh who was called "Rud". "And we takin' any trucks?"

"Six of each," Queho said. "No trucks. We can't spare the gas."

Gasoline was the one commodity the Cartel couldn't control in bulk. Despite a large concentration of refineries along the Gulf Coast and wet gas wells in the shale plays, they didn't have the manpower or skill to operate either on a large scale. Gasoline was, therefore, at a premium.

Electric or hybrid vehicles weren't a much better option. The hybrid vehicles still required gasoline. Both they and the electric cars required a reliable source of electricity for charging. That didn't exist in post-Scourge Cartel territory. Add to that the lack of maintenance and accelerated battery degradation from the Texas heat, and electric vehicles became obsolete. Most were cannibalized and melted at some of the high-temperature aluminum recycling plants that dotted the state. The lithium was used in making concrete when possible. Much of the metal product was repurposed for ammunition. All of it was subject to a functional power grid.

Hydrogen cars were just becoming popular when the Scourge took hold. Refueling stations were few and far between, as were reliable repair shops. The H-cars were even more obsolete than hybrids and electrics.

As a result, horses became the primary mode of transportation. The roads were mostly devoid of motorized traffic. Motorcycles were a distant second, behind the horses in popularity, and only the wealthiest of the Cartel hierarchy could afford them. The Cartel used cars and trucks for transporting goods and not much else.

"What about a motorcycle or two?" Rudabaugh pressed. "They could help with reconnaissance and speed things up for us."

"No," Queho answered. "We have directives not to use gas. It's too tight right now. This isn't important enough to take up the chain."

Rudabaugh tipped his hat back on his head. "You mean you don't want the brass knowing about this. That's why you don't want to ask."

Queho licked his teeth. "Six men. Six horses. That's the team."

"They wouldn't like it." Rudabaugh took a step toward Queho and leaned on the table, his hands flat on the map. "Your team lost the girl and got themselves killed. Who's got their guns now? Mad Max? Sounds like you're a triple loser, Queho. And why you're in charge of this miss—"

Pow!

Queho, having had enough of the criticism, pulled his six-shooter and, in one seamless move, grabbed Rudabaugh's wrist with one hand and used the other to jam the barrel into the back of his right hand before firing a slug through it.

Rudabaugh screamed and jumped back, grabbing his injured hand. "What the — why the — you mother — I'm gonna — " He stumbled backward, the pain burning through his hand and arm apparently rendering him unable to complete a thought. The momentum of his girth tipped him too far and he fell over the chair behind him.

While everyone else at the table stood in stunned silence, frozen in disbelief, Pico rushed to Rudabaugh's side. He knelt down to help the bleeding posse boss, but got a boot to his chest and fell back, hitting his head on the floor.

Queho stood over the two men and holstered his pistol. "Don't help Rud, Pico. You're not as smart as I just gave you credit for. This fat loser challenged *me, your* boss, and you're gonna help *him*? Go get me a beer."

Pico scooted backward on the floor until he was clear of Queho's reach. He scrambled to his feet and shuffled off to the bar, rubbing the back of his head.

"You believe that guy?" Queho said to Rudabaugh. He bent at his waist and put his hands on his hips. "Dude runs from a fight at Mad Max's but jumps to help you? Stupid."

Rudabaugh was sweating profusely and breathing through his mouth. He pushed himself straight against the wall, his legs still tangled with the chair. His hand was cradled in his ample lap.

Queho kicked his leg. "As for you, Rud, don't confuse your rank with my authority. You may be a posse boss, same as me, but you ain't got the power I got. I'm in charge. You question me again, it won't be your hand I make you see through. Got it?"

Rudabaugh grunted in between heavy, spittle-laden breaths. He started rocking back and forth against the wall.

Queho kicked his leg a little harder. "Got it, Rud? Don't make me ask again."

"I got it," Rudabaugh spat without looking up at Queho. "I got it."

"Good. Now get that hand fixed. You're leading the posse tonight."

CHAPTER 8

OCTOBER 22, 2032, 5:00 PM

SCOURGE +20 DAYS

EAST OF RISING STAR, TEXAS

Marcus was on the speakerphone in his home office. He was having trouble understanding his wife. She sounded like she was on the verge of hyperventilating.

"Slow down. Where are you?"

"I'm in town," she said. "Abilene is a mess."

"What do you mean?" Marcus spun in his swivel chair and opened the browser on his laptop. "Computer," he said, "show me *Abilene Newspaper*."

"First I went to the pediatrician," she said. "Wes had a well-check appointment today."

"And?"

"And they turned us away. They had too many unscheduled patients show up. They're three days behind schedule, so I've got to come back here Tuesday."

"Did they say why?" There was nothing obvious on the paper's home page.

"Vaccinations. They said they were overwhelmed with people demanding vaccinations. Then I went to the grocery store. There's barely anything on the shelves. Nothing. And the lines are ridiculous everywhere; gas stations, banks, the hospital parking lot is packed. I've never seen it like this, Marcus. And what's worse is…"

Marcus tuned Sylvia out as she explained the most frightening part of what she'd encountered. He was focused on the link he'd found under the business section.

ABILENE REGIONAL MEDICAL PREPS FOR PLAGUE, HIRES HELP

Abilene — It's a scene from a disaster film. Inside ARMC, the Key City's largest medical facility, administrators and healthcare workers are scrambling ahead of what they worry could be a local outbreak of the illness dubbed "The Scourge".

The illness, a highly contagious and potentially fatal form of pneumonia, has spread quickly from refugee camps in the Middle East and Eastern Europe.

The first cases in the United States hit New York and Philadelphia a week ago. There are now reported deaths in California, Kansas, Florida, Ohio, Michigan, and New Jersey.

The Texas Department of State Health Services has not received any reports of plague so far, but a warning late Thursday night from the Governor's Office has healthcare officials in cities throughout the state concerned about the implications of an outbreak here.

"It's coming," the governor's statement read. "We need all Texans to remain vigilant. The best protection is good hygiene. If you experience any of the early symptoms, we ask you immediately contact a healthcare provider."

ARMC has two hundred and thirty-one beds and has access to one thousand healthcare providers. However, should the bacterial pneumonia spread to Abilene, those resources won't be enough.

"We've already purchased one hundred fifty portable cots," said ARMC CEO Dr. Harry Newman. "And we've hired back many of our recent retirees. We don't know if it will be enough, but it's the best we can do right now."

"Did you hear me, Marcus?" Sylvia asked. "Did you hear what I said? Everybody is wearing those little surgical masks over their faces. Wes is freaked out. I'm freaked out. Is it here? Is the plague here?"

Marcus took a deep breath and exhaled. "No. It's not here y—"

"Then why is everybody panicking? Why is—"

"It's not here *yet*. But it's coming."

"How did we miss this?" Sylvia shrieked. "Your whole existence is prepping. How did you not know this was happening?"

Marcus could hear the stress in her voice, so he bit his lip before answering. "I'm a prepper, you're right. I've been preparing for this. And we are prepared, Sylvia."

"But you didn't know it was here." Her speech was ragged as she tried to regulate her breathing. "You didn't know everyone would be wearing masks or that the grocery store would be empty."

Marcus lowered his voice, trying to sound as calm as possible. "No, I didn't."

"I-I just…I…" Sylvia's words devolved into an indecipherable garble as she broke into sobs. "The masks…and Wes, I—"

"Sylvia," Marcus said sharply, "I need you to calm down. Understand, we are prepared. We'll stay isolated. Everything will be fine. Those people with the masks, the ones at the grocery stores, the ones panicking about vaccinations that won't help, they're not prepared like we are. Okay? I understand you're frightened, but I need you to calm down. Where are you?"

"The grocery store parking lot."

"Are you okay to drive, or do you need me to come get you?"

"I can drive," she whimpered.

"Get yourself together and come home. Drive the speed limit. We'll talk about what to do next when you get here."

"Okay."

"How's Wes?"

"Scared."

"Play some music. Take his mind off things. Assure him everything will be okay."

"Okay."

Marcus exhaled, sensing he'd talked his wife off the ledge. "I love you."

"I love you, Marcus."

"I'll see you in an hour."

Marcus turned back to his computer. On his home page was a preselected menu of items his computer's search engine intuitively selected based on his location and previous interests. He pressed "Plague Map" on the screen and then "images".

A series of maps appeared on the screen. The first was static and indicated known cases with black circles plotted on the global map. The larger the circle, the higher the number of cases in that region. A pinpoint indicated fewer than one hundred cases. The largest circle represented more than one hundred thousand.

The largest black dots covered most of the major cities in the Middle East, India, Pakistan, Ukraine, Western Russia, China, Japan, and other parts of Southeast Asia.

Medium-sized dots populated Western and Northern Europe: Rome, Milan, Paris, Marseilles, Frankfurt, Berlin, Stockholm, Geneva, Amsterdam, Belfast, and London.

The smallest dots were all over the United States. According to the map, the Abilene newspaper article published that morning was already outdated.

Marcus checked the key at the bottom of the screen. It indicated the map, a product of the CDC, was updated every thirty minutes.

Next to the static polka-dotted map was a full-color animated map. When initiated, the empty map bloomed with color. The darker the color, the greater the concentration of disease. Atop the map was a timeline. It began two weeks earlier, paused at present day, and extrapolated the data to predict future spread. Within another month, the entire map was dark purple.

Marcus leaned his elbows on the desk and ran his hands through his closely cropped hair. All of the preparation in the world wouldn't necessarily prevent them from getting the illness. They needed to isolate themselves. Once Sylvia and Wesson got home, nobody would be leaving for the foreseeable future.

He picked up his cell phone and called work. Marcus was a security consultant. He was his own boss and was incredibly well compensated for his expertise. It was that compensation that paid for the extravagance of their compound; however, it required a lot of travel. He wasn't traveling anymore.

"Hey," he said into the phone. His booking agent was on the other end. "I have to cancel the upcoming Los Angeles gig. Miami too. Take me off the books for everything until I call back."

The agent didn't like the idea of temporarily losing the ability to book his most sought after consultant.

"Too bad," Marcus told him when he resisted. "My family comes first. I'll be in touch." He hung up without waiting for the agent's response. It didn't matter to Marcus what he said. He was hunkering down. As much as he hated that characterization, it was exactly what he was doing.

He knew the next four weeks would be critical to their survival. If they could weather the storm that long, they'd be okay in the long term. He believed that. He had to believe that.

CHAPTER 9

OCTOBER 13, 2037, 1:47 PM

SCOURGE +5 YEARS

EAST OF RISING STAR, TEXAS

"Is it taut?" Battle called out. "It needs to be taut. No slack."

Lola looked up from the bottom of the tree trunk, her head poking above the high yellow grass. "It's as tight as I can make it."

They were fifty yards apart at the entrance to the property, both of them sitting beneath thinning oaks. The gravel driveway was mostly overgrown and barely visible from the highway.

Battle tugged on the green threaded fishing wire to check Lola's work.

"You're good," he told Lola. "Stay there."

Battle opened up a canvas bag he'd carried with him from the barn and pulled out his supplies. He flipped open a Spyder knife, sliced the top from a plastic party popper, held the plastic-sheathed fuse at the top of the popper, and poured in a vial of gunpowder. He slid a cherry bomb into the bottom of the popper top and then attached it to the fishing thread. He checked the knots at both ends and then wrapped it with electrical tape. He cut an extra foot-long piece of thread and knotted one end to the longer string.

"How many of these are you making?" Lola was leaning on the umbrella, standing a couple of feet from Battle while he worked on his explosive tripwire mine.

"Four."

"They won't kill them," she said. "A firecracker won't even hurt them, will it?"

Battle affixed the tripwire to the tree. "No, but the loud noise will confuse them and it'll give me a better idea of their position."

"I thought you had a motion alarm?"

"I do. It only lets me know someone has breached the perimeter, it doesn't tell me where. These will give me a much better idea of where they are."

"From the noise?"

"The noise and the flash. Plus, there's a good chance they'll open fire. The firecracker sounds like a gunshot. They might react before they think."

Battle reached back into his canvas bag and pulled out a flat metal contraption, a handful of nails, a hammer, and a plastic bag containing shotgun shells.

"What's that?"

"A twelve-gauge booby trap."

"What does it do?"

Battle looked up at Lola and sighed. He didn't feel like tutoring her. He held the plate low against the tree trunk, just above the tripwire, and hammered it into the oak with four thick nails. He took the free end of the foot-long string and knotted it into a firing pin on the side of the trap, being careful not to tug on it so as to activate the tripwire.

Once he checked the line, he thumbed one of the red shotgun shells into an opening behind the firing pin. "That'll do it."

"What will it do?"

"The shells contain pepper gas. At the same time the tripwire pops, the booby trap will fire the shell horizontally at the intruder. The shell will hit them with the gas. It'll make for a really bad day."

"It doesn't kill them?"

"No. It incapacitates them, giving me time to react. Incapacitating one or two of them has a multiplying effect. You get guys yelling and screaming for help, it occupies two or three more. If I kill them immediately, they can't help me mitigate additional threats."

"How many of these?"

"Four. One at each of the possible entry points."

"Have you done this before?"

Battle grabbed his canvas bag and stood. "No."

"Why not?"

"I only have enough supplies to do this once," he said. "I've never needed it."

"Will it work?"

"We'll find out. I've got other surprises too."

They walked toward the eastern edge of the property and a fence that separated Battle's fifty acres from a neighboring abandoned horse ranch. The fence was only waist high and useless for anything other than keeping lazy horses penned inside its perimeter.

There wasn't a spot Battle thought they might be more or less likely to penetrate the fence except for a point at which the fence swung northwest away from his house. He strung the tripwire for twenty yards on either side of that point, running the fishing line an inch above the top rail of the fence. That line was attached to a booby trap designed to shoot upward. Battle secured it to the fencepost nearest the center of the tripwire. He knew it was a crapshoot, but better to have the additional security than nothing.·

He placed the third tripwire/booby trap combination on a northwest-southeast diagonal stretching between his house and the barn. He repeated it along the covered walkway leading from the garage to the rear of the house.

Battle took a swig of water from a canteen on his hip and leaned against the side of his house facing the rear garden. "All right, now comes the fun part. You need to pay attention."

"What do you mean fun?"

"We're gonna set cartridge traps."

"What are those?"

"They're designed to break an intruder's foot. Make him even less mobile than you are right now."

Lola wiped sweat from her forehead and reached for the canteen. "Not funny."

"Wasn't meant to be," he said. "The idea is to maim, not kill. At least not at first. An injured man is a much bigger problem than a dead one."

"You've said that a million times."

"It's the truth. Follow me."

Battle retrieved a shovel and a stack of thin plywood boards from the barn and they trudged south through the grass toward the treehouse. Once they reached the tree, he tossed the boards to the ground, pulled a can of spray paint from the canvas bag, and shook it.

"What *don't* you have in that bag?" Lola asked.

"You're getting too comfortable."

"What does that mean?"

"Your sarcasm," he said, rattling the can. "It's indicative of someone who's comfortable. Don't get comfortable. You're not staying here. As soon as your ankle—"

"I'm anything but comfortable, Battle." She took a step back and her eyes narrowed. "My son is missing, maybe dead, my ankle's busted, and I'm not welcome by the one person who could help me. I'm uncomfortable. Sarcasm is also a coping mechanism. You're such an—"

"Fine," he cut in. "You're *not* comfortable. Now I need you to pay attention."

Lola huffed and tossed the umbrella to the ground. She folded her arms across her chest and shook her head as if he was wasting *her* time. "What?!"

Battle uncapped the paint can and sprayed a yellow square onto the weeds and dirt. He took five steps and painted another square. He repeated the process until he reached the gravel driveway at the gate.

"If you have to run from the house, make sure you're to the left of the driveway. If you're on this side, you could get caught." Battle stuck the shovel into the ground at the edge of the first spray-painted square. He kept shoveling until the top of the spade disappeared below ground as he dug.

It took him a half hour to hole out each of the squares. Lola was sitting under the treehouse, leaning against the trunk, sipping water from Battle's canteen. She pushed herself to her feet and joined Battle once he'd finished the dig.

Battle knelt beside the first hole. He took one of the plywood boards and lowered it to the bottom. It fit perfectly inside the square and provided a flat surface for the next step in the project.

"Can you hand me one of the large silver cylinders from the bag?" he asked Lola. "It looks like a big bullet."

She fished around in the bag and pulled out a pair of the silver cylinders. "What are they?"

"Big bullets."

"Sarcasm is a sign of —"

"They're fifty-caliber rounds, and they're the key component of these traps. Now hand me a handful of nails and the hammer, please."

She fisted a half dozen nails and handed them to Battle. He leaned over the hole and drove the nail into the board deep at its center. He took four more and hammered them lightly into a tight pattern around the center nail. Then he slid the fifty caliber cartridge into the center of the four nails, which held it upright on top of the center, deeply driven nail.

He took another balsa wood square, placed it on the top of the hole, and covered it with a thin layer of dirt and grass. The hole was concealed.

"That's a cartridge trap," Battle explained. "Somebody steps on the balsa wood, it can't support their weight, the foot drops onto the top of the cartridge, and that drives it down onto the nail. The nail acts like a firing pin and the bullet rips through the guy's foot or ankle. It's a bad deal."

"How'd you come up with this?"

Battle laughed. "I didn't come up with it, the Vietnamese did. This is a variation on what they put throughout the jungles of South Vietnam. They used them to injure and ambush."

"And you're putting them across the whole yard?"

"Only the wide side. It stops them from getting too close to the house. You need to remember, if you have to bolt, it's on the left side of the driveway."

"Let's hope neither of us have to bolt."

***

OCTOBER 13, 2037, 2:15 PM

SCOURGE +5 YEARS

ABILENE, TEXAS

The Cartel was bigger than anyone could comprehend. Even its leadership, who divided its power into large areas and regions, didn't know its true scope.

In the days after the Scourge, as civilization devolved and desperation trumped reason, disparate criminal elements seized control. After months of bloody turf wars and needless thinning of the unrighteous herd, the countless factions reached an agreement. Instead of fighting each other, they fought the existing, legitimate power structure and beat it back.

From small, disconnected enclaves, they consolidated their lands and held much of the space between the Mississippi River to the east, the Red River to the north, the Sandia Mountains to the west, and the Rio Grande to the south. The Rio Grande was a porous border, and the traditional Mexican drug cartels were considered brethren, if not patrons, of the new consolidated Cartel.

The men who rose to the top of the Cartel were the meanest, most morally bankrupt of its membership. They weren't elected to their positions, they grabbed them and choked the life from those who opposed their ascension.

One of those men was Cyrus Skinner, a ruthless self-preservationist who, before the Scourge, was a drug-dealing prison guard in South Texas. His thick neck and barrel chest matched the gravel rolling around in his nicotine-tainted voice. In his area he was king, judge, jury, and executioner.

Skinner was in his office, a back room in the corner of the HQ that used to house the hardware store employee break room. He was leaning back in a cracked leather chair, his boots planted on the edge of the black metal desk. Cigarette smoke swirled around his head, mixing with the dust dancing in the stale air. A fat man with a hand wrapped in gauze stood across from him, demanding action.

"He shot me," Rudabaugh whined. "That's got to break some sort of rule. You've got to be able to do something about it."

Skinner rocked gently in the chair, which creaked under his weight. He held half a cigarette to his lips between his thumb and forefinger, sucking the ashes red. "Probably," he said.

Rudabaugh tugged on his belt buckle, lifting up his pants. "Probably *what?*"

"Probably breaks some sort of rule. Frankly, Rud, I don't rightly care. You're two grown men. You fought. He won."

"There wasn't a fight, Cyrus. He hauled off and put a hole in my hand!"

"If I say it's a fight, Rud, then it's a fight."

"So you're not gonna do anything? You're gonna let it slide?"

A voice from the doorway behind Rudabaugh answered for Skinner. "Damn right, he's gonna let it slide."

Rudabaugh looked over his shoulder. Queho was leaning against the doorjamb, his hands stuffed in his pockets. His holster was slung low on his hip, and his brown hat was tipped back on his head, revealing a widow's peak.

"You weren't invited to this meeting," Rudabaugh sneered. "This is between me and Cyrus."

Queho chuckled. "Sounds like it's between you and me and you want to go bringing the boss into it." He craned his neck to look past Rudabaugh and catch Skinner's eye. "That what it sounds like to you, Skin?"

Skinner lifted his feet from the desk and leaned forward in the creaking swivel chair. "Yeah. It does. Honestly, Queho, I don't have time for this. You two need to work it out. You got a job to do tonight."

Rudabaugh turned, his wide frame open to both men. Sweat beaded on his upper lip. He tugged on his belt buckle. "I ain't done with this. This is not the end of it." Rudabaugh tipped his brown hat to Skinner, grunted, and elbowed his way past Queho, almost knocking him from the doorway.

Queho ignored the transgression and laughed as he sidled up to Skinner's desk. He sat on the edge of the desk opposite Skinner. "You believe that? He's gonna come to you?"

Cyrus Skinner rubbed his chin in thought. "I'm as much a bastard as the next man, but you can't go around shooting another posse boss. If it was anyone but you, I'd be putting a hole through *your* hand." He smiled, took another drag, and exhaled.

"Rud's not an equal, Skin," Queho argued. "He's a fat, lazy drunk who's only in the spot he's in because of connections."

Skinner's geniality dissipated with the smoke. His eyes turned dark and he leaned forward, pointing the remnants of his cigarette at Queho. "You're only where *you* are because of connections. Don't make me regret my decisions, Queho. Now get off of my desk, out of my office, and go kill Mad Max."

Queho immediately stood and stepped back from the desk. He tipped his hat to Skinner. "Sorry, Skin. My bad."

"It's fine. Just don't forget your place. Make peace with Rud."

Queho nodded and turned to leave the office.

"How you gonna do it?" Skinner pulled a cigarette from behind his ear and lit it. "You got a good plan? Pico give you good information?"

"We're not killing him tonight," Queho said over his shoulder. "We're testing his defenses. No need to risk killing more men tonight."

"Whatever you think is best, Queho. Don't let me down. Or I'll have to start listening to Rudabaugh." He sucked another drag from the cigarette and threw his feet back onto the desk.

Queho stuffed his hands back into his pockets and left the office for the bar. Skinner chuckled to himself as his right-hand man left in a huff. He'd never pick Rud over Queho. For anything. But he couldn't let Queho, an ex-con who'd worked for Skinner behind bars, ever think he was too big for a swift kick.

Cyrus Skinner had a gift for giving people enough rope to hang themselves. He'd work that noose up and down, toying with them. Just when they thought he was going easy on them, he yanked a little harder. Then, when they felt the life slipping from their pores, he let loose, giving them new purpose.

He'd dangle Queho enough to make the others uncomfortable. Every once in a while, though, when Queho got too comfortable with his swing, Skinner would wrap the rope around his fist and tug.

The post-Scourge world was meant for men like Cyrus Skinner. He was in his element. There were no rules except for the ones he created. And even then, he could ignore them if he was so inclined.

CHAPTER 10

NOVEMBER 3, 2032, 4:00 PM

SCOURGE +32 DAYS

EAST OF RISING STAR, TEXAS

The onions came out in clumps, the sharp smell sticking to Marcus's hands as he knelt in the thick black soil, harvesting the food-ready vegetables from the garden. Fall was always a tricky time of year. Other than the green onions, Marcus found he was limited to crops that grew underground. They needed the warmth of the soil to protect them from the cold wind and drop in temperatures that blew into Abilene every year at the same time.

He cursed himself for pulling the onions first, forgetting their pungency would rub off on the kale and chard as he plucked them from the ground. He should have done the onions last.

The garden had started as an experiment not long after they'd finished construction on the main house. There were leftover timbers and stone and, rather than toss them out, give them away, or pile them up behind the barn, Sylvia had suggested her prepper husband start a vegetable garden. He could build out the frame with the leftover construction supplies.

She'd already been canning her own jams and preserves as a contribution to their readiness and thought it would be therapeutic and productive for Marcus to give gardening a shot.

Marcus had hedged at first. "I don't have a green thumb. I can't even grow a weed."

"I believe you can do anything you put your mind to doing," Sylvia had encouraged him. "Plus, the smell of potting soil is a real turn-on."

He'd built the garden frame, complete with its own dedicated irrigation, in less than a week. His first crop of carrots, peas, and potatoes was paltry at best. But with each subsequent season, his skill improved, as did the yields.

Some of the vegetables they ate the day he picked them. Others they froze in bags and used before self-created expiration dates. They learned the hard way that snap peas weren't good after much longer than six months.

They'd packed their first summer crop of cucumbers in vinegar, water, and salt and had pickles for the better part of a year. With each crop, their pickling formula got better: a little less vinegar, a little more salt.

Marcus's bag was getting heavy. By the time he'd added the radishes to the bag, his knees and lower back needed a break. He stood at the garden's edge and brushed the soil from his knees. He knew he'd need to cut back the plants soon and start planning his next rotation, but it was getting close to dinnertime. He knew Sylvia was in the kitchen, awaiting the kale. They were having a salad to go with their meal of chicken and homemade sourdough bread. She'd cooked a lot in the last couple of weeks as they'd stayed isolated.

Marcus didn't want her in town, nor did he want Wes at school. He didn't take any trips. Despite the protests from his wife, his son's teachers, and his bosses, he was doing what had to be done.

The plague was coming. There was no stopping it. They could avoid the worst of it if they stayed to themselves, hidden from the rest of the world.

Sylvia conceded after week two, he'd been right. They were watching late-night cable news again. Instead of the mask-clad reporters telling stories from refugee camps in the Middle East, they were live outside of overwhelmed hospitals in Miami, Cleveland, Los Angeles, Chicago, Houston, San Antonio, and Dallas.

It was getting worse by the day. As the disease moved closer, it was strengthening, like a hurricane in the Gulf. People were dying in less than twenty-four hours after showing the first symptoms. The global death toll was becoming incalculable. Instead of reporting numbers, governments were issuing percentages. The 2032 presidential election was postponed until spring 2033 because of fears that gathering to vote could worsen the spread of the disease.

In their idyllic fifty acres, the Battles were safe, healthy, and prepared

Marcus trudged the short distance from the garden to the rear entrance of the house. He stepped into the mudroom, slid his shoes off with his toes, and carried the vegetable haul into the kitchen.

"Hey, Sylv —" Marcus stopped himself. They had a visitor. A woman was sitting on a barstool at their kitchen island. She was breathing their air; her hands were touching their granite.

Sylvia forced a smile. "Hi, hon. This is my friend Roseann."

The woman turned on the stool, looking over her shoulder at Marcus. She raised a hand from the granite and waved at him. "Hello. I'm so sorry to intrude."

Marcus didn't respond. He didn't move. He stood in the kitchen entry, gripping the heavy bag of vegetables. He shot a look at his wife.

"Roseann is looking for some help, Marcus," Sylvia said. Marcus recognized her sanitized tone. His wife was uncomfortable; something was wrong.

"What kind of help?" Marcus said, his eyes shifting back to the intruder.

"I know your wife from church," Roseann said. "She's such a good Christian woman. You're blessed."

Marcus didn't like where this was going. The woman wanted something he knew he wasn't going to give her. "I'm very blessed. In many ways."

"She's told me you served in Syria and Iran," Roseann said. "Thank you for your sacrifice, Mr. Battle." Her smile was genuine, though Marcus sensed the flattery was not. "She also told me your military training prepared you quite well. She told me you've built quite a place here."

"What kind of help do you need?" Marcus said bluntly.

"I have a husband and three children," Roseann said. "There's Billy, Jimmy, and Tammy. My husband is—"

"What do you want?"

"Marcus…" Sylvia chided.

"What do you want?" Marcus asked for the fourth time. "I don't have time for pleasantries and small talk, Roseann. I need to know what you want so I deny you and you can leave."

"Well," Roseann huffed, her dramatic glare bouncing back and forth between Sylvia and Marcus. "I'm not sure what to say to that, Mr. Battle. I understand I'm a guest in your home, but I don't see the need for—"

"You're not a guest, Roseann," Marcus said. "You're an intruder. My wife has a softer heart than I do. I wouldn't have answered the door, let alone allowed you into our kitchen. But Sylvia, being the good woman you say she is, wasn't about to turn you away."

"I—" Marcus held up his hand to stop the woman from saying another word. "You want our food. Am I right?"

"I-I—"

"You're wasting my time," he said. "Tell me what you want."

Roseann lowered her head and her cheeks flushed pink. "Yes. I am here asking for some food. Only enough for a day or two. We haven't eaten since Sunday night."

Marcus shook his head. "No."

Sylvia pleaded to Marcus with her eyes. "Can't we—?"

"No," he repeated. "And I'll tell you why. We give you food now and we create a bigger problem. You'll eat the day or two supply and then you'll get hungry again. A week from now, if not sooner, you're back. And then you bring your neighbors with you. They want food too. Do I say yes to you and no to them? Do I help all of you, shortening the limited supply I have for my family? I give you anything today and it begins a never-ending cycle of dependency on your part."

Roseann shook her head. "That's not—"

"If I say no to you today, you don't come back. You curse me, you hate me, your neighbors hate me—everyone hates me. But nobody comes here looking for a handout."

Roseann coughed into her hand and sniffled. She hefted herself from the stool and tugged on the bottom of her ill-fitting blouse. She stuck her chin up in the air and marched toward the hallway. She stopped at the entrance to the kitchen and spun around. "Matthew 19:21. Look it up."

A smile edged onto the corner of Marcus's lips. *"Jesus said unto him, If thou wilt be perfect, go sell that thou hast, and give to the poor, and thou shalt have treasure in heaven: and come and follow me."*

Roseann's eyes narrowed. "God have mercy on your souls, Sylvia. I'll show myself out." She bounded from the room, opening and slamming the front door behind her.

"Two things," Sylvia said. "Why can't we give them *something*? We have plenty."

"We have plenty today. We won't in a month or two or six. We don't know how long this plague will last. I don't want to create our own little welfare state."

"I still think—"

"Trust me," he said. "I know what I'm doing. What's the second thing?"

"How did you know that Bible verse?"

"I know a lot of verses. I read a lot at night when I was on a tour."

"I had no idea."

"I don't like advertising my faith. But when that self-righteous beggar tried to shame me, I couldn't help myself."

Sylvia moved from behind the island and walked to her husband. She put her hands on either side of his face. "I know you're not the proselytizing type, Marcus, but you could have shared that with me. I think it's wonderful you read the Bible when you were over there. It makes me love you even more."

Marcus thumbed the platinum cross hanging around her neck. "So you didn't love me as much as you do now?"

"You're ridiculous." She patted his chest. "But yes. And I'll love you even more tomorrow. Just don't hide something so important from me. We should be able to share our faith."

"Gotcha." Marcus wasn't much for emotion or sharing too much. He was strong. He was a man. He needed to project his unwavering stoicism, even to his wife. If he was vulnerable or perceived as weak, their world could crumble.

Sylvia took a step back. "You're being dismissive."

"No," he said. "I need to make sure Roseann doesn't steal from us. "Where's Wes, by the way?"

"Out front. In the treehouse maybe."

Marcus pecked Sylvia on the cheek, put the vegetables on the counter, and hurried out front. He stepped from the front stoop to the yard, saw Roseann's Chrysler minivan in the drive, and turned to his right. Wes was underneath the treehouse oak. He had a visitor. Roseann. And he was pointing her toward the barn.

"Hey!" Marcus called out, catching their attention. "Wes! Don't talk to her!" Marcus waved his hands and started running toward them. He slowed when he got close enough to see Roseann holding his son by the back of the neck with one hand. Her other hand was hidden behind his back.

"What are you doing?" Marcus approached with his hands up. "Roseann, this is not how to handle this. My son has nothing to do with my choices."

"Yes, he does!" she spat, venom dripping from her lips. She was shaking, pulling Wes backward toward the barn as Marcus moved closer. "He's your son. He has everything to do with your choices."

"Let go of him, Roseann." Marcus kept stepping toward her. "Let's work this out, you and me."

Roseann pulled her hand from behind Wes's back and stuck the muzzle of a semiautomatic pistol against the side of his head. She looked over her shoulder, watching her step as she tugged backward and closer to the barn.

"Dad!" Wes cried out, his face squeezed with fear. His shoes were untied, and his little feet shuffled heels first in the dry grass.

From behind him, Sylvia shrieked. She was calling out Wesson's name as she sprinted toward them. She was out of breath by the time she reached Marcus.

"Roseann?!" Sylvia's voice warbled. "What are you doing? This isn't you."

"Stop where you are, Sylvia!" She jerked Wesson's head with a shove of the gun. "Don't get closer. Tell your husband to stop too. Tell him to stop!"

Sylvia raised her hands and stopped. "Marcus, listen to her. Stop."

Marcus took a deep breath and, against his better judgment, stopped. "What do you want? How do we end this without anyone getting hurt?"

"Give me food from that barn," she said, coughing between words. "I have kids to feed too. They need food. I can't go back and tell them I don't have any."

"Fine," Marcus said. "Let go of Wes. I'll give you enough canned food to last a week. Deal?"

"A month," she said. "I want enough for a month. And I want meat too."

"Fine," Sylvia answered. "A month. And we'll give you some meat from the freezer."

Marcus nodded his agreement. "Let Wes go. I'll get you the food from the barn."

"You get the food," Roseann snapped, "then I let go of your son."

Her hand was shaky. She was jittery. Marcus didn't like it. "Pull the gun from his head."

"No!"

"Pull the gun down or you're not getting anything."

"Marcus!" Sylvia protested.

Wes whimpered as he kept shuffling backwards against his will. "Dad!"

"You're not going to kill him," Marcus said. "You kill him and I kill you. Then your kids get nothing and they starve."

Roseann pressed the gun against Wesson's head. "I don't—"

"Put down the gun! Otherwise we all lose. You don't want that."

Roseann's eyes darted back and forth between Marcus and Sylvia. She stopped moving. The four of them stood in silence. Marcus knew she was playing out the scenarios in her head and kept coming to the same conclusion. Her only option was to lower the gun, and she did.

"Thank you," Sylvia said. "Thank you, Roseann."

"Get my food," she snarled and coughed.

Marcus took a step toward Roseann and Wes. "You're sick, aren't you?"

Roseann wiped her nose with the back of her hand. "It's allergies, that's all."

Marcus took another step. "Look, let go of Wes. Put the gun on me. We'll go into the barn together and I'll let you pick the food. I don't want you coughing on my son again."

"You keep trying stuff," she argued. "We agreed! I put down the gun. You go get my food."

"You're sick," he repeated and stepped closer. "It's not allergies. You know it. How many of your kids are coughing?"

Roseann's eyes welled. Her face reddened. Her grip on Wesson's neck tightened and he winced.

"My hands are up." Marcus tried to reason with her. "I don't have a weapon, you do. Point the gun at me and let go of my son."

Roseann's chest started heaving as her breaths became more shallow. She was shaking. "No," she said. "I'm not doing that." She took another step backward. Her heel caught a shallow root from a young, dying oak and she fell, losing her grip on Wesson.

In a single bound, Marcus leapt forward, shoving Wes off to the right and out of harm's way as he tackled Roseann on the ground. He rolled onto her arm and yanked the gun from her hand before she could pull the trigger.

"Get Wes!" he yelled to Sylvia. "Get inside the house!"

Roseann struggled under Marcus's weight. She kicked and punched with her free arm. Marcus absorbed the blows and pushed himself free of her. He rolled over and onto his knees, pointing the gun at her head. She lay in the dirt and grass, coughing, retching, and wheezing.

"Get up, Roseann."

Her coughs and wheezes morphed into heaving sobs as she stumbled to her feet. She bent over at the waist. "I…food. My babies…food. Please. I'm sorry. So…sorry."

Marcus held the gun and looked back over his shoulder. Sylvia was standing at the front door, her trembling hands cupped over her mouth. Wes was hidden inside the house.

"I get it. You're desperate," Marcus said. "We're all desperate. But I can't have you coming back here for food every few days. I can't have your people coming here. I don't have enough. You understand?"

Roseann was looking at the ground, her hair in front of her face. She was drooling from the phlegm in her mouth and throat. Marcus couldn't tell if she was nodding or struggling to breathe.

"I'll give you food for a week, that's it. But I'm warning you. Anybody comes close to my property, my house, my family, and I'm killing them without asking questions first."

Roseann lifted her head, strands of hair sticking to her pallid, pained face. Her eyes were red and swollen. She looked fifteen years older than she had a few minutes earlier in his kitchen. Though he thought about putting a bullet in her head to end her suffering, he led her at gunpoint into the barn. He grabbed a bagful of canned food and loaded it into the back of her minivan.

She slowly rolled down the driveway and back onto the highway. It was already too late. She'd done her damage the minute she entered their home. She was infected and knew it.

CHAPTER 11

OCTOBER 13, 2037, 4:39 PM

SCOURGE +5 YEARS

EAST OF RISING STAR, TEXAS

Though the graves were marked, nobody aside from Marcus knew the importance of the people buried six feet beneath the headstones. He knelt to the side of the limestone brick. His hand rested on it and his thumb moved back and forth against its texture.

He was in the northeasternmost corner of the central two acres. The graves were inside the fenced perimeter, framed by a cluster of mesquite.

"I wish we were together," he said to the stone. "But I'm not ready to join you and your momma just yet."

He closed his eyes, trying to remember his son's face. It was getting harder. The edges of his features were blurring with each passing day, more opaque with each month.

"I may have made a big mistake," he admitted to Wes. "I let a woman onto the property and I didn't kill her. She's the first person inside the house since you and your momma left me."

Marcus ran his finger along the date chiseled into the stone. The chisel marks were darker than the rest of the stone, dirt, and mildew staining the thin but deep lines defining a life too short.

He traced the letters slowly. "She wants me to leave you. I told her no." Marcus awaited the imaginary question and answered, "Because, Wes, I built this place for us. If I leave, there is no us anymore. It's simply an empty house."

His finger reached the month of his son's birth and he ran it along the etching, listening to Wes's voice in his head. "I'm not being stubborn, son. I'm being smart. I'm surviving." He lifted his hand and balled it into a fist, squeezing the color from his hand.

"Fine. I'll ask your mother." Marcus shifted on his heels and turned to face the other stone. "Sylvia, what do you think? Was it a mistake to let this woman into our house?"

The oaks swayed in a slight breeze. Leaves struggled against it, gave up, and floated free of their branches. A couple of them landed on the stone marked for Sylvia Battle: Wife, Mother, and Friend. Marcus wiped the stone clean.

He chuckled. "I know you would have helped her. Maybe that's why I didn't shoot her on sight and why I let her in our house."

Another breeze, stronger than the previous one, whistled around him. He looked up and saw clouds building in the sky above him. "Yeah, it looks like a storm is coming. I'll be ready. I'm always ready."

Marcus closed his eyes and imagined his hands on the sides of Sylvia's face as he pulled her close. He could smell her jasmine perfume. "Her son," he said. "Her son is missing. That's why she wants me to leave you. She says she needs my help finding him. I can't do it, Sylvia. I already told Wes I couldn't do it. I—"

"Battle?" The voice was soft and feminine. For a moment, Marcus thought he was actually hearing Sylvia's voice.

"You're not supposed to be here." He pushed himself to his feet and stepped away from the stones.

"I'm so sorry," Lola said. "I didn't know…"

"Didn't know what?"

"That they…you…"

"That my family was buried here?"

Lola nodded. She looked at the stones and tears pooled in her eyes. She wiped them away with the back of her hand.

"How much did you hear?"

"Enough," she said, her eyes darting between the stones and Battle. "I didn't mean to eavesdrop. I heard you, and I didn't know who you were talking to. When I realized…"

Battle crossed his arms. "What are you doing out here anyway? You were sleeping."

"I couldn't sleep." She limped a step forward. "I went down to the kitchen and called for you. You didn't answer. I thought maybe you were in the garden. The back porch door was cracked open. I had no idea—"

"You're right," Battle snapped. "You don't."

"I'm sorry."

Battle looked at the stones and then at Lola. He took a step toward her and then marched past her, toward the back porch. "Forget about it. Let's eat. It's gonna be a long night."

Lola wiped her eyes clean of the tears that kept streaming. She gripped the umbrella and followed Battle back to the house. He was at the refrigerator when she slid the back door shut and found a seat at the island.

"We need protein," he said, bracing himself against the wide-open fridge. "We'll go very light on the carbs tonight. If we eat heavy food, it'll make us tired. That's not good."

"Okay."

"I've got some venison I killed a couple of months back. Thawed it two days ago. It's not a big portion, since I wasn't expecting intrud — er, guests." He turned and looked at Lola as he corrected himself. "You ever eat venison?"

"No."

"It's very lean," he said. "Not much fat. I let it age after I killed it. That tenderized it, so it should be okay and not too gamey. I'll dice it up and sear it in a pan. That'll be the fastest way to cook it. We don't have time for stew or a roast. I'll add some bush beans. It'll be good." Battle was trying to generate a conversation that had nothing to do with what had transpired outside. He wanted to move past it. Bury it.

Lola nodded again.

"Usually, I'd cook it with some dried prunes," he said, pulling the container from the refrigerator. "That's really good. But not tonight. For obvious reasons."

"So you hunt?"

"Yes." Battle slapped the meat onto a wooden cutting board. "It's the only way to get good, fresh protein." He flipped on the water in the sink and washed his hands.

"Did you before?"

"Before what?" He yanked open a drawer and pulled out a large serrated knife.

"Did you hunt before the Scourge?"

"A little," he said, drawing the knife easily through the thinly marbled meat. "Ooh, this is good. Nicely done, Battle!"

Lola chuckled. "You always talk to yourself?" Her face blushed crimson as soon as the words slipped from her mouth.

Battle stopped mid-slice. His expression flatlined and he clenched his jaw. His chest rose with a deep breath and he exhaled slowly. "Not always." He finished the cut.

"I didn't mean —"

"I would hunt boar occasionally," he said, his attention on the venison. "Some people call 'em peccary or javelina. They were overpopulated before the Scourge, and they could do damage too." He chuckled and crosscut a slice of meat to cube it. "I had no problem killing them with my bow."

Lola cleared her throat, her color having returned to normal. "Did you eat them?"

"Only in a stew," he said. "I never much cared for the taste. My wife liked it. She also liked quail."

"What's that taste like?"

"You haven't had quail?" He looked up at Lola, his nose scrunched in disbelief. "How have you survived this long and you haven't had venison or quail?"

"I told you, we haven't had good food in a long time."

Battle washed his hands again and plopped a saucepan onto the gas cooktop. He spun the igniter and threw a chunk of animal fat into the pan. It immediately popped and sizzled as it melted to a liquid. "It's deer fat. I save it and reuse it. I ran out of good cooking oil a year ago."

"Oil goes bad?"

"Yes. And you know it when it does. Olive oil is the best. It lasted me nearly three years. Since then, I've been draining fat, chilling, and reusing it three or four times before I toss it. Sometimes I'll use it instead of butter on my beans. It tastes pretty similar, especially when it's salted."

"I am sorry," Lola said. "I didn't mean to intrude."

Battle fought the urge to yell at her or uncomfortably change the subject again. He spooned the grease, tossed in the venison cubes, and covered the pan. "It's okay. I know you didn't. But I don't want to talk about it. We need to focus on eating and preparing for tonight. Got it?"

Lola exhaled. "Got it."

***

OCTOBER 13, 2037, 6:23 PM

SCOURGE + 5 YEARS

TEXAS HIGHWAY 36

BETWEEN ABILENE AND RISING STAR, TEXAS

The road was easier on horseback. Salomon Pico held the reins tightly as the recon posse clopped away from the setting sun. It was low in the sky, and he felt it on his neck as they moved in a caravan along the highway. He didn't have the benefit of a brown hat like the bosses. Up ahead, in the distance, pillows of clouds bloomed downward.

He tried licking his lips. They were dry. He curled them into his mouth and licked them with what little saliva he could muster. He wanted to save his water for the road back.

Rudabaugh slowed his horse and trotted alongside Pico's. "You better find this place," he said. He was holding the reins with one hand. The other, he held in a sling against his chest. "If you don't, I'm gonna put a bullet in both of your hands."

Pico thought about responding, about telling Rud that he'd had nothing to do with Queho's violent outburst. But he knew it wouldn't do him any good. He just nodded. "I'm pretty sure I do."

"Pretty sure?" Rudabaugh mocked. "Pretty sure? That ain't gonna cut it, *Sillyman.*"

Pico gritted his teeth. He hated the nickname some of the bosses gave him. "What I meant to say was that I'm sure. I know where it is. It's not easy to spot, that's all."

"We'll see about that," Rudabaugh snarled and spurred his horse forward. He joined a couple of men at the front of the caravan.

Pico couldn't count the number of times he'd been on "hunting trips" in the past five years. Several times a month, the posse bosses rounded up a handful of grunts and mapped out a search area. They'd pack for a few days on the road and leave in search of undiscovered homesteads, farms, ranches, silos, anything they could commandeer and ravage.

He always got a sick feeling in his stomach when a boss would call him in for a hunt. Queho was the most brutal. But Rudabaugh wasn't much better. When they'd find an untouched but developed piece of land, they were ruthless in their acquisition of it.

Pico lost himself in the long shadow extending ahead of his horse, his mind drifting from one raid to another. He shuddered.

He wasn't like so many of the men, or women, in the Cartel. It wasn't as if he was a good man. He wasn't. His proclivities and strong desire to live left him on the wrong side of history. But he wasn't morally bankrupt either. He had trouble sleeping. Voices and faces haunted his dreams.

He knew what he was doing and how he lived in the face of an apocalypse was wrong. But unlike most of the bosses, and so many of his fellow grunts, he didn't relish the opportunity to take a woman without her consent, make her man watch as he lay dying. He didn't laugh at the squeals of suddenly orphaned children herded into wagons so they could be put to work.

He also knew they'd seemingly combed every square inch of land for fifteen hundred square miles. So the idea that there was someone that close who'd escaped their detection and their wrath was surprising.

Pico thought back to the last hunting trip. He figured it had to have been at least six months ago. It was the worst of them to that point.

He knew, though, that this hunting trip was different. They weren't only looking to annex Mad Max's land and weapons. They were exacting revenge. Even if it was just to test defenses, there was the possibility it could end that night. Pico watched Rudabaugh bouncing in his saddle, chatting up the man riding alongside him. He knew Rudabaugh would do what he could to end it, even if that wasn't the objective. He wanted to prove to Cyrus Skinner he was more valuable than Queho. Pico could smell the jealousy on him. If Rud had his way, he'd ride back to Abilene with the woman on his saddle and Mad Max's head in a bag.

The fact that the big guy, Skinner, had personally okayed the hunt only amplified its importance. He'd seen the anger dancing in Skinner's eyes. Even through the thick blanket of smoke that followed the man everywhere, Pico knew this hunt was crucial. He imagined Rudabaugh had seen it too.

It was likely Mad Max was responsible for killing more than the three men Pico had seen him execute. There'd been other small hunting parties that had up and disappeared. Skinner, Queho, Rudabaugh, and the others always assumed missing men had died of natural causes or greed. Some of them, they guessed, had tried to run off and got lost in the vast, dry wilderness.

They'd never considered, until now, a single man had taken care of them. Maybe, then, Mad Max hadn't gone undetected. They'd found him. He'd just hadn't let them leave alive.

Pico swallowed hard and pulled his attention from the shadow, which grew longer by the second as the sun dipped closer to the horizon. He uncapped his canteen and took a swallow of warm water.

Within minutes, the sun disappeared and the sky darkened to a deep shade of blue before edging into black. There were clouds ahead of them. Storm clouds, Pico figured. They were still forming in the sky. A familiar nausea slithered from his stomach to his throat. He gulped against it and tasted its acidic burn on the back of his tongue.

Pico looked to the horizon ahead of them, his eyes drifting upward from the caravan to tendrils of lightning that forked through the clouds. Thunder cracked and rolled toward them, rumbling across the open land. It was getting colder. A fresh breeze was building into a wind. All of these were signs, Pico thought. It was nature's way of telling them to turn around. It was God's sentinel warning them of their enemy's strength.

He knew people would die in the coming storm. He wondered to himself if *they* were the ones who should be afraid.

CHAPTER 12

NOVEMBER 9, 2032, 11:00 PM

SCOURGE +38 DAYS

EAST OF RISING STAR, TEXAS

Marcus sat in the dark of his home office, staring at his computer, his head in his hands. He reread the same page over and again, searching for contradictory news on other websites. He couldn't find any.

The Centers for Disease Control has confirmed the pneumonic plague known as PP1, or the Scourge, is drug resistant. At a news conference this morning, Associate Director for Healthy Water, National Center for Emerging, Zoonotic, and Infectious Diseases, Mateo Negro, PhD, told reporters the outlook is grim.

"Despite early indications a drug protocol involving tetracycline and other broad-spectrum antibiotics was effective in diminishing the long-term effects of the disease, we now know this is no longer the case," Dr. Negro said. He is also the director for PP1 Emergency Response. "All indications are that the PP1 bacteria are adapting at a phenomenal rate. They are no longer responsive to any tested combination of existing drugs. This includes streptomycin, gentamicin, and a variety of cocktails involving the aforementioned drugs."

Dr. Negro, speaking for CDC headquarters in Atlanta, Georgia, added that those who contract the latest strain of the Yersinia pestis *bacteria are almost certain to die within seventy-two hours.*

"Historically," Dr. Negro said, "fatality rates for septicemic or pneumonic plague was at ninety percent without treatment. We're finding this latest incarnation of the bacterial disease is one hundred percent. Even with treatment, the rate is nearly ninety-seven percent."

The World Health Organization reported yesterday it is working on a vaccine cultivated from the blood of the early Syrian survivors of the disease. But development and testing could take months. There are also several American, German, and British pharmaceutical companies working on new, plague-resistant antibiotics. Those, experts caution, could take months to perfect on the fastest of approval timelines.

Both the WHO and the CDC have warned against air travel, attending large gatherings, and have advised those with the disease to isolate themselves for the sake of others.

The most recent census, in 2030, calculated a world population of 8.2 billion people. Three hundred and thirty million live in the United States. To date, the WHO estimates 2.74 billion people have died from the disease, seventy-five million are US residents.

The numbers are increasing exponentially by the day. Dr. Negro sees no end in sight.

"The only people who will survive this," he said at the conclusion of the news conference, "are those who have a natural immunity. And right now, there's no way for us to know who those people are. The incubation period is anywhere from a couple of days to a full month."

Marcus closed his laptop and sat in the dark. From the kitchen he could hear the hum of the refrigerator. The ice maker clunked. The house was otherwise quiet. And then Wesson coughed.

It was a wet hack that sounded croupy, full of phlegm, and was getting worse. In between coughs, Wes sucked in air as if he'd just surfaced from nearly drowning. Marcus hurried to his son's side to find Sylvia already there. She was rubbing his back with one hand and holding an empty popcorn bowl in front of him with the other.

"Get it out, Wes," she said. "Spit it into the bowl if it helps."

Wes was hacking, shaking his head as he struggled. Marcus flipped on the overhead light and moved to the other side of the bed. He patted his son's back and looked across to Sylvia. She was on the edge of the bed, wearing a loose tank top and baggy boxer shorts. She hadn't changed clothes in two days. Her eyes were swollen from lack of sleep and her cheeks drawn from a lack of food.

"Anything we can do to treat the symptoms?" she asked Marcus above the din of Wes's fit.

Marcus shook his head. The cough syrup, the lozenges, the analgesics, the ice packs—none of them had done anything in the last forty-eight hours to soothe the worsening signs of the plague.

Wes caught his breath and reached for a glass of water at his bedside. He gulped it down like a toddler and wiped his watery eyes. "It's hard to breathe," he said. His voice sounded as though his vocal chords were shredded. "If I take a deep breath, I cough."

"Don't take a deep breath," Marcus suggested. He put his hand on the back of his son's neck and gently squeezed. "Breathe in slowly through your nose." His son's skin was hot to the touch. His fever had to be above 102 degrees.

Marcus exchanged glances with his wife. He could tell she was struggling to maintain her composure. Her eyes were as wet as their son's. The puffiness, he reminded himself, was probably as much from crying as it was from sleeplessness.

"Can I get you anything to eat?" Marcus asked. "A popsicle maybe? We still have cherry and lime."

Wes nodded. "Lime, please."

Marcus tousled his son's sweaty head and smiled at him. "I'll be right back." He moved to the doorway when Wes stopped him with a question.

"Dad," he asked, his rasp making it difficult to understand him, "am I going to die?"

Sylvia immediately spun around, away from her son and toward her husband. She was quietly sobbing, trying hard to control the shudder in her shoulders.

Marcus put his hands on her shoulders. He looked at his son, who suddenly seemed more frail than he had a few seconds earlier. He couldn't lie to him. He smiled. "That's up to God, Wes. If he needs you more than us right now, then, yes, you will die. If he doesn't, you'll be fine before you know it. Either way, you win."

"I don't want to die, Dad," he whispered. "I don't think I'm ready to go to Heaven."

"Nobody is ever ready to go to Heaven, Wes," Marcus answered. He could feel his wife's tears dampening his shirt at his stomach. "That's why God makes the choice. He always knows the best time. I'll be honest, Wes, if God is calling you first, that must mean you're really special. It means you're important."

Wes nodded at his dad. He reached out and put his hand on Sylvia's back. He rubbed it back and forth. "Mom, it's okay. It's okay to be sad and scared. I'm scared. You don't have to hide from me."

Sylvia slowly turned back to her son and flung her arms around him. Wes reciprocated and waved his father toward them.

Marcus hesitated but sat next to Sylvia and joined the group hug. He pulled both of them toward him and took a deep breath. If his son was going to die, he might as well too. He willed the bacteria into his lungs with another deep breath. Sylvia kissed Wes's head repeatedly. Her nose was running; her eyes were shut and squeezing tears down her cheeks.

Marcus sat back, releasing his hold, and stood. "I'll go get the popsicle." He walked to the kitchen without turning around.

He opened the freezer door and stood in the blast of cold air. He reached into the popsicle box and fished around. He'd miscalculated. The box was empty.

CHAPTER 13

OCTOBER 13, 2037, 9:04 PM

SCOURGE + 5 YEARS

TEXAS HIGHWAY 36

EAST OF RISING STAR, TEXAS

Battle called out to Lola above the whistle of the intensifying wind. "Can you pass me Inspector, please?"

"Which one is that?"

"The long rifle. It's got a camouflage finish. The other shotgun, the Browning, is called Lloyd."

Lola stood at the base of the oak, looking up to the treehouse trapdoor. She raised Inspector up above her head. "Why do you name your weapons?"

Battle peeked through the trapdoor opening. It was dark, but with his thermal goggles he could see her leaning against the tree. He grabbed the weapon and set it inside the treehouse. "I just do."

"Please tell me," Lola asked, picking a couple of leaves from her hair.

Battle sighed. "Did you ever see that old movie *Cast Away*?"

"No. I don't watch movies. I haven't had a lot of downtime in the last few years, Battle."

"You asked. You wanna know or not?"

"Yes. Sorry."

"I watch a lot of movies," he called down to her. "I have a collection on a ten terabyte hard drive. *Cast Away* is like, I don't know, more than thirty years old now."

"What about it?" Lola shrugged, her orange glow flexing in the artificial goggle light on Battle's eyes.

"The main character, a guy named Chuck Nolan, gets stranded on an island after a plane crash. He's alone for four years. His only companion is a volleyball he names Wilson. He talks to the ball and becomes emotionally connected to Wilson."

"A volleyball? How'd he get a volleyball?"

"It washes ashore in a package," Battle said, "but that's not the point. The point is, he has no human interaction. He personifies the ball to stay sane, to simulate normalcy."

"So you have a relationship with the guns for the same reason?"

"More or less."

"You talk to them?"

Battle didn't answer. He regretted telling her. He shouldn't have told her. She couldn't possibly understand. She'd lived among people, albeit evil ones, since the Scourge had swept across the globe and left little standing in its wake.

She could poke fun, she could mock, she could question. But she couldn't understand.

There was a very thin line between sanity and...the alternative.

Lightning flickered in the distance, and the accompanying thunder was a low rumble.

"What happened to the ball?" Lola called up to him. Her voice was louder than it had been. She was closer.

Battle looked out the trapdoor. Lola was standing on her good foot halfway up the ladder. "I'm sorry."

"You say that a lot."

"Because I am. What happened to the ball?"

"He lost it. It floated off into the ocean."

Lola stood in the dark, her orange image dancing in Battle's thermal goggles, her bad ankle dangling in the air. Lloyd was strapped to her back.

Battle offered her a hand, reaching out in the darkness and grabbing her wrist. He pulled her up the ladder and into the treehouse. She sat next to him on the floor.

"What now?" she asked.

"We watch." He took off the goggles and handed them to her.

Lola slid the goggles over her eyes. "Whoa. This is weird. Everything is orange."

"Keep those on," he said. "They're thermal. You'll see people moving around no problem. Just don't kill *me*."

"What are you going to use?"

"I've got a scope on my rifle. I'll use that. Follow me."

Battle inched his way to the front of the treehouse, the perch from which he first saw Lola running onto his land. He looked through the scope. There was nothing yet.

"You're going to be here," he said. "I want you to point that weapon through this opening. It doesn't matter if you hit anything. You're here to confuse them and keep them away from the house."

A gust of wind howled through the pine slats. It was cold and damp. Lightning flashed, illuminating the stark inside of the treehouse. The thunder followed immediately and rattled the tree.

Lola lifted the goggles onto her forehead. "You're not going to be here with me?"

Rain started thumping against the roof. It was an intermittent patter before intensifying to a heavy, rhythmic beat.

"No," he said above the din. "I'm going to be on the other side of the yard. If you hear me open fire and then stop, that's your cue to pop off a couple of shots. I need you to distract them and draw their attention while I reload."

"You mean draw their *fire*?"

Battle shrugged. She wasn't stupid. "Put your goggles on," he said and backed away from the perch toward the trapdoor. "I'm closing this behind me. There's a latch on it. Lock it once I drop down."

"What do I do if…"

"If they kill me?"

Lola nodded. Lightning flashed and cracked an instant before thunder crashed around them.

"They won't."

Battle slipped down the opening and pulled the trapdoor over his head, descending into the rain. The drops were heavy and cold and they were relentless.

McDunnough was strapped to his hip, his canvas bag slung over his chest. It thumped his back as he jogged toward his position, the toys inside clacking and clanging as he moved. He held Inspector with both hands and pounded through the mud on his way across the yard. He moved north, closer to the house to avoid the line of traps, and then turned south once he crossed the driveway.

About thirty feet east of the driveway was a large oak tree. It had grown faster than most of the others he'd planted. He reached its trunk and looked up, rain falling into his eyes. He figured if he climbed halfway up the thirty-foot oak, he'd be in a good position.

He rubbed the bottoms of his rubber-soled boots on the base of the tree to free them of mud, slung Inspector over his head, and grabbed a pair of thick branches above his head. He hoisted himself with ease and navigated his way up the tree to the bottom of its dying canopy.

He set himself in a thick fork near the trunk and stuck his bag in a crook next to him. Satisfied it was secure, he pulled Inspector over his head and set it in his lap. His back was against the trunk and he had one knee pulled close to his chest.

The rain slapped against the branches above him, some of it pooling before streaming down like a small waterfall onto his head. It was miserable, but he was focused. His training came back to him like muscle memory. He was attuned to his surroundings but undistracted by them.

Battle thumbed the rain from both sides of the scope and pulled it to his eye. The rain distorted his view. The infrared scope wasn't the best in fog or heavy rain. Marcus cursed the weather.

He was essentially blind and they were coming.

***

Pico found the driveway with little problem. Despite the high grass, tall weeds, and intense rain, he led the posse straight to the area where it intersected the highway. Rudabaugh told the five other men to dismount and tie their horses to the fencing that separated the wide easement from Mad Max's land.

"Make sure you got enough ammo," Rudabaugh called out. "We don't want to run out and get trapped. Pico takes the lead. He knows the land, so he says."

"We staying together or splitting up?" asked one of the grunts.

"Two teams of three," he said. "Pico takes two and heads straight ahead. I'll follow with two more. Once we get past the interior fence, we'll split. I'll head left, Pico heads right."

The sky lit up and the ground rumbled as lightning forked directly beside them. A deafening boom shook them as they split into their teams. The men were armed with identical shotguns, the same model as the one he'd lost to Mad Max the night before. They also carried side pieces slung low on their legs, long-barrel pistols loaded and ready to fire.

"We get past that inside fence Pico talked about," Rudabaugh ordered, "we check it out, better figure out what he's got close to the house, and we pull back."

"What if he shoots first?" asked one of the grunts, wiping the rain from his face. "We supposed to hightail it, or are we staying and fighting?"

"Mad Max shoots first and we fight back, boys," Rudabaugh said, water pouring in sheets from the brim of his hat. "We ain't running if there are bullets flying. If we have to end him tonight, we do it."

"I don't think—" Pico started.

Rudabaugh grabbed Pico's collar, wringing the water from it with his fist. "You ain't supposed to think. You got us here. Now you do what I say."

Pico coughed and nodded. He regretted having said anything. He stumbled backward when Rudabaugh let go of his collar and shoved him in the chest.

"Screw it," Rudabaugh snarled. "I'll take the lead. Pico, you and your guys are behind us. When we get to the fence, we'll go left. You go right."

Pico pointed to the two men he'd take with him. They were grunts too, so they weren't gonna back-talk him or bust his chops. They'd do what he said because Rud told them he was the leader.

Rud and his two grunts disappeared into the sheet of rain and darkness. The only concept of how far they'd gotten was when a lightning flash gave away their position. Pico spit the water from his lips and waved his two men forward. He motioned for one of them to take his right and the other his left. He could feel the gravel crunching under his boots as they marched forward, but he couldn't hear it. The steady rain was too loud. They'd made it only halfway between the road and the interior fence when Pico saw a bright flash at eye level followed by a series of smaller flickers closer to the ground. A moment later came the crack of an explosion and the subsequent pops of gunfire.

***

Rudabaugh and his two men were walking shoulder to shoulder, traipsing through the high weeds and mud. They were off the gravel driveway and moving straight north.

In a flash of lightning, Rud saw the main house beyond a low wooden fence. To the far left, in the corner of his eyes, he thought he spotted what looked like a treehouse. He couldn't be sure. So he reached out and gripped the shoulder of the grunt to his left.

"Go ahead," he said above the percussion of the rain. "Walk a few steps to the left and then move to the fence. I think there's a fort or something in the tree."

The grunt nodded and moved to the northwest a few steps ahead of Rud and the other grunt.

Rudabaugh gripped his weapon and marched forward, turning his attention to the right. He was waiting for another flash of lightning to reveal more of the layout when a bright explosion boomed to his left.

He snapped his attention toward the explosion in time to see another flash and hear what sounded like a shotgun blast. The grunt wailed and started cursing. Rudabaugh responded by picking up his feet and running through the mud, splashing his way toward the grunt.

As he approached, his eyes, nose, and throat started burning. His eyes reflexively squeezed shut. He tried opening them but couldn't.

"I can't see!" screamed the grunt. "I think my eyes got shot. I can't see." The grunt's hands were covering his face. He was wandering aimlessly in circles and ran into Rudabaugh.

"What the—" Rudabaugh pushed back against the grunt and knocked him to the ground. The grunt rolled in the mud, unarmed and crying.

The sting was dissipating and Rudabaugh figured he was breathing in some sort of pepper gas or mace. The rain was lessening its effects. He blinked back tears and forced himself to surveil the area around him. The grunt was useless.

Rud raised his shotgun and spun in a semicircle, looking for whoever fired the gas canister. He still couldn't account for the initial explosion. He licked the rain from his lips and pulled his wet shirt above his nose. It exposed his belly to the rain but helped him breathe and made the air around him less torturous.

"Shut up," he called to the roiling grunt. "You're gonna get us killed." Rud took another couple of steps, the Browning held at eye level. He panned the fence line as he approached it.

Another flicker of lightning raised the hair on his neck and arms. Instantly a bolt cracked to his right, followed by another crash of thunder that rattled his teeth. For a split second he thought he saw someone perched in a tree outside the fence. He couldn't be sure. He thought maybe the sniper had a rifle aimed directly at him. It was the snap of a rifle shot and a bullet ripping into his shoulder that confirmed it.

***

Without the help of his scope, Battle knew he'd need to wait until somebody tripped a wire. The silent laser alarm he'd used the night before was useless in the rain. His watch, which connected to the alarm wirelessly, kept flashing false intrusions. He took it off and stuffed it into a pocket. He didn't want the light giving away his position.

A flash of lightning gave him the first hint that somebody was on his land. He saw three men walking side by side. He held his position and slowly raised the rifle. The scope was grainy, the rain blocking any accuracy it might have provided on a clear night.

Then one of the men tripped the wire. The firework exploded, as intended, and immediately triggered the gas-filled shell. Battle couldn't see what was happening, but he thought he heard a shriek and some yelling in the general direction of the trip.

He trained the rifle in that area, southwest of his position, and he waited. He knew the lightning would flash again, providing him a target. Battle held still, the rain pouring down his neck and back. It dripped from his head down his face. It was worsening.

Then there was a momentary flicker and a bright, ear-ripping bolt of lightning overhead. He saw two men in that instant. One was in the mud. The other was armed. He was large and was crouched with his rifle leveled. His head turned and Battle thought, maybe, the man saw him.

Battle deemed him the more immediate threat. He closed his eyes, the burned image of the man imprinted in his mind. He moved his aim incrementally to the left and fired a single shot. He then moved his aim downward and fired again. Twice.

Pop! Pop!

A distant strobe of lightning revealed he'd hit the gunman once, in the shoulder. He'd dropped his weapon and was holding the wound. The dude on the ground wasn't rolling around anymore. He was still. But in that flicker, Battle saw a third armed man joining the injured and dead.

Battle knew he had a split second to make a decision. He could stay in the tree, a position they'd likely identified, or he could jump down and assault them. The question he asked himself was how many more men were coming.

"There can't only be three," he mumbled to himself, tasting the cold rain. A shiver ran down his spine. He flexed his hands one at a time. They were stiffening in the cold, damp air.

He was about to leave his perch when a shotgun popped. The flash, however, didn't come from the trio near the tripwire. It was farther away, from the treehouse.

Lola!

A gust of wind blew the rain directly into Battle's face. He blinked past the water and raised the scope toward the treehouse. The infrared was still mostly useless.

Pop! Pop!

Lola again. Battle realized she was doing what he'd instructed, holding his place while she thought he was reloading. He'd need to act or she could be in trouble.

Rather than staying in the tree, he made the call to rush the trio and eliminate them before another wave of men attacked. He needed to move fast.

He grabbed his rain-soaked canvas bag, zipped it, and tossed it to the ground. Against another flash of lightning he slid out onto a branch and slipped. He tried to steady himself but couldn't and fell. But he caught himself with the crook of his right arm, Inspector slung over his back, and he held onto a thick branch twelve feet off the ground.

He was dangling from the branch by his forearm. He managed to reach up with his left hand and, despite the slickness of the oak branch, maintain his grip. His back was to the trio of men. Another flash of lightning lit up the sky, illuminating the milky clouds hung low and moving fast in the central Texas sky. Battle knew he was exposed.

Pop!

Another shotgun blast. But this one whizzed by Battle's head. He heard its whistle as it zipped past him. His hands were slipping.

Pop! Pop!

Two more shots whirred past him. One of them slugged the thick branch from which he was hanging. The wood splintered and shards exploded around him. A piece pierced the back of his arm, drilling deep. The jolt surprised Battle and he flinched, losing his grip.

He dropped to the ground below, splashing into the mud with both feet before falling onto his back and the rifle. His head slammed into the ground, disorienting him for a moment. But Battle struggled onto his stomach and swung around Inspector. His lower back was tight. His fingers were stiff. The back of his right bicep was thick with a searing pain.

He pitched himself onto his elbows, spread his legs behind him, and flipped open the bipod on the bottom of the rifle. He planted it in the mud and lay in wait.

Pop! Zip! Pop! Zip!

The shots were a good three or four feet above his head. They were coming from his ten o'clock. Battle shifted his weight and spun the rifle to the left. He slipped his hand onto the trigger and pressed, holding it there as Inspector did its job.

Rat tat tat tat tat tat tat! Rat tat tat tat tat tat tat!

Despite the steady, loud percussion of the rain, he could hear a man's sharp squeal followed by a grunt and the sound of a body splashing into the mud. A second threat was neutralized.

There was at least one more.

***

Pico could hear what sounded like a firefight, but the rain obscured his vision. He directed both of the grunts to follow him closer to the bursts of light.

The three of them moved cautiously but with purpose through the deepening puddles of mud. Pico felt his boots stick and worked hard to pick up his feet past the suction with each successive step.

The sky lit up for a moment and went dark again. One of the grunts caught Pico's attention and pointed off to the right. Pico nodded, giving him permission to move in that direction. The grunt stepped ahead, moving more quickly than Pico, and he slipped into the darkness.

The sheets of rain might as well have been a brick wall between Pico and whatever he was trying to see. He moved to the left with the other grunt. Together they forged a path toward the spot of the first explosion.

Pico kept his eyes up, despite the downpour, hoping for another fork of lightning to help him see his surroundings. A couple of shots sparked the blackness ahead of him. They came from maybe twenty feet off the ground. Somebody was there.

Rat tat tat tat tat tat tat! Rat tat tat tat tat tat tat!

The barrage of gunfire to his left threatened to draw his attention, but he kept his focus. Even as he heard a squeal and unearthly wail, he kept moving ahead. He crouched low, his weapon aimed upward. His eyes were set at the spot where he could best tell the shots emanated.

An explosion of thunder rocked the ground as the night turned to day with another prolonged concussion of lightning. He could barely see a treehouse set in the thick cradle of a large tree. He didn't see anyone. But he knew someone had to be there.

Pico worked his way west, making a ninety-degree turn to the left, and moved quickly, crouching as he ran parallel to the interior fence line. He knew better than to approach the treehouse from the front. He'd be an easy target. He thought it better to approach from the side. He gripped the Browning with one hand, holding it vertically, and he maneuvered his way to a fence that ran perpendicular to the highway. He climbed over it, into the neighboring property, and followed it north, past the treehouse. In another snap of lightning he saw a large barn on the other side of the fence. From this position, he could approach the treehouse undetected. He moved to the fence and grabbed the top rail to climb over. The instant his hand reached for the wood, he felt a wire tighten against his palm.

Boom! Pop!

A loud crack exploded to his left, knocking him to the ground. It sounded like a gunshot followed by a shotgun blast.

The successive blasts looked more like firecrackers to Pico. He immediately rolled onto his side and tried to push himself back to his feet when he sucked in a poisonous gulp of air. He stopped short and coughed out the burn. His eyes stung and he closed them. Pico dropped back onto his knees and tried covering his face with his shirt. He crawled in the mud, splashing like a hog as he moved on all fours away from the burn. His ears were ringing. He was disoriented. In the midst of the rain and lightning, mud and gas, Pico thought he might be dying. In that moment, he actually wished for death. The thought of it was strangely comforting.

***

Rudabaugh's arm hung uselessly from his ruined shoulder. His good hand was no better than the one with the bullet hole through it.

He was on one knee between two dead grunts. He bit down hard on his cheek, trying to mitigate the searing pain in his shoulder. He grabbed at it with his wounded hand and then planted the gauze-wrapped fist into the slop. He willed himself to his feet and stumbled forward toward a wrought-iron gate.

The rain poured off his head into his eyes as he staggered, his hat lost somewhere in the mud and blood. His heart pounded in his neck, his temples, and at the wound on both sides of his shoulder.

His breathing ragged and shallow, he somehow managed to flip himself over the fence where it met the gate. On his back, he blinked against the heavy drops slapping against his face. He'd lost track of Mad Max, or whoever it was who'd unloaded the barrage of semiautomatic gunfire.

Rud couldn't believe this was where he would die—in the mud belonging to some vigilante hermit. He'd survived the Scourge; he'd helped to build the Cartel's influence and risen through the ranks; he'd killed countless men, women, and even children to earn that brown hat. Damned if he was gonna go out like this.

He rolled over and again found his footing. The sky strobed white and he saw the treehouse straight ahead. Rudabaugh reasoned that was his best option. If he could make it to the treehouse, he could find cover and regroup. He still had his sidearm. It wasn't over yet.

Rudabaugh looked over his shoulder, but didn't see anyone. Still, he could sense Mad Max was there. He started walking, hobbling really, toward the treehouse. One step. Then another. Right. Left. Right. Left. His arm dangled limply, bouncing against his side. Another step closer. Straight ahead, beyond the treehouse, he saw an explosion of light and a smaller orange burst.

Then Rudabaugh, without any concept of what was happening, lost his footing in the mud, his boot slipping through the ground, into a hole, and onto something sharp.

His ankle twisted and snapped at the same moment he heard a gunshot and felt an instantaneous burning heat tear through the meat of his foot. He fell forward, his broken ankle and shattered foot still stuck at the bottom of the hole.

Without the use of one arm, his face slammed to the mud. Rudabaugh swallowed some of it when he gasped in shock and pain. He sucked in the mud, gagging on it as he grabbed at the wet earth. He coughed out the bilge water and cried out defiantly.

He was on his side, struggling like a beetle, when a pair of boots planted themselves in front of his face. Rudabaugh craned his neck, trying to look upward toward the owner of the boots. Before he could catch even the slightest glimpse of the hermit he knew as Mad Max, the man put the barrel of a Prairie Panther to the back of his head and tapped the trigger once.

***

Battle stared at the pitiful heap of a man in front of him. He knelt down and fished the six-shooter from the man's leg holster, flipping it over in his hands. It was a Cimarron Rooster Shooter, a single-action revolver that was essentially a rip-off of John Wayne's Colt single action. He opened the cylinder. It was fully loaded.

Battle stood and stuffed it into his waistband. He'd come up with a name for it later. "As far as the east is from the west," he whispered to himself, "so far has he removed our transgressions from us." He took a deep breath. There were more people to kill.

Just before he'd ended the lard in front of him, he'd seen the tripwire explode on the western edge of the property. Somebody was over there. He made a mental tally: three dead and at least one more alive.

He carefully walked back to the fence, hopped over it, and traveled along its edge toward the tripwire. The rain was lessening. At least the drops didn't sting as much as the wind blew them into his face. He was trying to get a good look at the treehouse and strained his eyes in the dark. He couldn't see much more than the rough shape of the fort lodged in the branches. He stopped and tried to focus when he felt something poking him in the back, right between his shoulders above where the canvas bag was hanging.

"Drop the rifle." The voice was jittery and sounded young. "I'm gonna shoot you if you don't drop it."

"Okay then." Battle raised his hands above his head, holding Inspector in one of them. "I'll put it down, but I'm not gonna drop it. It could fire and kill us both."

"Then put it down."

Battle felt a jab at his back. He imagined it was the same Browning shotgun all the intruders were carrying. He slowly bent at his knees and then his waist. He set Inspector into the mud.

Another man emerged from the darkness in front of him. He was marching with confidence, his Browning trained at Battle, who stood back up and kept his hands above his head.

"Where's the woman?" the new intruder asked. "What'd you do with her?"

Battle counted in his head. There were three dead, a fourth was likely rolling around in the mud, fighting the effects of the tear gas, and then there were these two. Six total.

"You guys only bring six people to this party?" Battle asked, clasping his hands behind his head. He was trying to buy himself time to think.

"We brought what we needed." Scarface stepped up to Battle and held the barrel inches from his face. The man, with a shaved head and long red scar down his cheek, looked past Battle. "You seen the woman?"

"No."

Intruder number five poked Battle again from behind. "Where is she?"

"Who are you talking about?" Battle shrugged and twisted his right boot heel deep into the mud. "What woman?"

Scarface inched a step closer, the shotgun pointed between Battle's eyes. "Don't be a—"

Using the mud to his advantage, Battle slid his left heel forward while keeping his right in place. Dropping into a quasi-split, he drove the heel of his left hand upward into Scarface's chest.

At the same time, he reached into his waistband with his right hand and pulled out the Cimarron Rooster and plucked the trigger three times at the man behind him. He then emptied the other three forty-five-caliber slugs into Scarface as he tumbled backward and dropped the Browning into the mud. The series of moves took a little more than two seconds.

Certain the two men were dead, Battle rolled onto his side. His groin hurt. And when he stood, it tightened. Battle worried he'd pulled a muscle or, worse yet, tore something. He tested his gait and limped toward the treehouse, staying on the outside of the fence. There was one man left, by his count.

He doubted there was another team. In fact, he worried there wasn't another team.

He hopped the fence, without his bag or weapon, and gingerly climbed the planks of pine toward the treehouse trapdoor. He banged on it, rattling the locking board on the other side.

"Lola!" he yelled. "It's Battle. Let me in."

He heard scurrying above his head and then the pounding of footsteps. "Coming!" Within a few seconds she had the trapdoor open, and Battle climbed through.

"Are they gone?" Lola asked. "Did you kill them? Did I kill them?"

"Let me see the goggles. I think there's still one out there." He hobbled to the right and slid the thermal goggles over his head. He leaned against the wall and peeked through, looking toward the fence on the western perimeter. He scanned along the fence line to the left and then back to the right.

Lola joined him at the wall. "Why do you—?"

"Shhh! Wait." Battle saw him. A heat signature glowed on the other side of the fence. At first, he couldn't tell if was an animal or a human. Then the figure stood and moved back and forth along the fence in a tight pattern. He was dazed or injured. Either way, he was vulnerable. "Stay here, I'll be right back." He ripped the goggles from his eyes and handed them back to Lola, stepping past her to the trapdoor opening.

She grabbed his shoulder. "Where are you going? How many were there? You're leaving me here?"

Battle put his hands on the sides of her face. "Chill. I will be back. You wait here."

"You're going to kill the last one?"

"No. I need to talk with him."

***

Battle's limp lessened the more he walked. The rain was shrinking to a drizzle and the flashes of lightning were moving north and west. He walked straight back toward the barn with McDunnough, the Sig Sauer, in his hand. He edged along the front of the barn toward the western fence line, crouching low. He barely picked up his feet as he slid along the mud, trying to be silent. When he approached, he realized the man was gone. He wasn't anywhere near the spot where Battle had spotted him a couple of minutes earlier. When he reached the fence line, he caught a glimpse of the man running south. He was headed for the highway.

Battle wasn't about to let another man escape. He hopped the fence and started running. His gait was like a wounded horse, but he kept running. The figure ahead of him was getting larger as he closed in on the man.

The rain was softening to a mist by the time they reached the cattle fence that ran parallel to the highway. Battle could hear the man huffing and wheezing as he leapt at him. He wrapped his arms around the man's spindly body, driving his shoulder into the man's back and plowing him to the ground.

The air was forced from the man's lungs as they landed and slid to a stop inches from the fence. Battle threw a battery of punches at the man's kidneys, pushing his head sideways into the mud. He grabbed at the man's waist and searched for his hands. The intruder was unarmed.

"Don't move," Battle spat into the man's ear and then shoved his back to push himself free. "Move at all and you're dead like all of your buddies."

The intruder groaned but didn't speak. His hand was twitching.

Battle rolled onto his knees and got a better look at the man's face. His face was long and narrow, and his mud-caked mustache seemed too big for it. The man's eyes were cracked open. Battle snapped his fingers and the intruder blinked.

"I'm not killing you," he said. "Not yet, anyway. We've got business to discuss." Battle stood, wincing against the pain in his groin, and ordered the intruder to stand. He got no response. A second order didn't yield different results.

"Okay then," he said. "Have it your way." Battle walked around to the man's feet, turned his back, and reached down to grab an ankle with each hand. "Watch your head," he said, and started pulling the intruder through the mud, belly first. The clouds were beginning to thin and the sliver of a new moon was fighting to shine through the milky blanket in the sky.

By the time they reached the treehouse, the intruder was unconscious. Battle called up to Lola. "C'mon down. I got him."

Lola climbed down the ladder and walked straight to the fence line. Remembering not to walk through the minefield of booby traps, she hopped the fence and met Battle on the other side.

She looked at Battle standing in front of the unconscious intruder, holding his ankles in the air like wheelbarrow handles.

"What are you doing?"

"I'm dragging him."

"Why?"

"He wouldn't get up." Battle dropped the man's feet into the slop. "Do you recognize him?"

"It's too dark," she said, shaking her head. "I can't tell."

"Let's get him to the garage."

"Why there?"

"I don't want him seeing what I have in the barn, and I don't want him in the house."

"Fair enough."

Battle reached down and grabbed the man's ankles, lifting them waist high. He looked over at Lola. "Grab his hands."

"*Please?*"

Battle rolled his eyes. Manners weren't a priority. "Grab his hands, *please*."

The two of them carried the intruder the rest of the distance to the garage. They dropped him onto the ground at the entrance to the bay doors. He grunted after his head hit the ground.

Battle tapped a code on a keypad adjacent to the doors, and one of them hummed to life, rumbling upward to reveal the cavernous garage inside. Gas vapor lights blinked on, intensifying as they warmed up. Battle dragged the intruder the rest of the distance and closed the door behind the three of them.

Though the garage was more than wide enough for three cars, only an old pickup truck sitting atop flat tires occupied the bays. Tool-laden pegboard covered the back wall of the garage. Underneath the pegboard was a long wooden workbench next to a four-foot-tall tool chest. Part of the workbench looked like a desk. A vented metal swivel chair was stored in the opening.

Battle grabbed the chair and rolled it to the center of one of the empty bays. He walked back to the pegboard and pulled two sections of bungee cord from their hooks.

"Let's get him into the chair." He nodded at Lola, who was preoccupied with taking in the size of the garage. "Help me, *please*."

They moved the heavy, limp intruder to the chair, and Battle bound him with the cord. He pulled the man's hands behind his back and wrapped the cord around his wrists, winding the excess around his chest. The second cord affixed his ankles and feet to the center cylinder, essentially tucking them up underneath the seat.

Lola was standing a couple of feet back, watching Battle work.

"We need to go get the weapons," he said. "We can't leave them out there. That'll give this guy a chance to wake up a little bit. When we get back, he starts talking."

The intruder grumbled something unintelligible and shook his hanging head. A viscous mix of snot and blood was nesting in his mustache. One eye was swollen shut and his upper lip was busted. He was caked with mud and tied to a chair. It didn't matter what he was mumbling.

He would eventually talk.

CHAPTER 14

NOVEMBER 11, 2032, 2:18 PM

SCOURGE +40 DAYS

EAST OF RISING STAR, TEXAS

"It's my fault." Sylvia was pacing back and forth in the kitchen. She was inconsolable. "I killed our son," she said.

Marcus tried reasoning with her. "You can't say —"

"Yes, I can!" she yelled, pressing her arms downward. Her hands were balled into fists. "I shouldn't have opened the door. She would have gone away. Wesson would still be here. He would be here!"

Marcus stepped around the island toward his wife. She backed away, holding up her hands. She shook her head.

"I don't want your consolation, soldier," she said. "The idea of you holding me only makes me angrier at myself. You smell like him."

Marcus shrank back a step and stuffed his hands into his pockets. Their son had been dead less than twenty-four hours.

Marcus had buried him in the backyard like a pet they'd had to put down. It wasn't worthy of Wesson, but it was all they could do.

Sylvia wouldn't come outside. She couldn't, she told him. But while he'd dug the hole, he'd seen her peering through a window. Her nose had been pressed to the glass like a child. He'd pretended not to notice her.

He'd had no idea whether she'd watched any of the short burial service or not. Marcus had wrapped his son's body in a large plastic blue tarp he'd found in the garage and helped him into the ground.

With a shovel, he'd filled the hole and patted it as flat as he could. Then, alone, he'd prayed for his son's soul.

On his knees, he whispered, "In a favorable time I listened to you, and in a day of salvation I have helped you. Behold, now is the favorable time; behold, now is the day of salvation."

Now he stood in the kitchen, feeling a disconcerting combination of guilt and anger. Sylvia was right. It *was* her fault. She knew better than to let anyone in the house. He'd warned her; she didn't listen. She didn't even wear the surgical masks he'd given her and Wes to wear if they inadvertently came in contact with someone.

He'd never said, "I told you so," after handling Roseann. He didn't have to. He knew Sylvia could see it in his eyes. And when Wesson coughed for the first time, he'd seen the apology in her eyes.

He was angry at her. Still, he also loved her. He regretted not having done a better job protecting them. Ultimately, Marcus believed it was exclusively his job to keep them healthy and safe.

He'd spent his entire post-army life prepping for the end of the world. Now it was upon them and his son hadn't lived more than six weeks. It was his fault more than it was hers. But that unspoken chemical, emotional mixture of conflicting feelings was like a wall between them.

"So if I can't console you," he said, "what can I do?"

"Nothing." She cleared her throat. "Nothing. It's too late."

"Too late?" he questioned. "That implies I could have done something earlier. But not now."

"No, it doesn't," she snapped. "This isn't about you anyway. Not everything is about you, Marcus." Sylvia cleared her throat again.

Marcus bit his lip before he spoke. He already regretted the tone of their conversation. He glared at her. "Really?"

"Yes, really." She crossed her arms across her chest and leaned in. "All of this is about you. You moved us here. You isolated us. You convinced me to live in a Winnebago for two years."

"Convinced you?"

"I did all of it, Marcus"—her eyes narrowed—"because you promised me it would work. You told me that if we did this, if we gave up normal lives, we'd survive whatever catastrophe came our way."

"I didn't—"

"You were wrong, Major Battle." The sarcasm oozed more thickly with each successive word. "It didn't work. Wesson is dead. None of your stupid planning saved him. None of it."

"That's not—"

"I put up with your eccentricity, your need to be some kind of hermit, because I thought it was therapeutic. I thought it would help with what I knew was PTSD. You came back a different man, Marcus. You're not the man I fell in love with. You haven't been since you deployed to Syria."

Marcus flinched at the jab. He could feel a thick lump building in his throat. "What does that—"

"Shut up and let me talk!" A thick vein in her forehead looked as though it might burst.

Marcus took a deep breath and held it. He put up his hands in surrender.

"For all of your — your — *crap* — I thought there was a pot of gold at the end of it." She waved her hands wildly. "I thought, 'Okay, so my shell-shocked husband is a freak now. What do I do with that? I guess I go along with it. Because, eventually, if anything bad ever happens, we'll be safe. Our *family* will be safe.'

"That's not what happened. That's…" She hitched and tears rolled from her eyes. She started sobbing. She leaned onto the island, dropped her head, and started coughing.

Marcus fought the instinct to move toward her and then succumbed to it. He slowly approached Sylvia and gently put his hand on her back before turning her toward him. She didn't resist.

He put his hand on the back of her head and stroked her hair. He didn't know what else to do. The pressure of the lump in his throat was painful. So he released it.

For the first time since returning from Syria, he cried. While he didn't moan or wail, he knew Sylvia could feel the shudder of his chest. Marcus wasn't sure why he was openly emotional. It might have been because he'd just buried his only child. It might have been because he could feel the congestion rattling in his wife's lungs as he held her back. He could hear it in her crying. She was sick too.

CHAPTER 15

OCTOBER 14, 2037, 1:27 AM

SCOURGE + 5 YEARS

ABILENE, TEXAS

Queho rolled over and fumbled around on the bedside table until he felt the tin case in which he kept hand-rolled cigarettes. "Want one?"

"No," said his girlfriend. "And I thought you quit." She got up from the bed and crossed the room naked.

Queho watched her slink toward the bathroom in the low, flickering glow of a pair of pedestal candles. His girlfriend had fashioned them from wax. She was good at two things. One was making and selling homemade candles. The other they'd just enjoyed together.

Queho regularly joked she could probably make more money at *that* skill. She never laughed, though she often countered by telling him she got more enjoyment out of making candles.

He dragged a lighter from the table and lit the cigarette. He puffed a couple of times and then tossed the case and lighter back onto the table. "I did quit."

"Doesn't look like it," she called from the bathroom. She was the only one, other than Skinner maybe, who could talk to Queho truthfully. She never genuflected or begged forgiveness for an indiscretion.

They lived together in a house on the corner of 9th and Butternut. It was a part of Abilene called Original Town South. Across the street were what used to be a liquor store and a library. The store was out of liquor; the library was empty of books.

The elderly man who'd lived in the home for sixty years before the Scourge was buried out back. Queho had tossed his stiff, bloated body into a hole after finding him dead in a recliner in the front room.

He took possession of the house. It wasn't much, but it was close to the HQ. He also knew he'd get the respect of his men by not choosing one of the fancier places in town. Respect was important to Queho. So was power.

"I'm stressed," he called back after a long drag. "It helps me cope."

She laughed. "I thought I just relieved your stress."

Queho chuckled to himself. He got up from the bed and walked to the dresser on the far side of the room. Atop the dresser, along with his holster and revolver, was his hat, his wallet, a large key ring, and an ashtray. He tapped the cigarette into the ashtray and carried it back to bed with him, his club foot thumping along the wood floor.

"What are you doing?" She emerged from the bathroom, wearing an open terry cloth robe, the tattoos that ran across her breasts and around her navel visible as she floated back to bed.

"Getting an ashtray."

"So"—she slithered under the sheets and ran her hand along Queho's leg—"what's got you stressed? I could tell you were…preoccupied."

"A woman." Queho sucked on the cigarette and waited for her reaction.

"Oh really?" She ran her fingers up his chest. "What woman?" she purred. It wasn't the reaction he expected.

"Some worker." He shrugged. "She owed us. She escaped. A few men got killed trying to find her."

Her hand moved down his chest and traced the scripted tattoo on his abdomen. "She killed them?"

Queho screwed the cigarette into the tray. "No. She found some ranch we didn't know about. Some guy was living there. He killed the men."

"And the woman?"

"Don't know. But the man is tough. That's what Pico says."

She laughed. "Pico? You trust what that little weasel says? He's scared of his own shadow."

Queho set aside the ashtray and slid his hand onto her thigh. "Yeah, he is. But I believe him. I think the guy's gotta be tough. He killed three men, one of them with his bare hands. At least that's what Pico said."

"Okay," she said. "So a woman goes missing. She gets away. Big deal."

Queho pulled his hand from her thigh and her hand from his stomach. He sat up straight and turned to look his woman in the eye.

"Are you kidding me?" he spat. "Big deal? Our power, our way of life, relies on fear. If people ain't afraid of us, we lose. One woman gets away and we do nothing about it? Word gets around. People start thinking they can do it. Next thing you know, we're getting hanged in the street by the common folk."

"I get that," she said meekly. "I just don't understand why it stresses you out."

Queho slapped the bed with his hands. His eyes widened. "Because we got this guy out there too. We're calling him Mad Max. He's a problem."

"Then take care of him. I don't get why this is such a big deal. You've taken care of plenty of people. What makes this one different?"

"I can't tell you that," Queho admitted. "I got a feeling about it, that's all. I don't think it's as easy as 'taking care of him'. He's probably been on that land since the Scourge. You could argue we ain't found him until now, but I don't buy that. We've had too many posses out looking for occupied ranches. We didn't miss him. I got a gut feeling we had more than one posse stumble on his place and *he* took care of *them*."

"So what are you doing about it?"

"We got a scout party out there tonight," he said, easing a pillow up the headboard behind him. "They're looking around, getting a better feel for the place. Then we'll go back with twenty to twenty-five men and end it."

"Okay." She shrugged. "Then that's your answer. No reason for the stress. No need for the cigarettes. No need to be…preoccupied." She slipped her hand under the sheet.

"Maybe," he said. "I don't know. I'm itching for the scout team to come back. Once I hear from them, I'll feel better. What time is it?"

"I don't know," she said. "Does it matter?"

"Yeah." He threw the sheet from his body, leaving his girlfriend alone in the bed. "It's late. They should be getting back soon." Queho thumped across the room to a pile of clothes on the floor. He reached down to get himself dressed.

"You aren't gonna wash up at least?"

"No," he said. "I gotta go talk to Skin. Don't wait up for me."

CHAPTER 16

OCTOBER 14, 2037, 2:00 AM

SCOURGE + 5 YEARS

TEXAS HIGHWAY 36

EAST OF RISING STAR, TEXAS

Battle twirled a brown cowboy hat with his hand. He was sitting opposite a man calling himself Salomon Pico. Lola was wrapped in a sleeping bag in the bed of the pickup truck. She was snoring.

"I appreciate the information you've given me so far, Salomon," said Battle. "But I'm gonna need a little more."

Pico asked for water. He licked his lips. His head hung such that his chin touched his chest.

"We've been at this for a couple of hours now, Salomon." Battle stopped twirling the hat and set it on his lap. "I'll give you water when we finish. You've given me your name. You've told me you're with the Cartel. You admitted you came here to kill me and take Lola. But you haven't told me where she can find her son. You haven't told me who sent you here or where you came from."

Pico shook his head back and forth without raising it. "I don't know where he is."

"Where did you come from?"

"I told you." Pico's voice was raspy. "I came from local headquarters."

"Which is where?"

"Near here."

"Wrong answer, Salomon."

He lifted his head. His lips were crusted white at the corners. "I can't tell you," he said. "They'll kill me."

"I'll kill you if you don't, Salomon," Battle answered. "But let's do this. I ask a question. You answer. I like your answer and I give you water or maybe something to eat. Sound good?"

Pico dropped his head again.

"If you don't give me an answer that I like, I'm gonna hurt you. I've been really patient. But I'm tired of being patient."

"Abilene."

Battle played coy and leaned forward in his seat. "What's Abilene?"

"That's where we have our HQ," Pico mumbled as if he didn't want Battle to hear him. "We came here from Abilene."

"Is the boy in Abilene?"

"I don't know. Can I have water?"

Battle reached down and picked up a canteen. He grabbed Pico's sweaty mop of hair and pulled back his head. "Open up." He held the canteen above Pico's mouth and poured in enough water to wet his whistle.

Pico slurped down the water like a baby bird in its nest. "Thank you."

"Where in Abilene are the headquarters?"

Pico shrugged.

Battle held up the canteen. "C'mon, Salomon, help me out here. Where are the headquarters?"

Pico pressed his eyes closed and cursed. "An old hardware store. Bible Hardware. That's where the bosses are set up.'

Battle nodded, working not to betray his disappointment at the fate of the old store. "How many?"

"How many what?"

"How many men are there? How many people in the Cartel?"

Pico hung his head and laughed before coughing. He shifted uncomfortably against the binds pinning him to the chair. "You really don't know?"

Battle put the canteen on the ground, sat back in the chair, and gripped the hat in his hands. He set his jaw and glared at the intruder.

Pico picked up his head and lost the smile on his face. He licked his mustache with his tongue. "Everyone is Cartel. Everyone. Even your woman over there. Lola? She's Cartel."

"What do you mean?"

"The Cartel controls everything," Pico explained. "If you're not in the Cartel, you pay the Cartel. If you pay the Cartel, you ain't gonna oppose them. So everybody's a part of it. There's no escaping it. You might be the only one in this part of the world who doesn't know that."

Battle leaned forward again. "So how many?"

Pico's eyebrows arched as if he didn't understand the question. He licked the thick white spittle from the corners of his mouth. "You can't kill all of them."

Battle didn't move. His gaze held Pico's.

"Ten thousand."

"Men?"

"Yeah."

"And that's Cartel regular, right?"

Pico blinked. "Yeah."

"And the people who aren't *in* the Cartel, but who *support* them?"

"A couple thousand."

Battle sat back in the chair, his eyes wide. "Abilene had a hundred twenty thousand people living there."

Pico shrugged.

"You're telling me nine out of ten people are gone?"

Pico shrugged.

"All right then," Battle said. He slapped his knees and stood from the chair. "You and me are heading there. I'm gonna thin out the herd a little bit and find that boy."

Pico shook his head. "Not a good idea. Not a good plan. You're gonna get us both killed."

"You're already a dead man, Salomon," Battle said, sliding the brown hat onto his head. "And I'm a boss now," he said, affecting Pico's Southwestern twang. "Ain't nobody gonna kill me."

***

OCTOBER 14, 2037, 3:04 AM

SCOURGE + 5 YEARS

ABILENE, TEXAS

Cyrus Skinner pinched the bridge of his nose and rubbed his eyes with his thumb and forefinger. The machine-gun knock on his door jolted him from his sleep, but didn't really wake him up.

He was sitting in the living room of his three-bedroom house. He called it the parlor. Not many visitors saw more of the house than that room. As an area captain, Skinner liked his privacy.

He sat in a high-back Fauteuil chair, his elbows resting on the exposed gilded wood-frame arms. He shifted against the quatrefoil fabric and blinked his eyes open to look at his early morning guest, Queho.

"So you're telling me that, after you decided to scale back and take a look-see before you attacked Mad Max, it was the wrong thing to do?"

"Yeah."

"And you want me to do *what* about it, seeing as how this mini-mission is already underway?"

Queho was sitting low in a chenille sofa that had seen better days. His knees rose above his lap. He felt like an adult in a kid's seat. He shrugged.

Skinner mockingly shrugged in return. "That's it? You wake me up at three in the morning for this?" He called over his shoulder, down the hall. "Woman! Get me a coffee."

"I thought it was a good idea to send a scout team," Queho explained. "We didn't know enough about this place or Mad Max to send an assault posse. We rushed exposing a lot of men without good intelligence. I mean, it *was* Pico giving us the information."

Skinner rubbed his chin and clicked his tongue against the roof of his mouth. He sounded like he was ticking off seconds as he thought about how to respond.

"I'm flummoxed," he finally offered. "I think that's the right word. Flummoxed. You doubt how good Pico's information is, so you trust his suggestion to send a scout team. Then you shoot Rudabaugh in the hand 'cause he questions you. So you make him the lead. And you don't go with him. Yeah, flummoxed is the right word."

Queho started to answer but stopped when a tall, thin woman walked into the parlor, carrying a tray with two cups of coffee and a pile of sugar packets. She was hunched at the shoulders, as if she carried a hump on her back. Her eyes were set deep in her skull, her lips oversized for her narrow jaw. She set the tray on a polished cherry table and slowly backed out of the room. She never looked either of them in the eyes.

Skinner reached for the coffee, and the lights flickered. "You were saying?"

"I didn't have the feeling in my gut before," Queho said. "I figured the guys could handle it and we'd minimize the risk of losing more men. Now, I don't know. They should be back by now."

Skinner pulled the steaming cup to his lips and sipped the scalding coffee. "This is where destroying cell phone towers doesn't sound like such a good idea, does it?" He didn't wince when the drink burned his tongue, the roof of his mouth, and his throat. He took a second sip and nodded toward the cup still on the tray.

Queho took the coffee. "I never understood that," he said. "It's like biting off your nose to spit in your face."

"Spite your face."

"What?"

"The saying," Skinner smirked. "It's 'biting off your nose to *spite* your face'."

Queho blew into his cup. "Whatever. It didn't make sense to me. We could have used cell phones to coordinate things, to communicate better."

Skinner set the coffee cup back on the tray. "The generals over in Houston and Dallas thought the risk outweighed the gains. They figured it was better that nobody had cells than for the early opposition to have them. Remember, in the days after the Scourge, we were fighting for control. We needed every advantage we could find. We had numbers. So it was better to level the technical playing field. Plus, those cells didn't work out in rural Texas anyhow."

"Have they talked about fixing them? I mean, now that we control everything from Louisiana to New Mexico?"

Skinner cracked his neck. "I dunno. Look, Queho, all of that's beside the point. And they reserve their two-ways for the cities. The situations are more unstable there. Instant communication is more critical. Out here, in the great open spaces with a bunch of farmers, they didn't see the need to share. They figured we could handle it without the creature comforts. And It doesn't matter. What's done is done. We need to figure out how we handle this potential mess you've created."

Queho took a tentative sip of the coffee. "Okay."

"You take ten men," he said. "Head toward the area Pico told you about. You got a general idea of where it's at, right?"

"Just past Rising Star."

"Good," Skinner said. "Head there. Get going before sunup. You'll either run into your search team…or you won't. Either way, we know what to do."

"What is that?"

"We end this guy. Mad Max. This is one guy, right?"

"According to Pico."

Skinner shrugged. "So it's one crazy guy. We end him. Kill the redheaded woman. She's too much trouble."

"And the boy?"

"He's where I told you to put him?"

Queho took another sip of coffee and swallowed it quickly so as to answer. "Yes.

"Leave him there for now," Skinner said. He leaned over, slid the cup from the table, and pulled it to his lips. He downed the rest of the coffee and licked his lips free of the stubborn sugar granules that refused to dissolve. "Once his momma's dead, you be sure to tell him. Describe it in detail. Even if you gotta make it up. That'll keep him in line."

Queho sipped from his cup and sank back against the worn cushion.

"Don't get comfortable," Skinner said. "You gotta get going."

***

OCTOBER 14, 2037, 5:40 AM

SCOURGE + 5 YEARS

TEXAS HIGHWAY 36

EAST OF RISING STAR, TEXAS

Marcus stood at the edge of the highway. He walked behind the six horses tied to his fence, his boots scraping across the cracked and pitted asphalt. He was far enough back from their hind legs to avoid a swift kick to the head but close enough, with the help of a flashlight, to inspect them and pick the best of the lot. He was wearing tactical cargo pants and a matching vest. The vest, covered with various-sized pockets, was stuffed with ammunition and first aid supplies.

"This is a good one." He aimed the light at a thick Appaloosa. It was dark with a black-spotted white blanket over its loin and hips. Its mane was black. It looked healthier than the others.

"I don't know a lot about horses," he admitted, sidling up to the Appaloosa, "but I know they have durable hooves. I like that." He turned off the light and came around to face the animal.

The horse looked at him with its human-esque eyes and nickered. It was a guttural pulse of a greeting that told Battle the horse liked him.

"I like you too." Battle patted the Appaloosa's forehead, lightly dragging his hand down to its muzzle. He carefully took the cheek pieces in each hand and tugged. The horse snorted.

"I think you're the one," he said. "What's it name?" he called over his shoulder to Pico.

Pico stood inside the fence line. His hands were bound together. His legs were tied such that he could walk but not run. "Aces," he said. "That was Rudabaugh's horse. You're wearing his hat."

Battle took off the brown cowboy hat and looked at it before replacing it atop his head. "Only makes sense I should take his horse if I already have the hat. Which one is yours?"

Pico nodded his head to a paint on the end. "That's mine. His name is Venganza."

"Okay," Battle said. "You're not taking him. I don't want you on a familiar horse. But thanks for the honesty." Battle pointed to another paint. "You can have that one."

"Lola, can you help me, please?"

She huffed, hopped over the fence, and moved next to Battle. She adjusted her T-shirt and folded her arms across her chest. "What?"

"I need you to help me load up the horses with the gear," he said, hanging a Kevlar vest on the fence post. "I'd appreciate it. *Please.*"

She grabbed a couple of saddlebags they'd retrieved from the barn while Battle worked on attaching his gear to Aces.

"I should go with you," she said, handing him one of the bags. "Let me wear the vest."

Battle rolled his eyes and checked the straps of the rifle scabbard then slid it under his saddle. He ignored her at first. It was difficult enough to leave the house, the barn, his family. It was even tougher to leave Lola in charge of the place. He didn't want to rehash an argument over leaving her behind.

"The sun's up in two hours," he said to Pico. "We should hit the road. I need you to change into some different clothes for me, and I'll need a lead from the back of my horse to yours."

Lola took a step toward Battle. "Did you hear me?"

Battle nodded. "I heard you," he said. "This is too dangerous. And I don't want the house empty. Plus the vest wouldn't fit you."

She threw her hands up. "*I* can't protect the house alone," she argued. "And you're going to find *my* son."

Battle adjusted the leathers. He was taller than Rudabaugh. The stirrups needed to hang lower. "I'm not going to argue about this. If you remember, a few hours ago, I wasn't ever going to leave my land. Ever. Now I'm doing it. Just stay in the house."

"But—"

"*Please.*"

Lola pulled her hair behind her ears and bent over to pick up a bag. She tossed it to Battle. "Fine. Please bring me back my son."

"You're not coming back alive," Pico said. He was kicking his toes into the mud. "They're gonna kill both of us. Then they'll come here and they'll kill her."

Lola's eyes flashed from Battle to Pico and back to Battle again. Her jaw tightened. She clenched her fist and took two big steps to the fence. She leapt over it, despite her injured ankle, planted her feet in the mud, and threw all of her weight into Salomon Pico. She drove her shoulder into his gut and knocked him to the ground. He unsuccessfully tried defending himself with his bound hands.

"Get her off me!" he wailed. Lola pushed her left hand onto his face and shoved his head deeper into the mud. With her right hand, she swung wildly with a closed fist. She connected with his neck and jaw.

"Help me!"

"I'll. Help. You. You mother—" Lola grunted between swings.

Battle took his time moving to the fence. He climbed over it one leg at a time and strode a few steps with his hands in his pockets. "Lola." His voice was soft at first, as if he didn't really want her to hear him.

"I remember you," she snarled and punched him in the throat. "I remember."

Battle's voice was louder. "Lola."

"My son. He's a *child*." She was crying, her arms flailing, but she kept connecting with the now bloodied Pico.

Battle grabbed her shoulder. "Stop." He squeezed, his grip tightening. "That's enough."

Lola pounded on Pico's chest twice more before sliding off him into the mud. Battle helped her to her feet and put his arms around her. He held her while she released the last of her outburst into his chest.

"It's okay," he told her, questioning his own compassion. "I'll find him. I promise." He regretted it immediately.

Lola's sobs slowed and she pushed away from Battle. "What did you say?" She sniffed and rubbed the snot from her nose.

"Nothing. Just that it'll be okay."

She pulled strands of muddied red hair from her face. "That's not what you said."

Battle bit his lip. He averted his eyes, choosing to look at the pitifully wounded punching bag lying in the mud.

"You promised to find him. You promised." She thumped his chest with the back of her hand.

He looked back at her and nodded. "I guess I did."

Battle couldn't account for the one-hundred-and-eighty-degree flip. He didn't know why he'd subconsciously relented to the emotional pressure of helping Lola find her son. But he had.

A shaky smile spread across Lola's face. She nodded and blinked back tears. "Thank you," she said. "I don't know what else to say."

Battle shrugged. "There's nothing *to* say. Keep an eye on the place while I'm gone. Let's get these extra horses into the barn."

CHAPTER 17

NOVEMBER 12, 2032, 5:18 PM

SCOURGE +43 DAYS

EAST OF RISING STAR, TEXAS

Marcus wiped the sweat from Sylvia's forehead. She was in their bed and barely conscious. She'd deteriorated almost as quickly as Wesson.

Her breathing was shallow and rapid, like a dog panting. Her cough was thick with mucus and a yellow pus from her lungs that had become pinkish from blood in the last few hours.

Marcus hadn't slept since their argument in the kitchen. He'd dozed off for a minute or two in the chair next to the bed, but that was it. He couldn't risk being asleep when she died.

"I love you, Sylvia," he'd said at regular intervals during his vigil. He held her hand and talked softly to her.

During her first day confined to the bed, when she'd become too weak to stand, she watched his eyes intently as he spoke. Occasionally she managed a hint of a smile.

"I remember seeing you for the first time," he'd recalled. "It was at graduation. The Goat had just crossed the stage and taken his money. We'd cheered wildly for him. I glanced into the crowd at Michie Stadium and noticed this adorable yellow sundress attached to a gorgeous woman. You glanced back."

"The ceremony ended and I looked for your dress. I found it. You were still attached to it." He'd chuckled. "Turned out the Goat was your brother. Hilarious. I pretended I was there to congratulate him, which I did. I introduced myself to your mom. And your brother introduced you to me."

Sylvia had interrupted the story with a violent cough. Marcus had patted her back and wiped her chin free of phlegm. Once she'd lain back against the mountain of pillows behind her head and back, he'd retaken her hand.

"So," he'd said, "I offered to shake your hand, but you saluted me. You insisted I give you my silver dollar. I said I couldn't. West Point tradition is explicit. The coin goes to the first enlisted person to salute a graduate. You argued that since your brother was in the army and your father had died in Fallujah when you were a young girl, you'd involuntarily enlisted."

"You gave me your coin," Sylvia had whispered through the rattle in her lungs.

Marcus had squeezed her hand, which he'd taken with both of his. "I did. There was no point in arguing with you. Especially since I wanted to see more of you."

Sylvia turned her head and looked at the ceiling. Above her a fan was spinning. Its pull chain whipping gently in its breeze was the only sound in the room. She tried to take a deep breath but couldn't. She wheezed and coughed again. With each percussive coughing fit, she emerged with less strength. Marcus could see the disease devouring her by the hour.

"You always kept me on my toes," he'd told her. "I was a fresh second lieutenant. You may as well have been my CO, the way you led me around. I was whooped. Still am."

Sylvia had turned her head back to him and rolled her eyes. There was no smile anymore. She couldn't manage the strength for it. But he'd seen the smile mixed with the sarcasm of the eye roll.

Now, he sat beside her in her final hours, contemplating, regretting all of the mistakes he'd made. There were so many.

When they'd married before his first deployment to Iran, he'd promised her everything would be okay. Her brother, who hadn't risen through the ranks as quickly as Marcus, was assigned to his company. When Sylvia had kissed her husband goodbye, she'd held his face in her hands.

"I know you'll come back," she'd told him. "You're too strong not to come back. But my brother, please take care of him. Please tell me he'll come back too."

"He'll come back too," he'd said. "Guaranteed."

He hadn't. His platoon had stepped into an ambush. Sylvia's brother was among the thirty-seven men who'd died. Only three survived. Marcus wasn't there, he was on a patrol some twenty miles away. He'd had to call his wife and tell her. He'd had to inform her that he'd failed to keep his promise.

Marcus regretted having made the promise to keep Sylvia's brother safe. He'd resolved not to make promises he couldn't be sure he'd keep.

When he resigned from the army and bought the land outside of Rising Star, he'd never promised Sylvia his plan would work. She'd pressed him to assure her that their sacrifices would pay off, that they'd survive whatever doom befell them.

"I'm doing everything I can to keep us safe," he'd told her repeatedly. "Nothing is certain. But if we follow the plan, we'll be in excellent shape."

Excellent shape, as it turned out, was a son in the ground and his wife on her deathbed. He'd failed even without making a promise.

Sylvia drifted to sleep. She was still breathing, albeit with difficulty. Marcus let go of her hand and reached for the television remote. He flipped to the cable news channel, turned down the volume, and read the captioning at the bottom of the screen.

"...estimates are at close to four billion," a news anchor read from behind a desk. *"The World Health Organization reports finding three different strains of the* Yersinia pestis *bacteria are now actively infecting populations in Europe, Asia, and Africa. In the United States, the CDC has reported only one drug-resistant strain of the bacteria. In all cases, patients are succumbing to the illness within seventy-two hours of the onset of symptoms."*

A man in a white lab coat appeared on the screen. *"We don't yet know the length of time between contraction of the illness and the onset of symptoms. It seems to vary from patient to patient. The best we've been able to determine is that it can take up to two weeks, but it could be as short as a few hours."*

"There are those who are exposed to the bacteria who survive," read the news anchor. On the screen was video of hospitals, their parking lots populated with large tents that served as triage facilities. It looked like a scene from a horror movie. *"Those survivors, however, seem to have immunity. At this point, overwhelmed researchers at laboratories across the globe have not determined what makes some immune and others susceptible. They estimate, however, that roughly only one in three people is immune."*

Another person in a lab coat appeared on the screen. *"We are working diligently to find the common denominator amongst the immune. But so far, nothing. As the bacteria continues to change its makeup and new strains materialize, that effort becomes more difficult."*

Video of sick people fills the screen and the anchor begins speaking again. *"Hospitals, clinics, even funeral homes are overwhelmed and cannot handle the incredible numbers of people who are dying. Some cities have turned to burning bodies at landfills rather than let them accumulate at morgues."*

The visual on the screen cuts to an aerial shot of a massive fire burning on top of what looks like a large hill. The camera zooms in to reveal the hill is a pile of bodies, smoldering and burning in the flames and heat. It then switches to a split screen of various cities in various states of collapse: a mob scene at a shopping center, masked gangs tossing rocks into the storefront of a big box store, a riot-gear-clad police force fending off protestors. *"But maybe more troubling than the deaths of so many people is the collapse of local governments and lack of first responders,"* said the anchor.

"Idiots," Marcus mumbled to himself. "Why in the world would you put yourself in a densely populated area when a single cough could kill you?" The more he watched, the less he judged. The people were desperate. They were panicking. They weren't prepared.

He looked over at his wife and took a deep breath. Preparation hadn't saved her. It hadn't saved their son. He was no better off than the desperate idiots roaming the streets, looking for food, water, and medicine. Marcus wiped Sylvia's forehead with the damp washcloth and turned back to the screen.

The anchor looked down at some notes on the desk. *"Joining me now is Professor Chris Blayney of Georgetown University. He is an expert in public policy and crisis management. Professor, it seems the infrastructure in so many large cities around the world has collapsed rapidly. Why?"*

The professor was wearing a surgical mask. His voice was somewhat muffled. *"The catabolic collapse of society is poorly understood. Whereas one complex civilization may survive a sudden or prolonged shift in its economic or social model, another may implode almost instantaneously. There is the well-known Tainter theory. It was proposed some fifty years ago and suggests that complex societies break down when increasing complexity, or stresses, fail to continue benefitting the population."*

"Can you dumb it down for us, Professor Blayney?" the anchor said off camera.

"Okay." The professor adjusted the mask on his face. *"There are some key things which keep order. If they don't exist, society collapses. And it can happen quickly. Those things are resources, capital, waste, and production. They create a chain that binds a society together. If any one of them, or all of them, weaken or disappear, the chain breaks. Society breaks."*

"What happens next," the anchor posed, *"for those who survive?"*

The professor blinked and then looked straight into the camera. *"That's grim,"* he said. *"Other entities, groups, or individuals seek to fill the void. They forcibly seek to reestablish the chain."*

"Anarchy?" The anchor appeared on the screen beside the professor.

"Or worse," said the professor. *"We'll likely find areas that fall under rogue rule. It's happened in destabilized places all over the —"*

Marcus turned off the television. He didn't need to hear any more. He'd been in those destabilized places. He'd seen the chaos. Marcus Battle knew what was coming and he didn't need a genius professor at Georgetown to tell him about it.

The world, as he knew it, was over. It would devolve into a place where the worst in people was revealed and the worst of people took control.

He resolved he would not become a part of that world. When Sylvia died, and he knew from the cadence of her breathing it would be only hours before that happened, he would isolate himself. No television. No Internet. No connection to hell. He couldn't do it again.

His fifty acres was his. He'd build his own world within the fences. He'd stay home.

CHAPTER 18

OCTOBER 14, 2037, 7:40 AM

SCOURGE + 5 YEARS

TEXAS HIGHWAY 36

CROSS PLAINS, TEXAS

His posse was at the intersection of Highways 36 and 206 in Cross Plains. A long ago abandoned Dairy Queen sat on the northeast corner. The faded sign still advertised burgers and ice cream.

"You ever have a Blizzard?" Queho asked a grunt riding alongside his right. He nodded toward the sign.

The grunt shrugged, a confused look on his face. "I guess so."

Queho sat higher in the saddle, straightening his back. "Either you have or you haven't. I mean, boy, if you had a Blizzard, you'd know it."

The grunt nodded. "I had it before."

Queho's eyes widened. "What flavor?"

The grunt pulled his collar up around his neck. "Butterfinger."

"Yeah." Queho nodded, a smile spreading across his face. "Butterfinger. Good one. I liked that one. I always got the candy stuck between my teeth. Same with the Heath Bar." He picked at his teeth with his finger. "Not worth the effort."

The grunt kept pace with Queho. The caravan was traveling more like an amorphous pack. The town's wide streets accommodated the disorganization as the posse clopped along. Queho was so preoccupied with Dairy Queen, he didn't notice.

"I always got the chocolate chip cookie dough," Queho said, licking his lips. "Oh, that was good. And remember? They'd hold it upside down?" He held out his hand to pantomime a Dairy Queen clerk holding a cup of ice cream upside down. "That way you knew how thick they made it."

The predawn chill was giving way to the sun. There was a fog blooming on the road ahead leading south and east toward Rising Star. Off to the left were the remnants of a used-car lot. The sign, which read Bi-Rite, was crumpled and rusted on its ends. It hung crooked on a mangled chain-link fence. An overhead power line drooped low to the ground, the large pole on the corner sitting in the ground at forty-five degrees. Queho pulled a canteen from his saddlebag and popped it open with his thumb. He took a long swig and pointed the canteen toward the dealership. The lot was cracked, empty of cars, and overgrown.

"I miss cars too," he said, adjusting his club foot in the stirrup iron. "I've only been in a car once since the Scourge. It was like floating on air."

The grunt's eyes stayed on the portable reader board as they passed it. It was missing all but a few letters. "You been in a car *since* the Scourge?"

"Just the once," Queho said. "Leather seats. Nice air-conditioning. I opened the vent all the way and cranked the AC to max." He closed his eyes and lifted his chin, imagining the cool breeze.

"I ain't been in one since...I can't remember, really," said the grunt. He grabbed the horn of his saddle and adjusted his lower back against the cantle. "I can't remember what it was like to have a lot of stuff before the Scourge."

Queho opened his eyes and turned to the grunt. "Like what?"

"Electricity."

"We got electricity," corrected Queho.

The grunt shook his head. "I mean, like, real electricity. What we got comes and goes. You never know when it's gonna be there. One second the lights are on, the next they're off."

"That's true."

"I miss the TV," said the grunt. "Streaming video. Binge-watching shows. I miss that. New music. When's the last time you heard a new song? I can't remember."

Queho nodded and looked out into the fog. The blanket was thickening on the horizon and it was rolling closer to them as they moved east and slightly south along the highway.

The grunt snapped his fingers. "I also miss pizza delivery. If I got hungry after a bender, I could call and get a pizza delivered."

Queho wasn't listening to the young grunt. His attention was up ahead. It was increasingly difficult to see as the fog billowed. The sun hadn't yet heated up the air enough for it to dissipate. It felt as if they were swimming in the opaque mist. He and the grunt were at the front of the pack. Queho looked over his shoulder. He could only see three others.

"You miss pizza?" asked the grunt.

Queho slowed his horse and eased back toward the rest of the pack. As he did, more of them emerged from the haze: six, seven, eight, nine. He could see all of the posse now. They were plodding along in the relative silence of the early morning, only the rhythmic clop of the shoed hooves on the asphalt giving away their numbers.

The grunt appeared beside Queho. He seemed oblivious to the lack of visibility.

"I liked anchovies," he said. "I think it was the salt. It always—"

Crack!

The familiar loud clap of a rifle shot ripped through the fog, slugging the young grunt in the center of his forehead, whipping his neck. His body fell back and then lurched to the side before he fell from his perch. His right foot was stuck in his stirrup as his horse leapt forward, its ears flat back against its head and it squealed with fear.

Crack!

Another shot was followed by a short moan and the sound of a man falling to the dirt. Horses squealed and reared.

Crack!

"My arm!" one of the men called. "Son of a—"

Crack!

The man cried out and fell silent. His body hit the ground with a thud masked by the sound of squealing horses. By now the cacophony of squeals and roars was almost deafening as they bolted from their rough formation.

Queho held his reins tight and tried to control his horse. He struggled against its fear and it shook its head wildly. The horse bucked and strained against the reins, galloping north of the highway and into the weed-laden dirt and mud.

Other horses moved in the same direction, kicking up a spray of mud from the previous night's heavy rain. The splatter blinded Queho as his horse raced north. The further away from the highway they traveled, the denser the fog.

He dug his spurred heels into the horse's sides and pulled back on the reins as hard as he could, coaxing the spooked animal to calm down as they crossed a cracked and pitted street adjacent to a grouping of trailer homes and sheds.

"Whoa!" he ordered and the horse stopped. It shook its head and snorted. Queho looked around. He could hear the snorts and blows of other horses, but he couldn't see much more than ten feet in any direction.

Queho's heart was pounding, his mind racing. In the years since the Scourge, nobody had ambushed them. Nobody was bold enough or stupid enough to try it.

Queho dismounted and tied his horse to the remains of a rotting wooden fence. He pulled a Browning shotgun he'd tucked underneath the saddle's billet straps and fender.

He guessed he was a good quarter mile from the highway. He'd be better off walking back and hiding amongst the buildings or waist-high weeds. He'd present a lower profile the attackers wouldn't expect.

He marched through the weeds south toward the highway and came across two grunts. He told them to dismount, grab their shotguns, and join him on foot. They obeyed without question.

"Who you think it is?" one of them asked Queho as they stomped through a water-filled gulley intersecting their path.

"Hell if I know," said Queho. "But they got three of us already. That leaves seven. Keep your heads on swivels. Don't let nobody get behind us."

"But they hit us from the front," the other grunt commented.

Queho stopped and grabbed the grunt by his collar. The brim of his hat bent against the man's forehead as he pulled him close. "Don't. Let. Them. Get. Behind. Us," he growled. That's your job now, grunt. You got it?"

The grunt nodded and stumbled back when Queho released his grip.

Queho grabbed the crown of his hat and adjusted it on his head. He wiped some mud from his cheeks and then grabbed the Browning with both hands. "Let's go. When we get close to the highway, turn left and head east. We need to use the grass for cover. We don't know how many of them there are."

It never crossed Queho's mind the attackers were, in fact, one man. And that man was the killer he knew as Mad Max.

***

OCTOBER 14, 2037, 7:47 AM

SCOURGE + 5 YEARS

TEXAS HIGHWAY 36

CROSS PLAINS, TEXAS

Battle adjusted the night-vision goggles on his head. Sweat made them uncomfortable around his eyes, but the heat signature they provided was invaluable.

He'd considered using the rifle scope on Inspector, but the intensifying fog made it useless. He'd managed to fire a couple of accurate shots off the shoulder without his eyes on the sight. That third shot had drifted on him, and Battle had to waste a second bullet on a single man. He blamed it on the fog and the rationalization that the Browning he'd nicknamed Lloyd wasn't as accurate as the semiautomatic Inspector.

It didn't matter. As best he could tell, he'd tagged three of them. He guessed there were a half dozen left. Though he'd tried to count them before opening fire, they were clustered such that the signatures blended.

Battle pushed himself from the roadside culvert in which he'd set up shop and walked back ten yards to the Appaloosa named Aces, the paint, and his guest Salomon Pico.

He set the Browning on the saddle and, still holding the rifle, hoisted himself into the seat.

"Same rule applies, Salomon," Battle reminded him. "You so much as eke out a fart and I'm putting a bullet in you. Got it?"

Pico cracked his neck and complained again about the garments Battle was making him wear. He shifted in the saddle.

"Got it?" Battle asked again.

"Got it," Pico said softly. "You've got a death wish. You know that, right? Even if you make it past this posse, you're not gonna survive Abilene."

Battle adjusted the depth of field on the goggles. He looked west into the fog and chuckled. "Death wish? That's laughable."

"I ain't kidding," Pico said barely above a whisper, wriggling his wrists against the bungee that bound them to the saddle horn. "You're gonna die. I'm gonna die. This is pointless."

Battle turned around, the leather creaking as he twisted to look at Pico. "Salomon Pico, you are far dumber than I gave you credit for."

"How's that?" Pico grunted.

"You tell me a single thing in this barren, evil-infested world that *isn't* pointless."

Pico shrugged, snorted through his damaged nose, and spat a blood-soaked loogie to the ground.

Battle turned back around to face the road ahead of them. "That's what I thought."

The sun peaked higher in the sky and the fog was lifting, albeit incrementally. Visibility was still nonexistent beyond fifteen feet. The horses had scattered on both sides of the highway, though Battle had no concept for how far off the road they might have galloped.

He tapped his heels into Aces's ribs and clucked his tongue against his teeth. The horse responded with a neigh and started west. Battle figured the posse didn't have thermal scopes or goggles. From what little he'd seen, they traveled like Spartans: a couple of weapons, rations, water, nothing else.

Aces clopped along the highway until Battle guided him to its edge. Pulling the paint with Pico aboard, they moved silently off the edge of the shoulder. The rustle of the high weeds was far quieter than the clink of shoes on the asphalt.

Battle forged ahead in the fog and neared a narrow concrete driveway that connected to the highway. It was shrouded by a cluster of bald cypress that had wrecked the drive. Their root knees kicked their way through the concrete, making the short path look as if it had suffered earthquake damage.

Battle turned onto the driveway and looped Aces's lead around the narrow trunk of a young tree. He looked over to Pico and held his finger up to his lips. Pico nodded.

With Lloyd in his hands and McDunnough in a holster strapped to his thigh, Battle left the horses and the grunt hidden amongst the trees. He walked north toward an aboveground pool and its neighboring house. Neither was in good shape.

He wasn't waiting for the posse to come to him. He was hunting them. He was a good fifty yards from the tree cluster when he changed his mind. He couldn't be sure which side of the highway was occupied and couldn't take the risk of choosing the wrong direction.

He certainly didn't want to get sandwiched between the half dozen men he imagined were coming for him once they regrouped.

Battle jogged through the mist back to the horses, the goggles bouncing against his eyes. He slowed as he approached the trees. Pico was sitting as he'd left him, tied up and quiet.

"Change of plans," he said to Pico. He took the bungees and loosened them from the saddle horn before helping Pico dismount. "I'm gonna tie you to the tree."

He looped the bungee around the young cypress, pulling it tight to remove its slack. He knotted it on the side opposite Pico. "Too tight?"

"Yes," Pico complained. He was sitting with his back against the tree, his legs bound in front of him. "I can barely feel my hands."

Battle rounded the tree and smiled at Pico. "Good," he said. "I won't be long."

"I'm uncomfortable," Pico whined.

"It's for your own protection," Battle answered. "I need you alive. I told you that."

"Alive until you kill me."

"Pretty much."

Battle untied the paint from Aces and led it out onto the highway. He adjusted his goggles, made sure he had a good grip on the Browning, and slapped the horse on its hindquarters. It snorted and took off, trotting west along the highway.

He waited about ten seconds and then started jogging behind the horse, running at a pace to keep his distance. His footsteps were masked by the clop of the iron shoes on the asphalt. It reminded him of running patrol on foot behind a Humvee.

Controlling his breathing, he listened intently and, with the help of his goggles, scanned both sides of Highway 36. The horse kept its slow trot west, staying on the asphalt as if it knew the plan.

Crack! Crack! Crack! Crack! Crack!

The shots came from the left, up ahead on the southern side of the highway. The horse snorted and squealed before accelerating into a gallop, disappearing into the fog up ahead. It had done its job as a decoy.

Battle dropped to a knee and focused on the southern side of the highway. He pulled the rifle to his shoulder and aimed, waiting for someone to move into his orange field of view.

He scanned to the right. Nothing. To the left. Nothing.

And then, a thick burst of bright color in the goggles. It was maybe thirty yards ahead, at his ten o'clock. Battle exhaled and pressed his finger to the trigger.

Crack! Crack! Crack! Crack!

He fished a pair of replacement shells from his chest pocket and slid them into the loading port at the bottom of the magazine. He took another pair and loaded them, ensuring they clicked when he pressed them up and inside the magazine.

He stood, walking deliberately toward the target area. He scanned to the right, checking the north side of the road, before panning across the highway to the original spot.

He knew from the number of shots fired there had to be at least two men. The Browning held four shells; there were five shots. The size of the orange glow in his goggles also indicated more than one person was standing at the edge of the highway.

His deduction was confirmed by the pair of bodies lying next to one another in the weeds off the shoulder. One of the men was dead. The other was twitching and grabbing his stomach.

Battle approached and then dropped to both knees next to the dying grunt. The man's eyes were wide. He was gurgling, gasping for air. Blood was leaking from his mouth and nose. He had both hands at his stomach, but there was another hole closer to his neck. Battle was struck by how young he looked. Despite his unshaven appearance, the fear in his eyes betrayed his youth.

Battle closed his eyes and prayed. "So far has He removed our transgressions from us." He unholstered the six-shooters from both men, stuffed them in a deep vest pocket at his side, and grabbed one of the Brownings. As he shifted his weight to stand, the dying grunt grabbed his wrist with a blood-soaked hand.

Battle looked the grunt in the eyes. He nodded, dropped the Browning, and pulled out one of the pistols. He pressed it against the grunt's forehead, turned away, and fired. He felt the warm spray of mercy along his neck and the grunt's hand released its hold on his wrist.

He slipped the pistol back into the long, wide pocket at his waist and stood with a Browning in each hand. Holding them at his waist, leveled straight ahead, he marched south into the weeds. He scanned the area from left to right. If he saw anything move, anything with a heat signature, he was ready to open fire again.

He looked left. Nothing. Right. Nothing. Left again. Nothing. He stepped deeper into the grass, the mud sucking at his boots as he moved.

Crack! Crack!

The shots came from behind him.

Crack! Crack!

Battle dove into the weeds, losing one of the weapons. He was face first in the mud. The goggles were coated with it. He spun around on his stomach and tore the goggles from his face. He didn't have time to wipe them clean. The shots, as best he could tell, were from the north. From their volume, he figured they were fired at close range.

He crawled forward on his knees and elbows toward a large tractor tire a few feet to his right. Once behind the tire, he caught his breath and listened. The shooter was probably reloading. If there was more than one attacker, he was in trouble. His only saving grace was the lifting fog and the incremental warmth of the early morning. It was still cool; the crisp fall air tightened his chest if he inhaled too deeply. He looked up through the mist to the sky. The thin clouds high above were tinged pink from the rising sun.

A few more minutes, and the fog wouldn't be a factor. That was both good and bad. Battle peeked around the side of the tire, still concealed by the grass. He couldn't see anything of value. He closed his eyes and listened. At first, there was nothing but the ambient sound of a slight breeze blowing through the lifting fog.

But in the subsequent stillness, he heard weeds brushing against something. It was close. Then the suction of mud slipping from a boot or a shoe to his right.

Battle slid his finger onto the trigger, shot to his feet, emerging from the weeds in time to catch the gun-toting grunt off guard. The man fumbled to aim, but Battle was too fast. He pulled the trigger twice and dropped the man where he stood before again dipping below the protection of the high weeds.

He crawled forward toward the grunt and found him on his back. Both shots had pegged him in the chest, blasting through him. His eyes were frozen with the same look he'd had the instant he realized Battle had the drop on him and he was about to die violently.

Battle rummaged through the man's pockets and took his extra shells. There was also a Leatherman multi-tool and an expired energy bar. Battle shoved the utility knife into his breast pocket and ripped open the energy bar.

It crumbled in his mouth and tasted like dirt, but he needed something. He'd not eaten since before the attack the previous night, and the food he kept in the saddlebag was on the other side of the highway.

Battle counted in his head. Six down. It was a good start.

***

OCTOBER 14, 2037, 8:08 AM

SCOURGE + 5 YEARS

TEXAS HIGHWAY 36

CROSS PLAINS, TEXAS

Queho heard the repeated shotgun blasts that sounded like they were coming from the other side of the highway. He was on foot with the two grunts, moving amongst the weeds and weaving between dilapidated mobile homes and trailers.

The rusted frame of a 2018 Dodge Charger was on cinderblocks. Queho moved next to the Charger and stopped when he heard a noise on the other side of a white double-wide that blended into the mist. It was its rust and black roof that made it visible.

Queho held up a hand to stop the two grunts walking behind him. He motioned for one of them to maneuver up against the double-wide and hold his position at the corner. Queho lowered himself to the ground and looked underneath the mobile home, but its foundation was too close to the ground for him to see anything. He could hear movement.

Queho pushed himself back to his feet. The clubbed one was throbbing from the walking, the cold, and the intensity of the moment. He motioned for the second grunt to join him and they made their way to the double-wide. He pointed for the first grunt to move around the trailer home to the left. He and the other grunt would go right.

The grunt nodded his understanding and checked the safety on his shotgun. Queho held up his hand with three fingers extended. Two. One.

They swiftly rounded the edge of the trailer, appearing on the opposite side. Queho had his shotgun pressed to his shoulder, his right eye glued to the sight. He swung from right to left and touched his finger to the trigger.

He located his target. Aimed. And, at the last moment, released his finger. "Hold up! Don't fire."

Queho and his grunts had found two more survivors of the initial ambush. They were astride their horses. They dismounted when they saw their posse boss on foot.

"Good to see you, boss," one of them said. "We got separated when our horses got spooked. We didn't know who was alive and who wasn't."

"It's just the two of you?" Queho asked. He looked over his shoulder and then past the men standing in front of him. The fog was burning off much faster now. It was turning into a clear fall morning. He shifted his weight onto his good foot. "You ain't seen anyone else?"

They shook their heads. "No," they said in unison.

Queho looked over the men, taking inventory. There were five of them together. He didn't know whether that was more or less than the attackers might have. He'd heard a lot of gunfire.

"So it's us, then." He shrugged. "We got to find our way outta here and make it east." He pointed at the two grunts they'd just encountered and told them to get back on their horses.

They remounted the animals and awaited their instructions. One of them offered water to the others.

"We need to stay close to the road," suggested Queho, "but far enough away from it that we can keep cover. You on the horses, take the lead."

The two nodded and got their horses headed east. They weaved through a maze of houses and low-slung grain silos, leading the group south, back toward the highway. They moved slowly, each of the men with their weapons at the ready. The fog was all but gone by the time they reached a cluster of bald cypress trees north of the road.

Queho stepped ahead of the group. There was a large horse tied to a tree. It turned toward Queho and nickered. The horse looked familiar. It was dark with a black-spotted white blanket over its loin and hips and a black mane. When he got closer, the horse nickered again and snorted. Queho placed his hand on the animal's poll, the spot atop its head between the ears and the run of the mane down its neck. He rubbed it then ran his fingers down its crest to its withers. He patted it gently.

"Is that Rudabaugh's horse?" asked one of the grunts. The group had gathered behind him under the wide canopy of the tree.

"I think it is," said Queho. "It's an Appaloosa and looks the same. The spots and such."

"What's it doing here?" asked the grunt. "That don't make any sense."

Queho was piecing it together in his head when he heard a noise from underneath a nearby tree. He raised the Browning and leveled it waist high, stepping around the horse.

Fifteen feet in front of him was a man tied to a tree trunk. At first, Queho didn't recognize him, though he knew it wasn't Rudabaugh.

The man's head was hung low, his face not visible. He was wearing a thick long-sleeved shirt. His arms were tied behind his back, attached to the trunk with a cord.

"Hey," he called out to the man. "Hey, you. What are you doing here? Who tied you up?"

The man shook his head but didn't raise it. He pulled his feet into his body as if he was trying to curl into a ball. As if that made him less visible.

"Hey, you." Queho aimed the barrel at the man's head. "I'm gonna shoot if you don't look up at me. I need to know why you're here and why you got a Cartel horse right next to you."

The four grunts held their positions while Queho inched his way closer to the man under the tree. All of them had their shotguns ready to fire.

Queho kicked the man's leg and shoved the muzzle into his chest, poking him with it. "Hey. Look up or I pull the trigger."

The man slowly raised his head, looking Queho in the eyes. Queho jumped back, nearly tripping over his bad foot. "Pico? That you?"

Pico nodded almost imperceptibly. He mumbled something Queho couldn't hear.

"What are you doing here? Where is Rudabaugh? What happened?"

"Can you untie me?" Pico asked. "I can't feel my hands. My arms are falling asleep."

Queho looked over his shoulder and motioned to the grunts. "Cut him loose." He looked back at the battered man he barely recognized. "You got the tar kicked out of you, huh?"

Pico nodded. Two grunts worked from the back of the tree, cutting the bungee cords. Pico fell forward when they snapped. He rolled onto his side, his hands and feet still bound.

Queho checked to make sure the grunts had him covered and set his weapon on the dirt at the edge of the driveway. He flipped out a switchblade and leaned forward to cut the ankle cords. He reached behind Pico and stuck the blade between his wrists, yanking it upward.

"Ahhh," Pico moaned and pulled his hands to his chest. "Thank you," he exhaled. He flexed his fingers in and out. "Thank you."

Queho grabbed Pico underneath his bicep and helped him sit upright. He was squatting like a baseball catcher a few inches from the mustachioed grunt. "Pico, what happened? Where's Rudabaugh?"

Pico swallowed hard. "Can I get some water?"

Queho studied him for a moment before snapping his fingers at one of the horseback grunts. He looked at Pico's wounds, the clothes he was wearing, the tree under which he was hidden. Something didn't sit right. They'd been ambushed less than an hour earlier, but Pico was acting as though he'd been tied to the tree for days.

"You come here with Mad Max?"

Pico nodded and looked at the grunt bringing him a canteen. He reached out for it and pulled it to his mouth, spilling as much of it as he was drinking.

"I asked you a question, Pico."

Pico wiped his mouth and handed back the canteen. "I did. And I know his name. It's Battle."

"Battle?"

"Yep. He killed Rud and the others. He attacked me. She attacked me. He—"

"Wait, wait, wait. Who exactly attacked you?"

"First he attacked," Pico said breathlessly. "I mean, he had booby traps. So we got caught, and everybody got killed."

"But he didn't kill you?"

"No," Pico said. "He tied me to a chair and asked me questions."

"What did you tell him?"

"Nothing."

"Nothing?"

"No," Pico said, backing up against the tree trunk. "I swear, Queho. I didn't tell him nothing."

"You said *she* attacked you. Who?"

"The redhead we were chasing the other day," Pico said. "I was all beat up. My hands were tied. She jumped me and started whaling on me."

Queho adjusted his hat. "How'd you end up here?"

"He put me on a horse and led me here," Pico said. "He wanted to go to Abilene and get back the redhead's boy. He's going to the HQ."

A knowing smile wormed across Queho's face. He rubbed his chin. "That's kinda funny, Pico."

Pico's brow furrowed. "What?"

"Twice now you're the only one to survive this Battle's violence," Queho said. "Twice. Everybody else dies. You live. Then you tell me, you swear to me, you ain't tell him nothing about nothing. But he knew we have an HQ in Abilene? How's that possible if you ain't tell him that?"

"I-I—"

"Yeah," Queho said, pushing himself to his feet. "That's what I thought."

Pico waved his hands in front of his face. "Please, Queho, I—"

"I should've killed you when I found you wandering the highway yesterday, Pico. You survive an Armageddon that kills men better than you and it's fishy. You do it twice? That's downright impossible."

Pico slid his back up the side of the tree and stood, his trembling hands raised above his head.

"Tell me this, Pico," Queho sneered. "How many men does Battle have with him? How big is *his* posse?"

"W-w-what do you mean?"

Queho bent over and grabbed his gun from the ground and then rebalanced himself on his good foot. "How many men does he have with him? How many men ambushed us?"

"It's just him."

Queho's eyes widened and he looked around at the other grunts. He didn't question Pico. For some reason, as ridiculous as it seemed, he believed him.

"Where is he?"

"I don't know. He left me here. I haven't seen him."

"Maybe he's dead."

"Maybe."

"Where is the woman?"

"She's at the house," Pico answered excitedly. "She's alone. I could take you there, Queho. I could lead you straight to her."

Queho pouted and considered the offer. "Okay," he said. "Why not? Hop up on Rudabaugh's horse. You can lead the way. Let's go."

Pico hurried over to the horse. He grabbed the saddle horn, set his foot in the stirrup iron, and heaved himself up into position. Another grunt untied the horse and Pico worked the reins to move Aces toward the highway. The horse trotted about ten feet when Queho raised his weapon to his shoulder, drew his eye to the sight, and pulled the trigger.

Crack!

The single shot exploded square into Pico's back, forcing him forward from the horse. The Appaloosa bucked as Pico fell, turned, and galloped west toward the center of town.

Pico was face down in the dirt.

"Let's go get the other horses," Queho said to the grunts. "We've got a woman to get and a house to burn."

***

OCTOBER 14, 2037, 8:23 AM

SCOURGE + 5 YEARS

TEXAS HIGHWAY 36

CROSS PLAINS, TEXAS

Battle heard the loud crack of a Browning shotgun to the east. A moment later, racing toward him down the center of Highway 36 was an Appaloosa. He could hear the rhythmic metallic clink of the shoes as Aces galloped toward him. Without considering how or why the horse was free, and what it meant about Pico or his plan to attack Abilene, he acted to gain control of it.

"Whoa!" he called out to the horse as it neared him. He started jogging and waved his arms. "Whoa! Easy, boy! Easy, boy!"

He knew he was giving up his position by calling out to the horse, but he'd already given up the paint. He couldn't afford to lose Aces too.

The horse turned south as it got close to him, slowing enough that Battle was able to run up to it and jog alongside it into the grass.

"Whoa!" he called again when the horse tried turning in front of him. It shook its head and snorted repeatedly, slowing to a stop. Battle grabbed the reins with his free hand and came around the front of the horse to face it. "Shhh! It's okay."

The horse whinnied and nickered. It was breathing heavily through its nose, gradually calming.

Battle looked back east, toward the direction from which Aces had run. He didn't see anything. The highway was empty. He pulled himself into the saddle with a swift move upward and clicked his heels into Aces's sides. He clucked his tongue against his teeth. The horse resisted at first but acquiesced and started its trot back toward the cluster of bald cypress.

Battle kept his reins in one hand, the rifle leveled in the other. He rode high in the saddle, his head whipping back and forth across the highway, his eyes scanning for trouble.

The sun was directly in front of him as he rode. It was bright and blinding. He took his reins hand and lowered the brim of the brown cowboy hat he wore. It helped a little bit, though not much. A few more gallops, and he saw the driveway to the left. The bald cypress towered high above it, their green a stark contrast to the overwhelmingly sepia-toned post-Scourge Central Texas.

Battle slowed the horse to a stop and dismounted. He wrapped the reins around his wrist, keeping enough slack so that he could effectively use the Browning if needed.

He inched off the highway into the shade of the trees and saw it immediately. Pico was face down in the dirt to the left of the concrete.

Battle looked to the right and saw the tangle of bungees near the tree where he'd left Pico. Someone had cut him free only to shoot him.

He inched forward toward Pico and immediately noticed the lack of blood. He smiled to himself.

"Salomon Pico," he said and kicked his leg. "Pico. It's me, Battle."

Pico grunted and turned his head to the side. "It hurts. It feels like my back is broken."

"You're fine. Bruised maybe. But fine. Roll over and take off your shirt."

Pico rolled onto his side and unbuttoned the tattered shirt. He sat up, groaning as he did, and pulled off the sleeves. Underneath the shirt was a black Kevlar vest, the back of it splattered with shotshell.

"I told you it would work, if it came down to it," Battle said.

"I still don't get why I was wearing it." Pico got to his knees and then stood. He unstrapped the vest on its side and pulled it over his head, groaning when he raised his arms.

"I needed you alive, until I didn't," Battle said. "I couldn't risk you getting hit in a shoot-out. You're my insurance policy."

"I don't know about that."

"Why? What happened? Who shot you?"

"A boss named Queho," Pico said. "He was with some other grunts. They found me here. I told them your plan. I told them you knew about the HQ in Abilene. They weren't happy."

"So they shot you and headed back to Abilene?"

"Not exactly." Pico pulled on the tattered shirt.

"What, then?"

"They're headed to your place," he said. "They're going to get the woman."

Battle's eyes widened. Nausea grew from his gut and settled in his throat. "Are they on horses?"

"Yeah."

"We gotta go. Now. Get on the horse."

Pico reached for the saddle horn. "You ain't gonna tie me up?"

"No need," Battle said. "They want you dead more than I do. I'm your best chance of survival now, Salomon Pico. You won't do anything I don't like. Scoot up."

Pico slid forward in the saddle and Battle hopped on behind him. "One more thing, Battle."

"What's that?" He took the reins and dug his heels deep into Aces's sides, steering the Appaloosa east, parallel to the highway.

"They said they're gonna burn down your house too."

CHAPTER 19

NOVEMBER 12, 2032, 1:17 PM

SCOURGE +44 DAYS

EAST OF RISING STAR, TEXAS

Battle shook the throbbing ache from his hand. Chiseling stone was not something he did frequently, if ever. His carvings were crude and not entirely legible without explanation.

He pounded the hammer onto the top of the chisel for the last time and then tossed both of them to the freshly dug earth beside him. He blew away the limestone dust and wiped the surface clean with a wet rag.

A breeze whistled through the branches in the oaks nearby. He looked up at the cloudless sky, noticing for the first time the absence of airplanes. He hadn't seen or heard one for weeks, come to think of it. The sun was to his left, casting his shadow across the stones that bore the names of his wife and son. He closed his eyes and inhaled the cold air, breathing it deep into his lungs before exhaling.

He ran his fingers along his wife's stone, feeling the rough etching under his fingers. A familiar lump grew thick in his throat.

"I failed you," he said. "I didn't protect you. I didn't protect Wes. In the end, all of the preparation, all of the sacrifice was worthless. You were right."

He'd buried her earlier in the day, speaking to her as he dug. He'd apologized, reminisced, laughed. Battle didn't know what else to do. The silence was too much.

Now, with the headstones in place and inscribed, it was time for the formal goodbye. He needed to repent. It was a Sunday, after all. The Lord's day.

"I was selfish," he said as much to God as to Sylvia. "I was so consumed by a fictional future that I neglected to live in the present. You were a selfless, giving woman I'll always love. You gave me our son. You gave me your life."

The wind swirled around him and shifted direction. It was growing colder.

"For the Lord himself will descend from heaven with a cry of command," he said, quoting the Bible, *"with the voice of an archangel, and with the sound of the trumpet of God. And the dead in Christ will rise first. Then we who are alive, who are left, will be caught up together with them in the clouds to meet the Lord in the air, and so we will always be with the Lord."*

Battle picked up the hammer and chisel and stood over the graves. He swallowed against the lump, suppressing it, turned from the graves, and walked slowly back to the house. He passed by the garden, looking at the still unripe vegetables his wife had planted.

He marched toward the sliding door at the rear porch and stepped into the kitchen. His laptop computer was sitting open on the counter. He set down the hammer and chisel and refreshed the browser:

Chaos Ravages Major Cities, Pandemic Reaches Critical Mass

The headline stared back at him, reaffirming what he already knew to be true. The world was devolving into a mosh pit, infrastructure was beyond its breaking point, and governments were collapsing. The inmates were running the asylum.

He'd seen it before on a smaller scale. Without a central government, without fear of reprisal, criminal elements would take hold. Violence would replace civility. Neighborhoods would become territories. Good would struggle against evil. There was no avoiding it now.

The only question for Marcus Battle was how long the chaos would rule. A year? Five? A generation?

Against his better judgment, he thumbed the mousepad, opening the doomsday article. He grew more nauseous with each sentence.

What's left of the United Nations Security Council held an online meeting this morning with surviving leaders at both the World Health Organization and the Centers for Disease Control.

The discussion, which participants accessed remotely via computers, revealed the dire circumstances developing in many of the world's largest metropolitan areas. Though reporters from the Associated Press and Reuters were invited to view the teleconference, they were not allowed to ask questions.

"The central governments in Berlin, London, Moscow, Paris, and Prague are unable to function or provide basic services," said UN Secretary General Lucius DeKaamp. "Much of Western Europe is under a facsimile of military rule. In Northern Africa and the Middle East there is essentially no military left. The Chinese," he said, "won't discuss the full impact of the Scourge on their people."

DeKaamp further said UN Security Forces were incapable of responding effectively to the scope of the unrest. He said much of the force had deserted.

The French representative, Ambassador Jacque Roget, confirmed first responders throughout his country had also deserted their posts. "We cannot effectively police our cities or villages. We cannot put out fires. We cannot transport people to the hospitals. There are no policemen. There are no firefighters. There are few doctors."

Russian Ambassador Vitaly Publichenko said Eastern Europe was a wasteland, overrun by disease, famine, and thuggery. He relayed anecdotal reports of a black market for uninfected children.

"It is most disturbing," he said from behind a surgical mask. "We have heard stories that criminal gangs are stealing healthy children from their homes. The parents are either too sick or too weak to fight back. If they do fight, they are slaughtered."

Representatives from the World Health Organization presented their latest casualty estimates, which are growing hourly. They predict two in three people will succumb to the bacterial pneumonia before only the immune are alive.

Economies have collapsed on every continent. The dollar, euro, pound, yen, and ruble are worthless, said Secretary General DeKaamp.

The council offered no solutions, advice, or comfort for survivors. They will meet again, via teleconference, tomorrow afternoon.

Battle slammed shut the laptop and slid open the sliding door with force. He stomped around the side of the house to the junction box on the exterior wall. He swung open its thick plastic cover and gripped a handful of conduit, ripping it from its delicate connection to the box. He grabbed another handful of wires and yanked them too. In an instant, he'd irreparably damaged his satellite connection to the Internet and television. He was cut off.

It was an impulsive, anger-driven choice Battle made. Without his family, he didn't want any part of the future. He didn't need the outside world. He wanted to disconnect from everything and everyone.

In his mind, it was a self-flagellating necessity. Without anyone to live for, he'd live alone for as long as he had left. He hoped he'd been contaminated. He prayed he wasn't among the immune. That would make everything so much easier.

For two weeks, he checked his temperature hourly, anticipating an imperceptible rise. He constantly cleared his throat, hoping it might show signs of an oncoming infection. With each passing hour of health, he further reconciled he was among the "lucky" ones, the one in three who survived the Scourge.

Battle couldn't kill himself, even though the thought crossed his mind. If he committed suicide, he wouldn't see his wife or child in Heaven. If he left his land with the intention of dying at someone else's hand, God would know his true intention.

So he would live in isolation for as long as his supply of food and water would allow. He would visit his wife's and child's graves every day. He would talk to them. He would seek forgiveness.

Only if someone came to him seeking help would he interact with others. That was his plan. Until it wasn't.

***

MAY 15, 2034, 3:21 PM

SCOURGE +228 Days

EAST OF RISING STAR, TEXAS

Battle didn't see a soul for one hundred and eighty-four days. Each of those days began with a short prayer before a sunrise visit to his wife and child. He spoke with them as if they would respond. After three months and ninety-three conversations, they did.

Wesson made suggestions about keeping up the property's defenses, cleaning the guns, taking target practice, and hunting for fresh meat.

Sylvia talked fruits and vegetables. She joked with him about his awful haircut and made fun of the old T-shirts with which he refused to part. She gave him advice about how best to use the rations they'd saved.

The conversations began at their gravesites. Slowly, they migrated from the plots to the garden, to the barn, to the house. Battle might spend half of his day talking to himself, to the ghosts of his family. It was an insanity that kept him sane, voices to break the never-ending silence of loneliness.

The silence ended, at least temporarily, some seven and a half months after Wesson and Sylvia died. He was sitting in the living room, his feet on the coffee table, a computer on his lap. He was watching *Raising Arizona* from the wireless hard drive he kept in the kitchen.

"That night I had a dream. I dreamt I was light as the ether, a floating spirit visiting things to come..." Nicolas Cage's character H.I. McDunnough was narrating the final scenes of the movie. Battle was unconsciously mouthing them from memory. He couldn't have counted the number of times he watched the film if he'd tried.

Movies were a daily escape for Battle, a reminder of his life before the Scourge. He had a couple dozen stored on the drive. He'd cycle through them every few days and start over.

The credits began to roll and Battle shut the laptop. He pulled his feet from the table and stood. He stretched his arms and his back. He needed to check his inventory and clean Inspector, so he trudged to the front door and swung it open. He stepped outside to see a woman standing on the stoop. He jumped back and pulled the door tight behind him.

He checked his waistband. The Sig Sauer was tucked into it. Battle never went outside unarmed. "Can I help you?"

"Yeah," said the woman through dry, cracked lips. Her hair was mouse brown and wild. She looked as if she'd stuck her finger in a working socket. Her face was painted with dirt. Her remaining teeth were more yellow than white. The river of wrinkles on her forehead smacked of long-lived desperation. "I need some help."

"What kind of help?" Battle looked past the woman onto his property. His eyes scanned the tree-dotted landscape. He didn't see anything unusual.

"I haven't eaten in a week," she said. "I haven't had water in two days."

"I'm sorry to hear that." Battle studied her clothing. It was tattered and stained at the various creases in her body. Her shoes weren't hers. The toes were cut away, revealing her toes hanging out the edge. Her long fingernails were thick with dirt.

"Can I come in?" she asked, her voice wavering. "For some water? It looks like you're doing okay."

"I can't let you inside," he said, paying close attention to her eye movements.

"Please, mister?" she begged. "Let me inside for a second? A sip of water?"

Battle was an instant from relenting, his defensive posture already relaxed infinitesimally, when he noticed her wrists. As she held her clasped hands to her chin in prayer, Battle noticed a bright red rash circling both wrists. The rashes looked like fresh rope burn or the raw blistering from handcuffs.

Either way, he knew she wasn't alone. He advanced, planted his feet shoulder width, and drew the handgun. "Where are they?" he demanded calmly with the Sig aimed at the woman's forehead.

She raised her hands and stepped back from the stoop, her eyes flittering. "Who?"

"The people who broug—"

Something collapsed on him from above, knocking him to the ground. The Sig Sauer went flying. He felt repeated, jarring thumps to the back of his head.

Somebody had jumped him from the roof!

Battle couldn't see him, but he heard the animalistic grunt emitted with every shot to his head. He was dizzy, but had enough sense to blindly jab his elbow straight up.

His elbow caught the attacker in his eye, forcing a girlish wail from him as he fell to the side, grabbing his eye. Battle turned to see blood pouring through the man's fingers.

Battle's head was throbbing and his equilibrium was compromised, but he managed a swift soccer kick to the man's nose. It knocked him unconscious, and the wailing stopped. His hand dropped to his side, revealing the swollen, bleeding hole where his eyeball used to be.

"Help!" screamed the woman. "Help!"

Battle couldn't tell to whom she was calling. He stumbled forward and tried to stand upright. His head pounded, blurring his vision. He reached for the back of his head and felt a pair of huge knots.

He tried to focus and find the Sig Sauer. However, as he blinked through the pain, a second figure emerged and stood beside the woman. They were ten feet from him, standing in the semicircular driveway.

The man held a rifle at his waist, aimed at Battle. The Sig Sauer was halfway between them on the ground.

The man motioned to it with the rifle. "Grab the gun, woman."

Battle raised his hands over his head but kept his eyes on the blurry semiautomatic rifle. The woman scrambled to grab the gun.

"What do you want?" Battle asked. His head was so thick with pain, he didn't recognize the slur of his own voice as he spoke. He felt awash with fatigue. He wanted to sit down.

"Whatever you got," the intruder spat. "You gotta problem, old man?"

Battle lowered his hands. He couldn't hold them up anymore. His ears were ringing. He looked at the rifle, tried to focus on it. He couldn't. He looked down at the unconscious cyclops.

"Any last words?"

Battle leapt to the side, diving behind the cyclops when he heard the rifle rat off a single shot. That was it. One shot.

He looked up to see the intruder struggling with the rifle. Battle used every ounce of strength in his body and pushed himself back to his feet. He lunged and stumbled forward, falling sideways into the rifleman. At the moment he hit him, the rifle discharged its second shot and then a third.

As they tumbled to the ground, Battle heard a scream and then the pop of the Sig Sauer. Battle felt warm blood on his neck as he tried to separate himself from the rifleman. Rolling away, he grabbed the back of his neck, expecting to feel a wound. Instead, it was just wet with blood.

The rifleman was staring back at him. He was on his side and his eyes were open and fixed. Blood leaked from his mouth. He was dead. The blood on Battle's neck belonged to the rifleman.

From the ground, Battle couldn't see the woman. He tried to get to his feet, knowing she held the pistol, but he didn't have the strength. He rolled onto his back and looked up at the sky. The world was spinning. He closed his eyes then squeezed them shut, trying to slow the vertigo.

He knew the woman, the bait, would step over him at any moment and empty the Sig into his chest. However, she didn't come.

He listened, straining through the high-pitched tone to get a sense of her whereabouts. Maybe she was ripping apart the house, guzzling water and chewing through his food. That was it. She was satiating her thirst and hunger first. Then she'd return to kill him. He welcomed it. He was ready.

For two hours, he lay there somewhere between lucidity and unconsciousness. The ache in his head throbbed with less intensity. The ringing in his ears diminished. He blinked open his eyes to find the sun had arced lower in the sky. There was a voice in his aching head.

"You can't do this," Sylvia said. "You can't give up."

Though Battle didn't want to hear it, he couldn't shut her up.

"We will wait for you," she said. "We will be here. When you join us, it will be for eternity. Right now, you can't give up. That's not you, Marcus. You're a fighter. You're *my* fighter."

Battle moved his legs, expecting they wouldn't respond, and swung himself onto his knees. He lifted himself up, the pounding in his head arguing with him, urging him to lie still. He looked across the rifleman's corpse and saw a second body. The woman was dead too. A pair of large red stains on her torso gave away the culprit.

Battle reconstructed the moments in his mind. He dove for cover behind the cyclops and a bullet missed him. A second pull of the trigger yielded nothing except a jam. When he lunged at the rifleman, the weapon cleared and he fired twice as Battle tackled him. The twin shots had hit the woman who, involuntarily, fired the fatal shot that killed the rifleman.

It was good fortune or serendipity or a blessing. Battle didn't care which. Nonetheless, he thanked God, rose to his feet, and carried himself inside. He collapsed on the sofa, convinced he had a concussion.

It was three days before he felt well enough to leave the house. By then, the headache had subsided, the ringing was gone, and the trio of bodies in the yard were putrefied.

Battle stood over the dead woman in a surgical mask, rubber boots, and gloves. Her mottled skin was marked by the decomposing blood vessels in her bloated body. There were maggots working at the stains on her shirt.

He dragged her body, then those of the two men, around the side of the house to a large hole he'd dug near the northern edge of his property. One by one, he dumped the stiffened corpses into the hole and covered them with dirt.

When he was finished, he pulled the mask down past his chin and prayed, choosing to believe the three were desperate victims of circumstance and not inherently evil. They'd become what their circumstances forged.

Battle walked back to the front of the house and retrieved the weapons. First, he picked up the rifle. He released the magazine and looked inside. It was loaded with cheap brass-encased ammunition. That explained the jam. The light, inexpensive ammo didn't always engage well with semiautos. That cheap crap had saved his life.

The rifle was okay, but Battle thought it nothing special. He held it with his left hand and picked up the Sig Sauer. "A lot of good you did me." He laughed. He flipped the handgun over and thought about the movie he'd finished in the moments before the intruders came to his door.

"McDunnough," he said to the gun. "I'm calling you McDunnough." He tucked it into his waistband and headed toward the barn. He still had weapons to clean.

"You could have died." Sylvia again. "You need to be more careful."

"I know," Battle responded. "It was a lapse in judgment."

"It was stupid."

Battle laughed and slung open the barn door. "What do you really think?"

"How's your head?"

"It hurts," he said. "I'll be fine."

"You have a concussion."

"Maybe."

"There's only one way to prevent this from happening again, Marcus," she said. "You know what that is."

Marcus took a deep breath and unlocked the gun case at the right of the barn. He looked around, the dust dancing in the high, overhead lights. The barn was bordering on stuffy. He set down the rifle and walked across the open space to a thermostat on the opposite wall, near the large refrigerators and freezers.

"It's what you have to do," Sylvia whispered in his ear. "You can't risk losing our home to anyone. Shoot first. Never ask questions."

Sylvia was right. She knew what was best. And he owed her. He could not let their home fall into anyone else's hands.

"Agreed," he said. "I'll do what it takes."

"I know you will," she said. "You'll keep us safe, Marcus. All of us."

CHAPTER 20

OCTOBER 14, 2037, 8:30 AM

SCOURGE + 5 YEARS

TEXAS HIGHWAY 36

EAST OF RISING STAR, TEXAS

Lola turned the handle and pushed inward, creaking open the bedroom door. She dismissed the voice in her head telling her not to snoop, but she couldn't help herself. The room was cooler and darker than the rest of the house. Ribbons of light snuck through the drawn slats of the wooden shutters. She blindly searched the wall for a light switch, found it, and flipped it up to illuminate the room from the trio of bulbs rattling beneath a spinning ceiling fan.

The walls were covered in a cheery floral wallpaper. Lola dragged her fingers across it, smiling at the idea of Battle, a man she knew as something akin to an emotionless killer, sleeping in such a feminine space.

The king-sized bed was made, its duvet pulled taut against the mattress. A pair of large decorative pillows that complemented the wallpaper sat neatly against the headboard. A pale blue chenille throw was draped across the foot of the bed.

On either side of the bed were matching nightstands that held matching glass lamps. A digital alarm clock announced the time. Opposite the bed was a large dresser. Atop the dresser was a flat-screen television. Lola took a couple of steps deeper into the room and noticed the television's screen was damaged. The large hole in the screen was matched by one equally as big in the wall behind it.

Past the dresser, in the corner opposite the bed, was an Eames chair and ottoman. The brown leather was worn and cracked. Lola moved next to the chair and pulled open the shutters. Sunlight poured into the room and Lola squinted until her eyes adjusted.

She peeked through the slats and saw the garden directly ahead. To the far right she could see the graveyard where Battle had talked to himself and prayed. A wave of guilt washed over her. She looked away and closed the slats. Lola turned to leave the bedroom when something caught her attention. On the floor to the left of the bed was a sleeping bag. It was unzipped. There was a pair of feather pillows at its head. There was a picture frame on the floor between the wall and the bag.

Lola walked the few steps to the bag and knelt down, careful not to tweak her ankle. The bag felt cool against her legs. She was tempted to crawl inside and zip it up. Instead she reached for the frame and held it up.

The photograph revealed a much-younger-looking Battle. His eyes were bright, his hair was shorter and less gray, he was tan, smiling, and his teeth gleamed. His strong arms were wrapped around two other people.

To his left was a beautiful woman with dark hair and penetrating eyes. She had a sly grin on her face. Her left arm was hidden behind Battle's back, her right hand on his chest.

To his right was a young boy, a remarkable combination of Battle and the woman. He had her intoxicating eyes, though his smile was all Battle. His arms were wrapped around Battle's neck. If she didn't know better, she'd have thought the photo came with the frame. The family looked almost too happy.

Behind them, framed carefully above them in the picture, was a treehouse. It was *the* treehouse. It was newer looking, the wood still had a hint of green to it in the picture. It wasn't the silvery gray of a weathered fort it was now, but she recognized it.

The perch from which Battle had killed countless intruders was built as a place for his child to play make-believe. Lola returned the photograph to its spot and blinked against the surprise flood of tears welling in her eyes.

She wiped her eyes dry, sniffed back the emotion, and moved to the other side of the room and the master closet. She flipped on the overhead fluorescent light and it clinked to life, casting a harsh white light into the space. It was a single walk-in closet shared by both husband and wife. To the left were his clothes; to the right were hers. The belongings hung and sat inside customized wood organizers measured to fit.

If Lola hadn't known better, she'd have thought Battle's wife was still alive. Her clothing was hung neatly and orderly, by garment type and color. Her shoes and boots were arranged in neat pairs on a shoe rack.

Lola's brows furrowed as she ran her fingers along the rows of women's clothing. She looked down at what she was wearing: an oversized men's Dallas Cowboys T-shirt and some large sweatpants rolled over at the waist and ankles.

There were plenty of women's clothes for Battle to have given her. He'd chosen his own clothing. First a T-shirt and shorts, then a T-shirt and pair of sweatpants.

Lola pulled up her pants, snapping the elastic. She left the bedroom and walked down the long hall to the kitchen, thinking about the man who'd saved her life. He was a killer. He was good at it. There was something disconnected about him, but deep down, at his core, she believed him to be a good man, a family man who was still bent on protecting what mattered most to him.

She pulled out the barstool at the kitchen island and sat down, her bad ankle dangling. In front of her was a Browning shotgun they'd taken from the Cartel, a box of shotgun shells, a cartridge bag, and an unusual-looking stainless steel knife. She picked up the knife by its black rubber handle and ran her fingers along the edge of its five-inch blade. At its tip, the blade hooked backward. Battle told her it was called a "gut hook". It was more devastating than a traditional smooth or serrated blade.

When he'd given it to her, he'd showed her the maneuver for a brutal thrust and rip. He'd said it was the knife equivalent of a hollow-point bullet. He'd also told her it was a last resort, because if she pulled it, the chances were even her attacker would use it against her.

Before he left, Battle had showed her how to reload the Browning. He'd reminded her it held only four shots.

"Once you fire the third shot," he'd explained, "you need to have a plan for reloading it."

She'd asked him why he was giving her one of the Cartel's weapons and not one of his own.

"It's better to use the weapon they're using," he'd said. "That way they don't know who's firing. They'll recognize the sound of the Browning and won't know if it's you or one of them. It's a little added camouflage."

Lola put down the knife and rechecked the shotgun. She counted the extra shells in the box. There were twenty-one. Plus, she had the four loaded into the Browning.

She took stock of her arsenal and stood from the stool. Lola knew there was a real chance she'd have to use them.

Lola tucked the knife in the elastic at her right hip. She took the cartridge bag and slung its strap over her head. She rested the bag on her left hip and stuffed it full of shotgun shells from the box.

She held the last of the twenty-five shells in her hand, looking at it closely and rolling it over in her fingers. She kissed it for good luck and dropped it into the bag. This was as ready as she was going to be.

Battle hadn't told her where to hole up while he was gone. She considered the master bedroom, the boy's room, the garage, and even the barn.

Ultimately she knew there was only one good spot from which to watch any approaching danger. The treehouse. She limped through the front door, her shoulders back. She turned right and crossed the driveway. Despite the pull of her injured ankle with each step, she pressed forward into the high grass and angled her steps to the left.

CHAPTER 21

OCTOBER 14, 2037, 9:35 AM

SCOURGE + 5 YEARS

TEXAS HIGHWAY 36

CROSS PLAINS, TEXAS

Queho figured they were about an hour from Battle's property. One of the grunts guessed the land was halfway between the almost nonexistent towns Rising Star and Comanche. That had to be twenty-five miles, they figured. The horses galloped at about ten to twelve miles per hour. Even Queho could do the math.

He bounced in the saddle, his club foot aching, but he ignored it as best he could. He was focused on the job ahead.

He recalled the crude map Pico drew at HQ. There was a house, a couple of other buildings, and a treehouse.

They'd have to attack from front to back, working their way from the southern edge of the property against Highway 36. He couldn't be sure how accurate the map was. Queho almost regretted blasting Pico. Almost.

He'd killed so many men since the Scourge. Really, he'd killed more than his share before the Scourge. His mind drifted with the rhythm of the gallop as he recalled the salad days.

Queho had made a living dealing meth and prescription drugs to the pitiful underclass in West Texas. He'd been careful to avoid the Mexican dealers and stuck to a very restrictive turf. That had only lasted so long.

Eventually, without much of a choice, he'd sworn allegiance to the Sinaloa Cartel, which controlled a narrow strip of land between Mexico and West Texas. It was one of the six major Mexican cartels before the Scourge. It was the only one to prevent the rival Zetas from holding the entirety of the Texas-Mexico border.

When Queho got arrested during a sting, the Sinaloas promised him protection in prison. They'd told him he'd be safe on the inside and he'd be rewarded when he got out as long as he kept his mouth shut. He'd obeyed.

It was in that West Texas prison that he'd met Cyrus Skinner. Skinner wasn't Sinaloa. He wasn't Zeta. He was his own man.

Queho remembered not being afraid behind bars. He knew the Sinaloas had his back. Nobody frightened, intimidated, or bullied Queho. Nobody except for Cyrus Skinner.

Skinner was a big man. Tall, broad shoulders, and a ridiculously strong jaw. He chain-smoked; a butt or blunt was always stuck to his lips.

Queho watched Skinner work the cell, the dining hall, and the yard. Other guards tried to act tough. Skinner actually was.

When the guard came to him with a proposition, Queho knew he couldn't refuse. Together, with the full knowledge of the Sinaloa Cartel, they initiated a complex and successful drug trade within the prison walls.

If anyone challenged them or shorted them, Queho was the enforcer. Skinner was his alibi.

Queho couldn't remember how many men they'd killed and maimed. It was a tenth of the number he'd murdered since the Scourge.

Queho looked ahead at the rising sun. It was shaping up to be a beautiful day. He had a good feeling about it and regripped the reins, urging his horse to run faster.

He hadn't killed a woman in weeks. He had an itch.

***

Battle wasn't sure how much harder he could push the Appaloosa. He worried it might give out on him, but he couldn't afford to stop for water. Every second wasted was an advantage to the men racing toward his home.

Battle looked past Pico toward the road ahead. They were drawing closer with every gallop.

"The only way she'll be alive is if they take their time," Pico said. "Sometimes they take their time."

Battle clenched his jaw.

"Why are you taking me with you?" Pico asked, changing the subject. "Why didn't you just leave me there?"

Battle looked at the side of Pico's face. "I need your help. I told you that already."

"Doesn't make sense," Pico said. "I'm one of them. I get that you kept me alive as a bargaining chip when we were headed over to Abilene. But now? I don't get it."

Battle laughed. "You're not that thick, are you, Salomon Pico? You're not one of them. They killed you once already. They'd do it again."

Pico turned his head forward. He didn't respond. Battle guessed the grunt didn't want to reconcile his plight.

"You're better off helping me," Battle said. "I give you a chance at living. They don't. And I need an extra hand. I need someone who knows how the Cartel works. I need a guide."

Pico didn't respond.

Battle decided it was time for a full-court press. He needed Pico on his team before they got home. "They don't trust you anymore. Well, they didn't. They think you're dead. And I guarantee if they killed you once, they'd do it again without blinking. You know them better than I do. Am I wrong? Would they let bygones be bygones? If they let you live initially, wouldn't you always wonder when the bullet was coming? Wouldn't—"

"Yes," Pico snapped. "You're right, okay? You're right. They'd kill me again. It'd be near impossible for me to prove myself."

Battle didn't interrupt. He let Pico vent.

"I did everything I could do for them," he said, his voice fighting against the wind. "I took orders, I killed, I stole— whatever they wanted. It wasn't ever good enough, though. They always wanted more. And I wasn't ever gonna be anything but a grunt. Didn't matter. Once a grunt like me, always a grunt."

Battle took one hand off the reins and gripped Pico's shoulder. He flinched. "I won't make you a grunt, Salomon Pico," he said. "You'll have a stake in things."

Pico looked back at Battle and then turned forward. He nodded but said nothing, his body bouncing in the saddle.

Battle hoped his talk had worked. If it didn't, Pico's admonition would prove right and they'd both die.

CHAPTER 22

OCTOBER 14, 2037, 10:39 AM

SCOURGE + 5 YEARS

EAST OF RISING STAR, TEXAS

Lola heard the horses before she saw the men. They were coming from the front of the property, south of the treehouse. A breeze kicked up and whistled through the pine slats in front of her.

Lola cursed herself. If she'd been in the house, the laser alarm at the front fence would have alerted her instead of her guessing and straining to hear.

She looked down at the Browning shotgun in her hands. She understood Battle's logic, but regretted not having insisted on a longer-range weapon. Even with her lack of experience, she knew a shotgun wasn't going to be accurate from a distance.

She wiped a cold sweat from her forehead with the back of her arm and pressed her eyes closer to the opening in the treehouse wall. The tall grass was rippling against the breeze, the oaks swaying. Leaves twirled to the ground with every gust.

The skies were clear. The early morning fog was gone. Her pulse was racing. She could feel it in her chest and as she breathed. Lola cursed Battle for leaving her behind, for leaving her alone. She didn't like being left alone.

Her husband left her alone with their son, Sawyer, when he got himself killed. He'd promised to come back. He was only going to look for water. They were low and maybe had a couple of days left in their Shreveport efficiency.

"We can go together," she'd suggested. "We should stay together.

He'd refused. He didn't know exactly where he'd find water or what he'd have to do to obtain it. He didn't want Sawyer with him, and they couldn't leave him alone in the apartment.

He'd left with a kiss on her lips and a tousle of Sawyer's red hair. "I'll be back," he'd promised.

Four hours later he'd kept his promise. He came back with two gallons of water and a stab wound under his left arm. He'd never explained how he got the water or the fatal wound.

He'd died on the floor of the apartment, his wife and son watching him take his final breath and exhaling it with a rattle.

Now, sitting in a treehouse alone, she feared her solitude even more. Somebody was coming for her. She narrowed her eyes and focused south, toward the main gate. In the distance, she could see something or someone. There was movement. The oak branches blocked much of the view between the treehouse and the highway.

She tightened her grip on the shotgun and scanned the horizon as best she could. She was lying on her stomach, her elbows bracing the weapon. Lola checked her position and scooted backward into the treehouse a few inches. She didn't want the muzzle sticking too far out through the opening.

She heard the snorting again. It was definitely horses. Somebody was at the front gate, and it probably wasn't Battle. He would have bounded into the property by now.

There were men talking. She couldn't hear what they were saying, but picked up at least three voices.

***

"This is it," Queho said.

The men hopped off their horses and tied them to a cattle fence along the edge of the highway.

"You sure?" one of the grunts questioned.

"Yep," Queho said and pointed to clumps of dark brown manure dotting the grass around them. "This is it. There's a bunch of horse crap right here and the grass is trampled. Our guys were here."

Another grunt reached for the Browning strapped to his saddle. "What do we do?"

Queho looked at him incredulously and hocked a loogie into the grass. "You serious? We attack. Load up everything you got."

The grunt imitated Queho and spat onto the ground. "Are we taking the woman alive?"

"Depends on what kinda fight she gives us." Queho shrugged. He looked up into the blue October sky. There were a few high wispy clouds speeding along. An intermittent breeze swirled around them as they prepped. A couple of black birds circled above.

Queho bent over, leaning on the fence for support, and adjusted the boot on his bad foot. His ankle was sore and felt swollen from the ride. He tested his weight on it, winced, and then bit the inside of his cheek to counteract the pain. He'd suffered through worse.

"Let's go." He nodded to the four surviving grunts. "I want this done. I want to be back home in Abilene by sundown."

The five marched through the opening in the perimeter fence and trudged through the grass.

Queho had his shotgun at his belly, sweeping it from left to right. He had six-shooters on both hips and a double-edged bowie knife tucked into his belt.

He had two men on either side of him. They worked the ground in the same manner, checking each step, careful not to get stuck in the sucking muck left behind by the previous night's heavy rain.

As they moved closer, weaving between the oak trees large and small, Queho could see the buildings. To the left was a treehouse. Behind that was a large barn. Straight ahead was a house. To the right was a large garage. There was no sign of anyone, no obvious movement.

The closer they got to the fence, the air filled with a pungent, sour odor. Queho recognized it. It was unmistakable. It was the odor of death. He slowed his approach to the interior fence line. The black birds were directly overhead; there were three of them now.

Above the top wisps of grass, he could see what looked like a hand. Maybe it was a bare foot. He couldn't tell at first. The closer he got, the more apparent it was a hand.

He stood above the corpse and saw there were two men there. They were heaped together in death. Both of them were a purplish color, stiffened, and unrecognizable. Not that Queho would have known their names anyhow. But they looked more like ghouls than men. He could tell the birds were already working on the bodies. Only the cool weather prevented the odor from being worse.

Queho gritted his teeth. Two more men dead at the hands of this man named Battle was too much. Anger rose from deep within his gut, searing his throat as he screamed at the top of his lungs every foul word his mother had taught him.

The birds flapped and crowed and circled away from their meal. Queho's cries reverberated, falling flat against the breeze.

***

Lola jumped at the outburst from the man below, worried at first she'd blown her cover. Thankfully, none of the men looked her way.

From her perch, she thought she knew the angry one. He wore a brown hat, which separated him from most of the Cartel. She knew only some of the leaders called "bosses" wore the brown hats. Though she couldn't clearly see his face, she recognized his limp. He had a bad foot. He was among the more ruthless of the bosses. She'd seen him beat his own men for amusement. He'd hit her once. His shirt had a crease along the sleeve. He hadn't liked it, so he'd backhanded her at the front counter of the laundromat. She couldn't remember his name.

Lola touched her cheek, recalling the sting of it, and narrowed her focus through the single sight. She couldn't hit him from this distance. He was still outside the fence.

She counted the men huddled around the dead bodies of the men killed the night before. There were five of them. Only one boss, the rest were grunts.

Lola wiped her hands on the hip of her sweatpants one at a time. Her mouth felt dry. Her pulse quickened. She worked hard to breathe in and out slowly through her nose.

Five men. All of them armed. She'd need to choose her moment. If she attacked too soon, it could be fatal. If she attacked too late, it might not be fatal enough.

She ran her hand through her red hair, mixing in the sweat from her palms and forehead. She peeked through the opening in the pine boards and shifted the aim of the shotgun. The crippled one with the hat pointed at the interior fence, guiding his men through the gate. They slowly trudged through the opening one at a time.

The brown hat rubbed his chin, scratched his neck, and then looked to his left. His gaze shifted upward and stopped directly at the treehouse. He was looking right at Lola. Her pulse told her he was looking *through* her.

He stayed outside of the fence line and worked his way west, closer to her. His eyes and his shotgun pointed at the treehouse.

Lola held still, careful not to move at all. She didn't even train the shotgun downward to match his movement. Sweat dribbled into her eyes. Her nose itched. She wiggled it, knowing she couldn't scratch it. The more she wiggled it, the worse the sensation became.

He moved to within fifteen yards of the treehouse, his eyes narrowly focused on her position. Lola licked her lips. She was ready to jerk the shotgun down and fire off a volley of shots. Her finger moved to the trigger. She blew the itch from her nose.

"Boss!" one of the grunts called from the driveway, drawing the brown hat's attention away from Lola.

She exhaled and watched him limp away from her. Two of the men were to the right of the driveway, closer to the garage. The other two were on the drive itself.

One of them pointed at the ground in front of him with his Browning. "Ain't that Rud?"

"Where?" Queho picked up his pace through the open gate until he joined the pair of grunts. The other two grunts worked their way back to Queho and joined the group.

One of them pointed again. "There."

"Yeah," Queho said. "That's him." He tipped the hat back on his head and rubbed his face before he chuckled. "This is a sick dude we got here. Surprised he ain't workin' for us."

"That looks like a booby trap or something, right?" said one grunt.

"It is," said Queho. "We gotta be careful. There could be more of them. You need to move slow or you're gonna get caught in a hole like Rud here."

"He looks messed up," said the other grunt.

"'Cause he is," said the boss. "Like I said, be careful." He nodded with his chin forward, as if to point out the invisible traps.

Lola held her position. She scratched her nose and wiped another stream of sweat from her face.

***

Battle slowed his horse to a full stop about one hundred yards from his front fence. He knew the Cartel was already there. He could see their horses fixed to the posts.

"I don't want them hearing us," he told Pico. "We get off here."

Battle jumped off first and helped Pico down. "Remember," he told his unrestrained prisoner, "they killed you. I didn't. You need to trust me."

"You gonna give me a gun?" Pico asked.

"No. I don't trust you yet."

"That don't seem fair," Pico argued. "You need my help, but you gonna bring me into a gunfight with nothing to defend myself?"

Battle tipped his hat. "I'll defend you."

Battle walked the Appaloosa to the eastern edge of his fence and tied up the horse. He whispered thank you into its ear and pulled his shotgun from the saddle scabbard. He checked his waist for McDunnough. All was good.

He stood against the fence, his fingers curled around the barbed wire, and listened. The only sound was the breeze whistling through the oaks.

He waved for Pico to join him, and they walked through the fence opening. The mud wasn't as thick as when they'd left earlier in the day, but it made moving with speed a tricky proposition. If Battle's boots weren't sucked into it, they were sliding on top of it.

"Be careful once we get to the interior fence," he warned Pico, who was a step behind him to his right. "Between the driveway and the treehouse, there are a half dozen traps. They'll break your ankle."

Pico shook his head. "You don't play."

Battle moved a step at a time closer to the interior fence, pushing his way through the grass. The trees obscured a clear shot to the house, but he could see the tops of the roofs.

To the left he caught sight of the treehouse and decided to approach from that side of the property. He crouched low and picked his way west to the edge of his land before cutting back north toward the interior fence.

As he drew close, he stopped and dropped to a knee. Pico followed Battle's lead and hid in the grass. They were virtually invisible from their position, though Battle could see the treehouse clearly. He searched the thin openings in the slats until he saw a hint of a muzzle poking through the southeast corner of the pine walls. Lola was there.

She was alive!

The sensation of relief and the resulting exhale surprised Battle. He shook himself back to focus and poked his head up above the grass. He saw a group of men to the right. They were at the edge of the driveway near where he'd killed the man whose hat he now wore.

Without thinking, Battle stood up and yelled out to the men while racing back toward them at the fence line. He had the Browning pulled to his eye as he bolted, trying to keep his footing in the mud.

None of the men saw him until he'd reached the fence and he called out to them. "You shouldn't have come here. This is my land. I didn't invite you."

The men turned in unison, swinging their shotguns in his direction. As they spun around, Battle could see there were five of them. He was maybe thirty yards away, well inside the weapon's effective range. He picked the one on the left and pulled the trigger.

Crack!

The shot exploded from the Browning and hit the grunt in the throat. He grabbed at the spray, his blood spewing through his fingers. Battle dropped to a knee and moved his aim to the right.

Crack!

The second blast struck the target in his shoulder. He moved just as Battle pulled the trigger, growling with pain and dropping his shotgun. His arm went limp when another blast hit him in the chest. He crumpled to the ground, his head slapping the driveway with a thud.

Battle moved his aim again, knowing he had one shot left in the Browning. The remaining three men had reacted now; they were separating. He couldn't keep all of them within his range of sight.

One of them made a fast approach straight at Battle, running to the right of the dead boss trapped in the hole. Battle pulled the trigger on his last shot.

Crack!

The target screamed, a guttural, unearthly sound echoing uncomfortably in the cool air, and Battle thought he'd hit him. But he hadn't.

His shot sailed over the man's head as he fell knee deep into one of the remaining dozen traps. Battle knew it as soon as the man called out in a warbled voice.

"Help!" he cried. "I'm stuck. I think my leg's broke. Help!"

Battle dropped the Browning, pulled his Sig Sauer, stood, and fired two shots into the man's forehead. He slumped forward. His crying stopped.

Crack! Zip! Crack! Zip!

A pair of shotgun blasts powered past Battle from his right, some of the pellets catching his side when he turned to react. He resisted the urge to grab at the sting and dove to the ground. There were two left, and they were close.

Battle scrambled to reload the Browning, but couldn't find it in the grass. He rolled over onto his back, gripping McDunnough with both hands. He was a sitting duck. He knew it. The best he could hope for was taking them out as they pumped him full of shotshell.

***

On his back, he couldn't see anything beyond the grass and the sky above him. He sensed the tangled branches of a younger oak to his right. The fence, he knew, was to his left. A cold sweat bloomed on his forehead. If he risked getting to his feet, he'd get his head blown off.

He slowly inched backward in the mud and grass, using his heels to slide along on his backside. The pain in his side was intensifying as if he'd been stung by a swarm of wasps. It made it increasingly difficult to move, demanding his focus and attention. He stopped pushing with his heels and sucked in a deep breath. He lay still and listened.

Nearby, maybe a few feet from him, there were footsteps. One of the men was walking slowly toward him, his boots sticking and pulling from the mud, his legs were brushing against the grass.

Battle thought the man was coming from his right. Or was it the left. No. It was the—

Crack! Crack!

The twin shots shocked Battle. He shuddered and then winced against the burning ache in his side. He heard the low moan and raspy breath of a dying man in the grass to his right.

"Battle!" It was Lola. "Battle! Are you there?"

He started to raise his arm, but stopped. He knew there had to be one man left. And where was Pico? He couldn't trust Pico yet. He stayed flat on the ground.

"I'm alive," he called out. He was only fifteen feet or so from the fence. The treehouse was another twenty feet beyond that.

"There's one left," she called back. "He's in the house. And there's the one you brought with you."

"Salomon Pico?"

"He's in the house too."

Battle wasn't sure he heard her correctly. "What?"

"He's in the house. Both of them. They bolted for the house when you killed those first three guys."

Battle rolled over onto his stomach and pushed himself to his feet. He moved to the fence, trying to ignore the thick heat on his right side. He looked up at Lola peeking through the slats.

"You stay up there," he said. "I'm going to get them."

Battle found the Browning he'd tossed to the ground and started reloading it as he walked along the fence line toward the open gate at the driveway. He was walking straight toward the house, scanning the windows for signs of life, when the front door swung open. He hadn't finished with the Browning.

A worn-looking man with a limp emerged from the house. He was wearing a hat. He had his shotgun aimed at Battle's head as he shortened the distance between them.

Battle realized he'd lost his hat, and his weapon wasn't loaded and ready to fire. The cripple had the drop on him.

"So you're Mad Max," the cripple called, his bad foot almost dragging behind him. "You're Battle. Is that it? Battle?" Half of his face was hidden behind the Browning.

"Yeah," Battle said.

"And this is your land, you say?"

"Yeah."

"Tell the woman in the treehouse to get down here or I blow your head off right now."

Battle raised his hands over his head, one of them holding the partially loaded shotgun. McDunnough was tucked into his back. If he could only —

The brown-hatted cripple snapped, "Drop the weapon and get the woman to come here. I ain't up for games."

Battle lowered his arms and tossed the Browning onto the ground. "Lola," he called. "C'mon down."

"Good boy," said the man. "Now, I reckon you killed a lot of my men. That so?"

Battle shrugged. To his left, Lola was scrambling from the treehouse. The brown hat called over to her without taking his eyes or his aim from Battle.

"Leave your weapon over there, darlin'. You ain't got no use for it. You hear?"

Battle could sense Lola moving from the back side of the treehouse to the driveway. He glanced to his left. She was slowly moving toward them, her hands above her head.

"This'll be over for you in a minute, Battle," said the brown hat. He shifted his weight from one foot to the other. "I ain't gonna keep you long, but I'll be taking the woman with me."

A breeze swirled past Battle and he caught the smell of smoke. He looked past the cripple to the house. His eyes drifted to the roof. There were wisps of white smoke curling up into the sky. His eyes darted between the intruder and the smoke.

A grin as wide as the brim of his hat spread across the cripple's face. "You smell that, huh?" He inhaled deeply through his nose, puffing his chest. "Yeah." He snickered. "Your place is burning."

The white smoke was darkening in color, blooming into a grayish black. Battle's neck stiffened. His hands balled into tight fists. His jaw set.

"It's the least I can do for you," he said. "Like I said, you killed a bunch of my men. I can't let that go unnoticed. What kind of boss would I be? What message would that send if I let you get away with that?" He motioned with his head to Lola. "Come closer, woman."

Black smoke poured from the roof. The hint of orange flames began licking at the sky, growing in intensity. Battle could feel the heat.

Lola limped to within a few feet of the cripple. Her hands trembled. Her shoulders hunched.

"Get over here!" he snarled.

When she refused to move closer, the man stepped to her. He pulled her in front of him, pressing himself against her while managing to keep the weapon leveled at Battle.

"You're gonna help me kill him, woman," he spat. He grabbed her hand, and despite her effort to free herself, he pulled her hand to the trigger. "Now just aim like so and—"

Lola raised up her injured foot and slammed it down onto the cripple's club foot. He shrieked and let go of her. She jabbed her elbow into his gut and he fell backward onto his tailbone. The shotgun flew into the air and landed some five feet from them and slid across the driveway.

Battle pulled McDunnough from his waistband and aimed it at the brown hat. He leveled the Sig at his face.

The cripple crossed his arms in a futile attempt to block however many nine millimeter slugs Battle decided to unleash. He shook his head, protesting his impending death when a voice called from the western edge of the driveway.

"Battle. Stop." It was Salomon Pico. He was carrying Inspector and had it aimed at Battle.

***

"What are you doing?" Battle snarled. He kept the Sig aimed at his target. He wasn't letting him move. From inside the house, glass was breaking, wood was snapping, and smoke was leaking from the front windows and from underneath the door.

"Put down the gun, Battle," Pico said forcefully. He licked his mustache and repeated himself. "Put it down now."

Battle cursed at him and tossed McDunnough to the ground. He was sick of giving up his weapons. It was almost comical.

The cripple pushed himself to his feet, struggling to stand on one foot. "Pico? That you?"

"It's me." Pico nodded. "I ain't dead." His eyes narrowed. The smoke was blowing in waves.

The brown hat chuckled nervously. "I can see that," he said. "I'm thankful you ain't dead."

"C'mon, Pico," said Battle. "He will kill you."

Pico held the rifle like an amateur. He adjusted it against his shoulder and aimed it at Battle's chest. "I don't think you should be talking right now." He walked closer to Battle.

"All right, Pico." The cripple sucked in air through his teeth and tottered on his good foot. "You got 'em. You redeemed yourself. You proved it."

Pico looked over at the man. "What do you want me to do to him, Queho?"

The crackle of the flames inside the home was nearing a roar. Smoke was pouring from the house. It was stinging Battle's eyes and intermittently obscuring his view of the others. He couldn't act; he was unarmed and beaten.

Pico wiped his own eyes and cleared his throat. "You tell me where to shoot him. You want it slow or quick?"

"We ain't got too long," Queho said and coughed. "This house is gonna blow. Shoot him in the knee first."

Lola coughed too. She stood, her hands in the air and trying to balance on her uninjured ankle and foot. "Don't," she said. "You don't have to—"

Thump! Thump! Thump!

Lola screamed. She rushed the short distance to Battle and grabbed him through the smoke. "Battle!" she cried. "Battle!"

It was Queho who took the three shots. The first was in his left knee, splintering the kneecap into nasty shards. The second hit his left thigh, boring through the femur and expanding as it nestled inside the thick bone. The third drilled into his gut. He dropped onto his knees, crying out. He fell onto his side, roiling with pain and the knowledge that he was about to die. He grabbed at the hole in his abdomen, thick dark blood leaking uncontrollably from the wound.

Pico offered Battle the rifle and walked over to Queho. He crouched down into a catcher's position, squatting in front of the boss who'd tried to end his life. He looked into Queho's eyes but said nothing. He watched the once-powerful boss, hatless, gasping for air like a grounded fish. The color was fading from his face. His lips were blue. His nostrils were flared.

He blinked rapidly, tears draining from his eyes.

Battle stood next to Pico, as did Lola, and they watched Queho take his final breath. His body shuddered, twitched, and went limp. His mouth fell open, his eyes fixed. He was dead.

"Thank you," Battle said. He offered his hand to Pico.

Pico took it and pulled himself to his feet. "You were right. He'd kill me the minute he got the chance."

Battle coughed against the thickening smoke and heat. He pulled Lola with him away from the house. Pico followed. Battle directed the two of them toward the barn, and he stood in the driveway, watching the flames consume his home.

He cupped his hands around his mouth. "Go to the barn! I'll be right there."

Pico put his arm around Lola and led her away.

Battle wiped his eyes clear of smoke and ran around the right side of the house toward the garage. He rounded the corner into the back of the house and was met with a wall of thick, black smoke. He pulled his shirt collar up over his nose and mouth and stepped back to the eastern side of the home. There was a window leading into the master bedroom. The shutters were drawn, so he couldn't tell if the flames had consumed the room yet. He touched the glass with his hand. It was hot, but not searing. Battle leaned the rifle against the side of the house. He turned his head away from the window, drew back his elbow, and drove it through the glass.

Smoke spilled out of the jagged opening. Battle tried to take a deep breath but couldn't because of the shotgun wound in his side. He closed his eyes, pulled up a mental image of his bedroom, and climbed through the window.

He landed awkwardly on the floor, knocking over a bedside table. He felt a tear along his thigh followed by the deep sting of a cut. He pressed forward along the floor. The room was black with smoke. It didn't help the shutters were drawn on all of the windows.

As best he could tell, the flames hadn't yet engulfed the bedroom. Though, through the darkness, he could see an orange glow outlining the bedroom door. He could taste the smoke.

Battle slid along the floor, trying to hold his breath in between filtered sips of air through his shirt. It wasn't really working. He couldn't see. His nose and throat were burning.

He felt the edge of the bed and yanked on the duvet. He tugged on it twice more until he popped a pillow from atop the mattress. Battle put the pillow over his face and sucked in as deep a breath as he could muster. It was only slightly better, but it helped.

He pulled himself under the bed and crawled flat against the floor to the other side. To his left he heard an explosion. It sounded like a mortar. His mind flashed to Syria, but he brought himself back, emerging from underneath the bed. He felt around blindly with his fingers spread wide, his eyes squeezed shut. Under his hand he felt the nylon sleeping bag in which he'd spent five years' worth of nights.

He groped around aimlessly. He was coming up empty.

Battle felt the concussive force of another explosion, and a blast of heat poured into the room. He'd been inside the house for less than a minute. He had seconds left. He coughed and felt the dizziness in his head. He was about to black out.

He extended his arm as far as he could reach and felt what he'd come to get. Battle gripped the picture frame and slid it across the floor. He held it with one hand, pushing himself backward along the floor.

The orange glow had spread. The room was on fire. His skin was burning from the ambient heat. He scrambled out from under the bed and opened his eyes, only to close them against the sting of the smoke, and pushed himself to his feet. He held his breath and scrambled for the window, pulling himself through it.

He spilled out of the window, landed on his shoulder, and hit the ground with a thud. He rolled onto his back, coughing and gagging involuntarily. His chest hurt; he was cut and burned and no doubt had sucked in too much smoke.

He crawled to the Inspector he'd left against the side of the house, struggled to his feet, and stumbled away from the house to the garden. He tripped over a thick root exposed from the rain and fell forward, sliding face first onto the ground.

He couldn't catch his breath. His skin hurt. His side ached. His leg stung.

Battle lay there in the grass and felt the waves of heat from his burning home. He was sinking into the ground from exhaustion. He couldn't get up. He didn't want to get up. He opened his eyes and looked at what little was left of the home he'd built with his own hands. It was collapsing in on itself. Despite the care, the planning, the craftsmanship, the security, the home was lost. All it took was a spark, an unconfined spark.

"I'm sorry," he whispered. He couldn't have managed more than a whisper if he tried. "I'm. So. Sorry," he wheezed.

"You need to get up, Marcus," Sylvia's voice implored. "You need help. Get up. Make it to the barn."

Battle tried to swallow. He couldn't. He couldn't muster enough saliva.

"Marcus," the voice repeated. "Get up. Get to the barn. I need you to get to the barn."

"Dad!" Wesson's voice joined his mother's. "Please get up. Please, Dad."

Battle clenched his jaw. He didn't want to move. He couldn't move. He would rest here. This was a good spot. He closed his heavy eyes and sank deeper into the ground.

"Get up, Battle!" It was another voice: Lola's. "Get up! You need to get away from the house."

Battle was slipping into unconsciousness. His breathing was shallow and ragged. Lola and Pico stood over him. They bent over and grabbed his arms, trying to drag him toward the barn. Slowly, they trudged backward until they reached the edge of the driveway where it met the barn.

"We can't pull him across the driveway," Lola said. "He's already bleeding. His skin looks burned. His breathing doesn't sound good. We need to pick him up."

Together they managed to lift him up and draped his arms around their shoulders. Battle was in and out of consciousness, his wheezing more pronounced by the time they crossed the threshold of the barn.

Along the back wall of the barn, Lola found a folded military cot on the bottom shelf below the first aid supplies. She gingerly walked back to the middle of the open space and unfolded the cot.

Pico lowered Battle onto the cot, and the warrior's injured body sank deep into it, stretching it nearly to the floor. Pico looked at Lola and shrugged. "What now?"

"We need to help him breathe," she said. "He's having trouble breathing. Check the freezer for drugs. I'll check the shelves."

Lola limped back to the shelf and rifled through the selection of first aid supplies. She found plenty of things that would help the burns on his arms, neck, and face. There was antiseptic and Polysporin for his shotgun wounds. She grabbed handfuls of what she could carry and lugged it back to the cot.

"Did you find anything?"

Pico was opening and closing freezer doors. He stopped at the third one on the right, leaning into the freezer and calling out over his shoulder, reading labels. "Tetracycline, imipenem, ciprofloxacin. Will any of those work?"

Lola shook her head. "No," she said. "He needs a steroid. A steroid will open up his lungs. It'll help him breathe."

Pico turned and looked at her sideways. "How do you know that? You a doctor or something?"

"No," she said and knelt beside Battle. "I'm a mom, remember? Every child who gets bronchitis takes steroids to open up their lungs."

Pico turned back to the freezer. "Ibuprofen? Naproxen sodium?"

"Those are painkillers," she answered. She struggled to pull Battle's shirt over his head. "He'll need those if he survives this."

Despite the first-degree burns, his skin looked pale. The smoke inhalation was damaging his lungs, and he wasn't able to breathe beyond gulps of air.

"Albuterol?"

Lola nodded, her eyes wide. "Yes! That'll work."

Pico slammed shut the freezer and returned to the cot with the painkillers and the steroid. "What is it?"

"It's a bronchodilator," she said. "Not quite as good as a steroid. It won't last long, but it'll help him breathe. My son used the liquid for breathing treatments. I haven't seen the pill before. It'll have to do."

"We don't have any water," Pico said. "There are jugs in the freezer, but they're ice."

"Don't worry about it," Lola said. She lifted up Battle's head and his mouth dropped open. She popped two of the pills into his mouth, shoving them as far back as she could. He gagged and coughed. His body shuddered. "Go thaw a couple of the jugs. We'll need the water."

Battle stopped coughing and Lola laid his head back onto the cot. She took his hand in hers and, for the first time in a very long time, prayed. She asked God to save her friend. She asked Him to bring Battle back. She needed him to help her. It was a selfish prayer. She knew it was. But she hoped God would reward her prayer and reinstall the faith she'd lost with two-thirds of the world.

Lola squeezed Battle's hand. It was hot from the burns and lifeless.

CHAPTER 23

JUNE 13, 2023, 8:40AM

SCOURGE -9 YEARS, 4 MONTHS

ABILENE, TEXAS

The doctor held the transducer probe in his gloved hand. "Do you want to know?" He looked at Sylvia before glancing at Marcus. "I can tell you."

Sylvia squeezed her husband's hand. Her faded "Make America Great Again" T-shirt was pulled above her belly, her maternity jeans unbuttoned. "What do you think, Marcus?"

Marcus returned the squeeze. "It's up to you," he said. "I'll paint the room blue regardless. If it's a girl, she'll live with it."

Sylvia giggled. She was a beautiful pregnant woman. She radiated joy. Even on the worst of the days, when the baby gave her horrific nausea and debilitating exhaustion, she was as happy as she'd ever been. She'd told Marcus more than once that the only thing better than being married to her hero was having his child.

Marcus remembered the moment she'd told him she was pregnant. It was the last Monday in February. He was in Raqqa, more than two hundred miles from Aleppo, Syria. American, French, and Russian forces had taken control of the city after a month-long siege versus ISIS and antigovernment forces who'd assassinated the previous three Syrian presidents.

Marcus, barely six weeks into a three-month deployment, had been on the verge of earning a battlefield promotion to lieutenant colonel. His CO had handed him a satellite phone. Sylvia had said two simple words. They'd changed everything.

Marcus had finished the tour. He'd gone home. He'd requested an honorable discharge. Within days, a buddy from West Point had offered him a lucrative consulting job. He'd taken it, along with the cash he'd squirreled away, and they'd moved to the middle of Nowhere, Texas.

"Let's do it," Sylvia said, snapping him from his daydream. "Let's find out."

The doctor nodded to the nurse. "Gel, please."

"Are you excited?" Sylvia looked up at Marcus. "Or are you going to vomit?"

"I'm so excited I think I'll vomit," he deadpanned.

Sylvia squeezed his hand again. "You're hilarious, Major Battle."

The doctor squeezed warm gel onto Sylvia's belly. "*Major* Battle?" He smirked, with one eyebrow drawn higher than the other.

Marcus rolled his eyes. "Yes. Army. You serve?"

"Semper Fi," the doctor said. "Annapolis Class of '10."

"My condolences." Marcus winked. "West Point '19."

"Good for you." The doctor took the probe and touched it to Sylvia's belly. He turned his attention to the ultrasound monitor and kept talking. "I've got a joke I think you'll appreciate, Major."

"I'll bite," said Marcus. "I wasn't aware Marines had a sense of humor."

The doctor touched a button on the ultrasound and swirled the probe. He stopped near Sylvia's navel and pressed. "An army officer is standing at the bottom of a hill with a platoon of soldiers. He looks up the hill and grabs one of his men by the shoulder. With a ridiculous amount of seriousness he says, 'Soldier, there's a drunken Marine at the top of the hill, talking about our mothers. Go get that Marine and bring him here to me.' The soldier obeys the order but minutes later comes rolling back down the hill, beaten to a pulp. So the officer sends a fire team up the hill. He shouts, 'Bring that Marine to me now!' Three soldiers come rolling down the hill, bloodied and embarrassed. The officer sends the rest of the platoon up the hill to bring down the Marine for a good army whooping. The whole platoon returns humiliated and without the Marine. The officer grabs an injured soldier by the collar of his filthy uniform and demands an explanation. 'What is your problem, son? Why can't you bring me that Marine for a good army whooping?' The soldier, out of breath, says, 'Sorry, Colonel. It's a trap. There are two of them.'"

The doctor kept his eyes on the monitor, his shoulders shuddering with laughter. The nurse chuckled. Sylvia pursed her lips and looked at her husband.

Marcus didn't laugh. "I think we may have the wrong doctor," he said. "Then again, if he tells us it's a girl, we could use him for a reference when she applies to Annapolis."

"That's sexist," said Sylvia, pausing for effect. "Women are stronger than most Marines."

The doctor turned from the monitor and looked straight at Marcus. "I like her," he said. "How she ended up with a dogface is beyond me." A smile snaked across his face.

"I'll agree with that assessment," Marcus said. "So is it a boy or a Marine?"

"Just a second more," the doctor said. "I need to check some measurements. We'll let you listen to the heartbeat and then I'll let you know it's a boy."

"A boy?" Sylvia's eyes welled instantly. She looked back at Marcus. His eyes were as glossy as hers. "Did you hear that, Marcus? A boy?"

Marcus nodded and blinked back the unexpected pool of tears in his eyes. "I love you," he said to his wife and moved his hand to her shoulder. He leaned over and kissed her on the lips. He could taste the salt on her warm lips.

"He's growing well," the doctor said, wheeling the ultrasound machine closer to the bed. "You can see his head here." He ran his finger across the screen, circling the obvious three-dimensional representation of their son's melon-shaped head.

"He's got an enormous head," Marcus said. "Is that normal?"

"For a Marine." The doctor chuckled. "Actually, yes. It's just fine. Everything is developing normally. And here is where we can tell he is, in fact, a boy."

"That's enormous too," said Marcus. "Like a soldier."

"You wish." Sylvia giggled.

The red-faced nurse cleared her throat. "Any names?" she asked.

"Wesson," said Sylvia. "It's my maiden name."

"Wes for short," added Marcus. "His middle name will be Isaac. It's my middle name too."

"Beautiful name," the nurse said. "Wesson Isaac Battle. Very nice."

"Did you have any girl's names picked out?" the doctor asked.

"We were down to two," Sylvia offered. "Marcus liked Lilly."

"And you?" the nurse asked, handing the doctor a damp cloth to clean Sylvia's belly. "What name did you like?"

"I've always liked Lola," she said. "If our baby had been a girl, I would have picked Lola."

CHAPTER 24

OCTOBER 14, 2037, 3:57 PM

SCOURGE + 5 YEARS

EAST OF RISING STAR, TEXAS

Battle slowly regained consciousness, struggling against the paralysis of sleep. His neck and back were drenched with sweat. He blinked open his eyes and felt a deep, muscular pain pulsing throughout his body. He shifted in the cot and felt the sting of burned skin.

He turned his head and looked at his surroundings. He was in his barn. He didn't remember getting there. The last thing he remembered was the fire. There was too much smoke. It was too hot.

He struggled to sit up, but a hand caught his shoulder and gently urged him back onto the cot. It was Lola.

"How are you feeling?" she asked. "You've been out for a couple of hours. Your breathing sounds better, though."

Battle tried to speak, but nothing came out. He licked his lips and shook his head.

"Pico," she called, "I need a cup of water."

A moment later, Salomon Pico appeared next to Lola, holding a Solo cup.

"Lean up slowly," Lola suggested. She took the cup and drew it to Battle's lips.

The water was ice cold. It soothed the dry scratch that ran from the roof of his mouth to deep in his throat. He was too eager and coughed up a swallow of it, spraying it all over himself. Pico patted him on the back. Lola withdrew the cup.

"Small sips, Battle. You nearly died. You probably did some serious damage to your lungs."

Battle coughed, gasped for air, and motioned for more water. He took smaller sips, relishing the relief.

"Take these." Lola handed him a pair of red capsules. "Advil. It'll help with the pain from the burns."

He took the pills and shook them down his throat, gulping past the pain. His throat felt sunburned.

Battle sat up on his elbows and looked at the large six-inch-square bandage on his side. It was stained with blood and ointment.

"I cleaned it out and put Polysporin on it," Lola said. "It's not as bad as it probably feels. Everything was pretty superficial."

Battle swallowed and winced, managing to eke out a few words. "Thank you, Lola," he said. "Thank you, Pico."

"You saved us," Pico said. "Well, I mean to say you saved her. You kinda saved me. You almost killed me. But—"

Lola shot him a disapproving glare. "Pico," she said.

"You're welcome," Battle said.

"What were you doing in the house?" Lola took a damp cloth and draped it on Battle's neck.

"I needed something," he said, his voice full of gravel. His eyes widened and his body tensed with the panic of sudden recognition. "Wait. Where is it?" He tried pushing himself from the cot, but Lola stopped him.

"The photograph?" she asked calmly. "I have it. It's on the shelves over there." She pointed over her shoulder to the storage racks along the back wall of the barn. "The frame is broken, but the photograph is okay."

Battle's body relaxed and he lowered himself flat onto the cot. He exhaled and closed his eyes. "Thank you," he whispered.

"Why the hell would you risk your life for a picture?" said Pico, stuffing his hands into the pockets of his ill-fitting jeans. "That don't make no sense. I mean, you done killed all those people and then you run into a burning house for a picture?"

Battle opened his eyes and stared at the high wooden beams that framed the barn's roof. He slowly inhaled as deep a breath as possible through his nose and then exhaled through his mouth. With each breath he was able to inhale incrementally deeper.

"What's he doing?" Pico asked Lola.

She put a finger to her lips. "Give him a few minutes," she said as if Battle weren't in the room. "He's lost everything. That house was his connection to his family. It was the only thing that kept him sane, kept him grounded. It was his castle. He spent every day since the Scourge protecting it. Now it's gone."

"What's that got to do with a picture?"

"It's of his family," she said. "Don't you understand that?"

Pico shook his head. "I ain't never had one. Not that I remember."

The three were silent for a long time, each of them lost in their own minds. Each of them likely mourning the lives they'd lost as much as dreading the days to come. Finally, Battle broke the silence.

"We need to find your son," he said. "And we need to find him before the Cartel finds out what happened here."

***

OCTOBER 14, 2037, 5:14 PM

SCOURGE + 5 YEARS

EAST OF RISING STAR, TEXAS

Marcus Battle looked at the open gun cabinet along the eastern wall of the barn. All twenty-five feet of weapons and ammunition were exposed. There was an empty spot where Inspector usually hung.

"Tell me again how you broke into this and took the rifle?" He folded his arms across his chest, his skin stinging as he did.

"I have a knack," said Pico. "I just…I know how to open these things."

"Huh," Battle said. "Good to know. Where is Inspector, by the way?"

"The what?"

"The rifle you took?"

"It's over by the door. You left it in the yard. I figured you'd need it later. Why'd you call it Inspector?"

"Long story," said Battle. "All right. I need you to grab a couple of backpacks off the shelf. Stuff them full of whatever you think we're gonna need. Food, supplies, extra socks."

"Socks?"

"Nothing's worse than wet feet."

"Okay."

"What are you doing?"

"I'm taking inventory," he said. "I'm deciding what weapons we're taking with us."

"And Lola?"

"She's feeding the horses," Battle said. "They need to eat and drink before we head out."

Pico left Battle at the armory to do what was asked of him. Battle pulled out a clipboard on which he kept a meticulous inventory of all weapons. He ripped a sheet of paper in half and marked it with a pencil.

What we need

3 Brownings – loaded, one box of ammo

3 9mm – three boxes ammo – armor piercing

dozen hand grenades

3 smoke grenades/flash bangs

XM25, ammo

Inspector, ammo

slingshot

He held the pencil above the piece of paper as he reviewed his list. It was good.

They'd use the Brownings to mask their identities from the Cartel once they reached Abilene. They were easy to carry on horseback and fire on the move if necessary.

They'd each get a sidearm. He'd keep McDunnough for himself, and he had a couple of Glocks with which he'd happily part. The ammo was the same for the Glocks as it was for his Sig.

The hand grenades were good for getting them out of a jam or providing additional cover. While he'd learned Lola could handle herself, he still wasn't sure about Pico. There was a weakness, an insecurity in the man that made Battle question his fortitude.

The smoke grenades, assuming he had room for them, would be a nice bonus should they have to gain entry into a guarded or heavily armored building. He'd used them more times than he could count in Syria.

The XM25 was a unique piece of the arsenal and Battle shouldn't have had one. It was one of the weapons the army used to replace the long-used M16.

A gas-operated semiautomatic air-bursting assault weapon, the XM25 was initially too heavy. In the early 2000s, Special Forces units refused to deploy with it. At fourteen pounds and capable of only five shots at a time, it wasn't a viable option for the elite teams who relied on ease of movement and stealth to execute the most critically sensitive missions.

Battle had procured one through questionable methods. He'd paid through the nose for it and five rounds each of three different types of ammunition. The twenty-five-millimeter color-coded rounds were task specific. Yellow rounds were the most important. They were the high-explosive air-bursting projectiles. The red were armor-piercing. The orange were door busters.

He'd saved the weapon for the right moment and chose never to deploy it on his own property. Battle feared an errant shot, especially the air-bursting rounds, could damage or destroy his house, barn, or garage. It wasn't worth the risk. Now, on the road with unforeseen challenges and obstacles in their way, he believed it was worth it despite the added weight to his horse.

The last item on his list was a slingshot. It wasn't a normal slingshot. It was tactical and could fire ball bearings capable of inflicting maiming or deadly penetration. The steel shots could travel up to five hundred fifty feet per second, a velocity much slower than a firearm. But the slingshot was silent. It was an outstanding close-range weapon for a sneak attack.

He laid out the supplies in three separate piles on the long worktable in front of the weapon cabinet. Pico returned and dropped a backpack on the table.

"I'm loading them up with the same stuff," said Pico. "We each have our own share. That way if one of us goes down, the other two are good."

"Perfect," said Battle.

Lola limped through the barn doors, carrying a basket full of radishes and green onions she'd pulled from the garden.

"I figure it can't hurt to take some fresh food," she explained, plopping the basket on the floor next to Battle.

"Go ahead and ration it into plastic bags," Battle instructed. "Give everybody the same amount. Horses are ready?"

"They're ready. So we're good to go?" Lola asked. "We need to go."

"I'm good," said Pico.

"Almost," said Battle, raising his hand. "You two get loaded up. I'll meet you at the horses. I've got one more thing I gotta do."

***

Battle walked past the charred remains of his house. His eyes were drawn to the lingering hot spots, where flames continued to gnaw away at his home. It wasn't really his home anymore; it was a burned heap of nothing now and not recognizable as the place where his family had lived and died. He took a wide berth around the char and walked straight for the gravestones at the rear of the interior acreage.

Though the pain in his side was acute, he did his best to ignore it as he knelt in front of the limestone markers. He leaned over and wiped them clean of the soot and ash covering the etched lettering. The acrid smoke still hung in the air, and he could taste it in the back of his throat.

"I'm leaving," he said, his eyes drifting between the markers. "I can't stay. The house is gone. Lola needs my help."

He rubbed his chin and ran his hand through is hair. Neither his wife nor his son responded.

"I'm not only doing this for her," he assured them. "It's not just about her kid."

The air was colder than it had been earlier in the day. He felt it in his fingers as he clasped them in prayer.

"I'm doing this for us," he promised. "These people, the ones who came here and invaded our home, it wasn't their choice. They were sent here. Somebody gave them orders. I'm going to find who it is. I'm going to tell him who I am. I'm going to tell them who you were. I'm going to kill him."

"Revenge isn't the answer," Sylvia said, breaking her silence. "It won't bring us back. It won't rebuild the house. That's not who you are, Marcus."

"I need to do this," he said. "I can't let this go without punishment. I can't leave you here, leave our home without a real purpose."

"Saving that boy is your purpose," Sylvia said, her soft voice filling his head. "That's all it needs to be."

Battle balled his fists and worked to control the rage he felt building in his core. All he'd wanted after Syria was to leave the violence behind. He wanted a simple, private life with his wife and child. He'd prayed to God for it and built it with hard work and faith.

The Scourge and the Cartel had stolen it from him. They'd returned him to the bloody existence he'd lived for so long. He'd fallen into the very world he'd spent years trying to avoid.

"Romans 12:17," Sylvia said. "'*Repay no one evil for evil, but give thought to do what is honorable in the sight of all.*' First Peter 2:23, '*When he was reviled, he did not revile in return; when he suffered, he did not threaten, but continued entrusting himself to him who judges justly.*' Matthew 5:7, '*Blessed are* – '"

"I get it," Battle said. "I get it." He hung his head, knowing his wife was right. But he didn't want to hear it.

"God understands," he said to her. "He has a sense of justice. He knows good and evil. He knows I am good. He knows I will do His will by extinguishing the evil."

Sylvia didn't respond; Wesson didn't speak. Battle nodded at their silence. He kissed his fingertips and pressed them to his son's name. He kissed them again, tasting the ash as he did, and touched his wife's name.

"'*Eye for eye, tooth for tooth,*'" he said, pushing himself to his feet. "'*Hand for hand, foot for foot, burn for burn, wound for wound, stripe for stripe.*' Exodus 21: 24-25."

Battle looked at the stones one final time. He looked at the space between the garage and the shell of his house. Through the thin wisps of remnant smoke, he saw Lola and Pico. They were already on their horses. Pico was holding the reins for Aces. The Appaloosa was alternately snorting and nickering.

"You coming?" asked Pico. "We should get going before dark. It'll be easier to travel at night. We could hit Abilene by first light."

Battle marched forward through the smoke toward his horse. He resisted the strong urge to turn around, to look back one final time.

He reached Aces and slung himself into the saddle. "Let's go," he said and dug his heels into the horse's sides. He grabbed the reins, pulling the horse south toward the highway.

The sun was low to their left and cast long shadows of the trio as they began their trek. Battle knew he'd never return. There was nothing for him here now. His future, whatever it held, was in the wilderness of a post-apocalyptic world. He was a traveler without a home.

CHAPTER 25

OCTOBER 15, 2037, 2:14 AM

SCOURGE + 5 YEARS

ABILENE, TEXAS

Battle didn't recognize the city. It didn't help it was a cloudy, moonless night, nor that he hadn't been there in five years. Abilene wasn't Abilene anymore. It was a far-flung outpost for a large concentration of the Cartel, which he'd learned was the nasty criminal organization that had taken over most of Texas since the Scourge.

He shifted in his saddle at the intersection of Highways 36 and 322. He ran his hand along the mane of his commandeered horse and looked south to the primary runway at the city's airport. A single blue guidance light flickered on and off like the neon sign of an old boxcar diner. The horse nickered and backed up a step.

Battle looked up into the milky sky and thought about how he'd not seen a plane in the skies for years. It was the kind of thing he didn't notice until he noticed it.

He and his traveling companions had just trotted past the airport's main terminal. The former Taylor County Expo Center was lit from the inside. A soft yellow glow told the trio it wasn't empty.

"That's where they keep a lot of supplies," said Pico in between slugs of water from his canteen. "It's guarded, but we could get in, I reckon."

"We'll dismount here." Battle hopped off his horse and slipped the reins through the opening in a rusting chain-link fence that surrounded the runway. He walked over to grab the reins of Lola's horse and help her down.

She took Battle's hand and dropped to the ground, tying her horse next to his. "You think this is a good idea?" she asked.

Battle opened up his saddlebag and started grabbing mission-critical supplies. "What?"

"Attacking their supply storage? Aren't we only announcing our arrival?"

"She might be right," said Pico. "If our goal is to find her boy and get him, why do we care about the supply store? What do we gain?"

Battle pulled a tactical slingshot from the bag, rolled it over in his hand, and stuffed it into a lightweight backpack. "We're not just here to get her son," he said. "We're here to hurt them too."

"That's not what you said," Lola said, stomping her foot. "You said rescuing Sawyer was your number one priority."

Battle shook his head and moved closer to Lola to quiet her. "I said that was *your* priority and I understood it. I also told you we were leaving a mark here. We're not some special ops team sneaking in and out unnoticed to extract a target."

Lola crossed her arms, held her chin up, and set her jaw. "And what if your revenge plot stops us from getting my son?"

Battle looked in her eyes. He was expressionless. "That's not happening."

Pico shrugged. "We don't even know if the boy is here."

Battle and Lola turned to him and in unison said, "Shut up, Pico."

Pico held up his hands in surrender and went to work on his saddlebag, mumbling and cursing under his breath.

Battle zipped up his backpack, grabbed a Browning from the saddle scabbard, checked his Sig Sauer at his hip, and started marching southwest toward the Expo Center's main hall.

"You two," he said to Lola and Pico, "leave your gear here. You won't need it."

Though they looked surprised, and a little wary, they scrambled to follow him. Battle hopped a waist-high fence and started jogging across the wide-open, weed-infested lot that separated the hall from the intersecting highways. He carried the shotgun in the two-handed ready position and, from habit, started a Jody call and chanted his cadence as he moved.

"My honey heard me comin' on my left right left," he said to the rhythm of his footsteps. "I saw Jody running on his left right left. I chased after Jody and I ran him down. Poor ol' boy doesn't feel good now."

Battle glided along, unaware Lola was on his right as they approached the main hall. He stopped about ten feet from the northeastern wall and flinched when he spotted her so close.

"You're faster than I expected," he said, crossing a concrete embankment that framed the building.

"And you can't sing," she replied without a smile. "What was that?"

Battle cleared his throat. "Nothing."

Pico joined them at the wall between two large windows. "Inside this building," he huffed, out of breath, "they keep trucks, generators, some trailers. It's mostly big stuff."

"All guarded?"

"Yeah," Pico said. "Maybe a dozen fellas. All of them have the Brownings. Some probably also got themselves six-shooters. Maybe there's a rifle. Maybe not. Depends on who's on duty."

"What's our best entrance?" Lola asked.

"I'm gonna suggest going in through the front," Pico said, pointing toward the main entrance. "It's the fastest, easiest way into the arena. That's where they keep the big stuff."

"You said that," said Battle. "The big stuff. It all works? It's mechanically sound?"

"I reckon." Pico pressed his face to the window. "I can't say for sure."

Battle pinched the brim of his brown cowboy hat and tilted it back on his head. "So we go in through the front."

"And you're the only one who's armed?" asked Lola.

"For now."

***

Battle walked along the edge of the building to the set of tall, aluminum-framed glass doors at the main entrance. When they rounded the corner to the front, Battle told Pico and Lola to put their hands above their heads and walk in front of him.

They were standing at the doors for less than a minute when a young, wiry grunt noticed them and came running. He stopped short of opening the locked door and eyed the threesome through thick black-rimmed glasses.

The grunt raised his Browning, aiming it at Lola through the glass. "Who are you?"

"I'm a boss from Fort Worth," Battle said. "Caught these two trying to steal horses back near Cisco. Been a pain getting them here. I need some help."

The grunt's eyes darted amongst the three uninvited guests. "I ain't got notice of this. Nobody told me you was coming here."

Battle chuckled. "That's because nobody knew I was coming," he said. "I've been on the road with these two for two days. I'm tired. I need help."

"You should take them to HQ," said the grunt, his shotgun trembling in his hands. Battle surmised he was an overnight depot guard for a reason.

Battle's voice deepened. "That's another four miles, grunt. I'm exhausted. Now open the door and help me with these thieves."

The grunt hesitated, then opened the door cautiously and stepped aside. "C'mon inside," he said. "I gotta check you for weapons."

"They don't have any," said Battle. "I'm the only one who's armed."

"Gotcha, boss," said the grunt, his big eyes blinking through his thick glasses. "But I got rules. I gotta do it."

"No problem," he said. "You alone?" Battle stepped to the side and the grunt started the pat downs.

"No," he said. "I'm the only one up front. We got a bunch of guys in the arena. They're playing cards."

Battle's eyes lit up. "Poker?"

The grunt smiled. "Texas Hold 'Em." He was on his knees behind Lola. His shotgun was on the ground, and he held a revolver to her back as he patted the insides of her legs. "I won a couple packs of cigarettes earlier tonight."

"Good for you," said Battle.

"She's a skinny one," said the grunt, his hands lingering on the inside of her thighs. "I bet she's feisty, being a ginger and all."

Lola looked back at Battle with a steely glare but didn't resist the unwanted groping. It wasn't the first time hands were places she hadn't invited them. She closed her eyes while the grunt slid his curious fingers upward along the curves of her body.

Battle gripped the grunt's shoulder. "That's enough. I told you they're not armed."

The grunt studied Battle's face. "You got a claim to her? That it?"

Battle stuck his tongue into his cheek and laughed. "No. I don't have a claim. But like I already told you, I'm tired. I need to get some help and some sleep."

The grunt walked around the other side of Lola. "All right then," he said. "You're good. I still gotta check the dude."

Battle sighed. "Hurry up."

The grunt performed a cursory, essentially useless backhanded sweep of Pico. "All right, follow me. We got some rooms to put them in. I'll get you some food. Maybe you can join the game before you get some sleep."

Battle leveled the shotgun on Pico and shifted it to Lola. "Sounds good. Lead the way."

The grunt turned his back on the trio, directing them with his pistol in one hand and his Browning in the other. He walked with the confidence of an older, more experienced man, strutting across the concourse.

The concourse was warm. There was little, if any, air-conditioning. Battle looked up at the high ceilings as they walked. For every bulb still lit, one out of three was flickering with weakness.

As they moved further into the building, the stronger the odor of gasoline and oil became. The odor confirmed Pico's intelligence. There was some sort of large gas-powered equipment in the arena.

They approached an opening into the arena, but rather than pass through it, the grunt stopped and opened a dented metal door. He spun the knob without using a key and shouldered his way inside a small room.

"They can stay in here for now, boss," said the grunt. "You can take a load off and then grab 'em again at sunup and take 'em to HQ."

Battle poked Pico in the back with the shotgun and forced him into the darkness, then Lola. From the light leaking into the room from the concourse, Battle could tell this was once a concession stand. To the right, on the concourse side of the room, was the service counter. To the left were a sink, a microwave, and an empty popcorn machine. That was as far as he could see.

The grunt stood at the door, his foot holding it open. "Door locks from the outside," he said. "They're stuck here."

Lola shot Battle a look, her brow furrowed in confusion. Battle knew he hadn't shared this part of his plan with them. That was partially because he was winging it and partially because he didn't want tactical input from either of his companions.

He winked at her, spun around, and left the concession stand without saying anything to either of them. They'd be safer here and he could focus on the task at hand.

The grunt locked the door, and Battle followed him back through the opening into the arena. Dust danced in the moderately lit air that hung in the large, open bowl. He could almost taste it as they descended the aisles between stadium seats that wrapped the arena on all four sides of a dirt floor.

One end of the floor looked like a collision repair shop. There was a box truck, a pickup, a military Humvee, and a pair of black SUVs. One of the SUVs was attached to a landscaping trailer. Whatever was in the trailer was covered with a blue plastic tarp. All of the vehicles were in various stages of disrepair.

"Got a motor pool down there, huh?" Battle asked.

"Yeah," said the grunt. "They look like hell, but they all work. A couple of the guys here are mechanics. They keep 'em running for whenever the bosses feel like using something faster than a horse. They're pretty stingy about it, though. Gas is hard to come by."

"Those the mechanics?" Battle nodded to the group of men sitting at a round wooden table at the end of the floor opposite the vehicles. They were engrossed in their game. Battle counted four.

"Yep," the grunt said. "Hey!" he called down to them. "I got us a visitor. A boss from Fort Worth."

The men looked up at Battle and the grunt. One of the men waved. Another toasted them with a beer bottle. A third laid his cards on the table and stood. He set his hands on the hips of his torn, ill-fitting jeans and watched Battle approach.

The grunt led Battle to the floor and introduced him to the group. The only one who seemed remotely interested was the one on his feet. His name was Hedgepath.

"Fort Worth?" he said, his eyes giving Battle the once-over. "You're a long way from home."

"Yep," Battle said.

Hedgepath's eyes narrowed. "What's your name, boss?"

"Marcus."

Hedgepath frowned. "Huh. Boss Marcus."

Battle kept his eyes on Hedgepath's. The grunt was suspicious.

"He's got a couple of prisoners with him," explained the wiry grunt serving as Battle's host. "I got 'em locked up while Marcus takes a load off."

"What kind of prisoners?" Hedgepath asked. "And why'd you bring 'em here?"

Battle chuckled and lowered the brim of his hat. "One, they're thieves. Two, 'cause I've had them with me since Cisco. I'm tired and need a break. Three, you ask too many questions for a grunt in a garage."

The other grunts laughed at Battle's assessment.

"He's right," said one of them. "Sit down, Hedge. Let the boss play a hand."

Hedgepath blushed, his eyes darting from grunt to grunt. He pulled out his chair and dropped into it. He picked up his cards and slid a couple of chips into the center of the table. "That's my blind. I ain't put it in yet."

Battle leaned his Browning against the table, pulled his Sig Sauer from his holster, and set McDunnough onto the table. He found an empty seat and leaned in on the table with his elbows. Battle was comfortable at a poker table. He'd spent many long, sleepless nights in Aleppo and the outskirts of Tehran playing cards with his comrades. Be it Texas Hold 'Em, Spades, Hearts, or Five Card Stud, he'd played. And he was good.

Battle begged off the next couple of hands. He assessed each grunt as they played their cards. Hedgepath was the best of them. He didn't have any tells. He sat stone faced whether he'd drawn an empty hand or a straight. His stack of chips was the biggest among the four players.

"What are the chips worth?" Battle asked as he watched Hedgepath slide another pile to his side of the table. "Cigs? Liquor? Women?"

"A little bit of everything," said Hedgepath. It was his deal again. He started shuffling the cards. Battle watched his technique, which he instantly recognized as an overhand or stripping shuffle.

Hedgepath took a group of cards on the bottom of the deck and held them between his thumb on one side and fingers on the other. He lifted them sideways out of the deck and then placed them on the top, repeating this multiple times.

Unlike the riffle or the Hindu shuffles, which almost always produced a random order of the cards, the overhand shuffle was a cheater's best friend. It was easier to control card placement on the top and bottom of the deck.

Battle paid close attention to Hedgepath's fingers as he moved them. The kid was stacking the deck.

"I'll play," Battle said. "What'll it take for me to get in?"

"That gun," Hedgepath said. "It'll get you a hundred chips."

Battle looked at McDunnough and then back to Hedgepath. "Fair enough."

One of the other grunts reached into a bag and pulled out a stack of ten chips. "These are ten each. It's minimum."

Battle looked at the dozens of chips in front of Hedgepath and nodded at them. "You're doing well tonight, then."

"He always does well." One of the others laughed. "I dunno why we even try."

Hedgepath licked his index finger and started the deal. He slid a pair of cards facedown to each player. "All right," he said. "You got your hole. Bet or fold."

They worked their way around the table. All but one of the grunts checked. He folded.

Battle peeked at his cards. He had a queen and a ten, both of them spades. He checked; Hedgepath checked.

Hedgepath dealt the flop to the center of the table. The three cards lying face up were a nine of spades, a king of hearts, and a six of diamonds.

"I'm out," said one of the remaining grunts. The other checked with a chip.

Battle looked over at Hedgepath and then back at the flop. He tossed a chip into the pot. "Check."

Hedgepath dropped a pair of chips into the pot. "Raise it ten." The other grunt matched it, as did Battle.

"Here's the turn," said Hedgepath. He dealt another card face up to the center of the table. It was a ten of hearts. "A pair of tens."

Battle looked at his cards again. The grunt folded. "Guess it's just you and me," he said to Hedgepath.

"Whatcha gonna do, Boss Marcus?" Hedgepath sneered. He rapped his fingers on the table, tapping out a rhythm. "Whatcha gonna do?"

Battle slid two chips into the pile. Hedgepath matched him.

"Here's the river," said Hedgepath. "Let it flow, Boss Marcus." He flipped the final card into the center of the table. It was a jack of clubs.

Battle checked his cards again. He looked at the pot. He looked at Hedgepath. "I'm all in." He slid his remaining chips into the center.

"Oooh." Hedgepath sat forward in his chair. "A player. Nice." The kid had a ridiculous amount of confidence for a grunt, especially since Battle was selling himself as a boss.

That was his tell.

Battle concluded that somehow Hedgepath knew *Boss Marcus* wasn't who he claimed to be. It was that conclusion that forced Battle's hand. Despite holding a king high straight, he figured the cheater's hand was better. His only option was to go all in and lose McDunnough to the pot. That would give him a chance to get it back into his hand.

Battle looked over his shoulder. The wiry grunt was leaning against a railing that separated the arena floor from the stadium seating. He was chewing on his fingernails and not really paying attention to the game.

"I'll match you," said Hedgepath, sliding more chips across the table. "Should we do this?"

Battle quickly checked the other grunts. They were preoccupied with the game. None of them was on alert; none of them suspected anything. One of them yawned, revealing his lack of teeth. "Sure," Battle said, his eyes returning to the cheater. "You first."

Hedgepath narrowed his eyes and looked at the cards, the handgun, and the other grunts. He shrugged. "Cool," he said and flipped his cards. He revealed a pair of jacks.

"Full house," said Battle. "You got me." Battle flipped his cards. "I had a straight."

A smile wormed its way across Hedgepath's stubbled cheeks. He reached for the pot and drew the chips to his side of the table. "I'm gonna need that Glock," he said. His right hand moved to his hip, disappearing under the table.

Battle tensed in his seat, his quick twitch muscles ready to fire. He slid one foot back and planted it in the dirt floor. "Sure thing," he said. "But it's not a Glock. It's a Sig Sauer. See?"

Before any of the grunts could react, Battle pulled McDunnough into his hand and, with it still lying on its side on the table, pulled the trigger twice.

A pair of slugs ripped into Hedgepath just beneath his sternum. His body pulsed and jerked, his eyes popped wide with shock, and he fell to the side. By the time he'd slumped and the blood leaked through his gray T-shirt, Battle was on his feet, taking target practice. The shots echoed one after the other in the cavernous arena.

One of the grunts fumbled at his hip as a hollow-point round drilled into his throat and settled there. He abandoned the holster in favor of grasping at the hole in his neck, blood spurting through his fingers with each fading carotid pulse.

Battle popped another pair of shots between the eyes of the second grunt. His hand was so steady, both of the shots traveled through the same hole in the man's skull. His jaw dropped and his head slapped onto the table before his body hit the floor.

The fourth grunt had his hands raised. He was shaking his head, pleading unintelligibly when a single shot exploded through his chest. He grabbed at the wound and stood, stumbling and tripping face first into the floor. He grabbed at the dirt, trying to claw his way to safety. Battle stopped him with a final shot to the back of his head. No sense in making him suffer.

All four card-playing grunts were dead within three seconds. Battle spun to check the wiry grunt as a shot zipped past his head. He dropped to a knee, turned, and leveled the Sig at the spot where he'd last seen him. The grunt wasn't there; he was halfway up the stadium. The grunt fired another errant shot before lowering his revolver and running farther up the stairs. He lost his balance, tripping over his own feet as he scrambled toward the concourse. His Browning was still leaning against the railing.

Battle leapt to his feet and jumped over the railing into the first row of seats. He bounded over another set of seats until he found his footing in the aisle. The wiry grunt reached the top of the arena. The kid aimed, but pulled back the pistol and disappeared around the corner.

Battle sprinted up the steps, his lungs protesting. They weren't at full strength after inhaling too much smoke in his burning home just hours earlier. He made it to the concourse seconds after the grunt, sliding into the wide-open hallway on both feet in time to hear a loud crash and a woman's shriek.

He turned left to the concession stand and saw the door open, the wiry grunt's legs on the floor and extending into the hallway. Battle could only see the bottom half of his body, a pool of dark red fluid leaching across the floor.

Battle gathered his momentum and ran to the doorway. "Lola! Pico!"

He reached the opening and saw Pico leaning over the popcorn machine, which covered the wiry grunt's head and torso. Pico looked up as if he'd been caught with his hand in the cookie jar, as if killing the grunt wasn't the right thing to do.

Battle caught his breath and stood over the body in the doorway. "You okay?"

Pico stood and nodded. "We heard the gunshots. We didn't know what was happening."

"We grabbed the popcorn machine," said Lola, appearing from the darkness of the room. She had her hands over her mouth. "When he opened the door, we heaved it onto him. It knocked him over into the door and then fell on his head."

"We didn't think we'd kill him," said Pico. "We didn't even know who it was. We were trying—"

Battle put his hand on Pico's shoulder. "You don't owe me an apology. You did what you had to do."

Pico shook his head. He was pale. "Yeah, but—"

Lola gagged. "His head popped. We didn't—" She retched again and turned around to vomit.

Battle looked down again and, for the first time, saw the damage. There was a disgusting mix of hair, skin, bone shards, and brain matter on the floor. He grabbed Pico's shoulder and yanked him clear of the body. He offered his hand to Lola and waved for her to take hold. He helped her step over the wiry, headless grunt and into the concourse and noticed that some of the grunt was on her clothing. He couldn't understand the physics of it as he looked at the mess. It didn't seem possible they could have crushed his skull with the machine or that he would have fallen face down like that. But there it was. Everywhere.

Lola bent over at her waist and put her hands on her knees. Her back was heaving, her breath hitching.

"You're hyperventilating," Pico said. He too was splashed with gray matter. "Slow down your breathing."

Lola shook her head, working to catch her breath.

"It could have been you," Pico said, wiping sweat and blood from his brow. "I think that's what has her spooked. We didn't know if it was you until you called out to us. For a split second we thought we killed you."

"You didn't, though," Battle said. "I'm good. We're good. The others are dead."

"Now what?"

"Yeah," Lola said in between gulps of air. "Now what?"

Battle adjusted his Stetson and gestured with McDunnough toward the arena. "We steal a truck and get your son."

EXCERPT FROM CANYON:
THE TRAVELER SERIES BOOK TWO

JANUARY 3, 2020, 3:02 PM

SCOURGE -12 YEARS, 9 MONTHS

ALEPPO, SYRIA

The IED ruptured without warning, blasting pieces of pipe, shards of glass, ball bearings, red synthetic fur, and carpenter screws into three of the six soldiers on patrol near Abdul Wahhab Agha Hospital on the city's western edge.

The concussion blew Captain Marcus Battle from his feet, slapping the back of his helmet on the cratered pavement of Assultan Suliaman Alqunoony Avenue. He was dazed, a sharp ringing in his ears overpowering his thoughts.

Staring into the cloudless, pale blue sky, for an instant he thought he was in Killeen, lying in the grass with Sylvia. As quickly as the delusion formed, it evaporated. The muted sounds of shrieks and pained screams accompanied the high-pitched tone of the ringing.

He rolled over onto his side, facing the spot where the tattered Elmo doll had exploded. Two of his comrades were on their feet, tending to what was left of the other three. Then he saw one of them spasm. He shuddered, his head snapped backward, and he went limp in a spray of red.

The second soldier dropped to his chest, quickly engaging his HK416 rifle, thumping random targets as he searched for the source of the gunfire and took two shots in his left leg.

Battle, still dazed, rolled over and found his HK416 on the ground next to him. He dragged it into position, pulled himself to one knee, and started firing.

He couldn't hear and could barely focus. He didn't know who was dead or alive. Regardless, he stood and started moving toward the gunfire. Bullets whizzed past his head and ricocheted off the ground around him. He took one in the side that slugged his Kevlar. It knocked him back for a second and felt like a thick punch to his gut. Battle kept moving forward, fully exposed, until he emptied the thirty-round magazine and found some protection behind the overturned charred frame of a pickup truck.

"Battle!" the wounded soldier called during a momentary lapse in gunfire. He'd managed to find adequate protection behind a concrete road barrier, having dragged himself there with one good leg. "Get out of here. I'm pinned. The others are gone. Get out of here. Try to find us help."

Battle couldn't hear him. Though his vision was clearing, the dog whistle piercing his ears hadn't subsided. He exchanged magazines and looked through the holes in the truck's frame. Behind him was a three-story building, most of the windows shattered or cracked. He couldn't tell from which spot the sniper was taking shots. Battle looked back toward his patrol partner. It was only a matter of minutes and he'd be dead. He couldn't leave him.

His back pressed against the underside of the truck frame, Battle said a prayer and spun around free of the truck. He aimed up at the building and pulled the trigger, releasing a quick burst for cover. He dashed across a short field of debris to the building's entrance and bolted through. He found himself inside a narrow concrete stairwell that stank of urine.

Battle bounced up the first flight of stairs. Feeling the vibration of gunfire against the stair rail, he knew it was coming from a higher floor. He pressed his eyes closed against a searing headache and clenched his jaw, climbing the second flight of steps. He stood still and felt the vibrations of the gunfire, not able to distinguish from which direction they were coming.

He was about to move to the third floor when, through the ringing, he heard a garbled, guttural-sounding discussion between two men. They were on the second floor.

Battle stood to the left of the door, his back against the wall, and with his left hand pulled on the handle to swing the door wide open. He guessed he had maybe twenty-five rounds left in the magazine. He took a deep breath, moving into the open doorway with his HK416 leveled at whatever lay on the other side.

Nobody was there. It was an empty hallway. It was dark from a lack of power, except at the far left end. From the corner of his eye, he saw movement in that light. An open door led to the two men unleashing the barrage onto his fellow soldier.

The men were preoccupied with reloading a Kalashnikov AK-103-4. One of them was pacing back and forth with a pair of binoculars. He was pointing wildly and yelling at the other man, who was manually loading a new clip. That explained the long pauses between volleys. Behind them was a window devoid of glass and an armoire pressed up against it they were using for cover.

This was his chance.

Battle took off in a full sprint. Bounding along the hallway, yelling at the top of his lungs, he tapped the trigger.

Thump! Thump! Thump! Thump!

The spotter turned to face Battle just as the bullets slapped into his chest. He dropped the binoculars and stumbled backward. Battle pressed the trigger again when he reached the open doorway.

Thump! Thump! Thump! Thump!

The second volley found the man's neck, throwing him against the corner of the room in a violent heap. Battle burst into the room, shifted his momentum, and slid toward the dead spotter. To his right, the shooter was still on one knee, trying to engage the magazine. He was too late. Battle held down the trigger.

Thump! Thump! Thump! Thump! Thump! Thump! Thump! Thump!

The bullets tore through the shooter, rattling his body, knocking him onto his back. Battle lowered his weapon, aiming it directly at the shooter's head, and tapped the trigger for good measure.

Thump! Thump! Thump! Thump!

Battle checked the rest of the room, which he figured was once a dorm room or student apartment for the medical school or nearby university. There was a mattress on the floor. A desk was on its side. The bullet-riddled armoire blocked half of the window. On top of it, Battle saw a crude detonator. He looked to his right. The wall was adorned with Arabic graffiti he couldn't read and bullet holes from return fire.

Battle pinched the bridge of his nose and loosened his helmet's chin strap. The ringing was subsiding. He could hear yelling from across the street, but he resisted the urge to move to the window. It could subject him to friendly fire.

He fished around the back of his neck for his earpiece and found it, plugging it into his right ear. He pushed the button on his comms. It didn't work, so he yelled from inside the building, hoping his voice would carry far enough.

"This is Battle. All clear. Threat neutralized."

"Battle. This is Buck. I'm injured. Need assistance."

Buck. Rufus Buck. That was who survived. The men liked him. He was a natural leader and a fellow Texan, but he wasn't one of Battle's favorite people. He didn't always adhere to the rules of engagement. He liked to bend the rules in his favor. However, he was an American, he was a soldier, and he needed help.

"On my way." Battle cleared the room, raced back down the stairwell, and maneuvered through smoking debris into the street.

He crossed the crumbling asphalt to its opposite side, for the first time seeing the full impact of the IED Elmo. Bile rose in his throat. He couldn't distinguish arms from legs or one man from another. Only the names on the ragged, bloodied strips of the digital camouflage uniforms told him who was who.

"You're it, huh?" Battle asked Sergeant First Class Buck.

"Roger that." Buck was still leaning against the concrete barrier. "I don't know for how much longer."

Battle saw the extent of the sergeant's injuries. He had a tourniquet tied above his knee. Below his knee was a bloody mess. His foot was wonky, turned at an unnatural angle.

"I'm gonna need your help." The sergeant was pale, his eyes sunken. Battle knew he'd lost a lot of blood. "I've called for help. Nobody's coming. Our comms are busted."

"I know. Can you walk?"

"What do you think?"

"Had to ask." Battle turned around and scanned the debris field. "I'm guessing the medic's kit is gone."

"Good guess."

Battle put his rifle on the ground and stood over Buck. "I'm gonna carry you."

"You're what?"

"We've got no choice. I'm gonna put you on my back and carry you back to the checkpoint. Then we can get help."

"That's gotta be an hour away."

"At least."

"You're not gonna make it," Buck said. "I'm gonna bleed out."

"Give me a better option."

"Go get help. Come back for me."

"That'll take too long," Battle argued. "And clearly, the faction we thought was controlling this part of the city isn't really in control. You'll be dead before I get back."

Buck unstrapped his helmet and tossed it to the ground. "All right. Let's do this."

31999828R00155

Made in the USA
Middletown, DE
18 May 2016